ALL SALES FINAL

Sea Legs

KG MacGregor

Bella
BOOKS

2009

Copyright© 2009 by KG MacGregor

Bella Books, Inc.
P.O. Box 10543
Tallahassee, FL 32302

All rights reserved. No part of this book may be reproduced or transmitted in any form or by any means, electronic or mechanical, including photocopying, without permission in writing from the publisher.

Printed in the United States of America on acid-free paper
First Edition

Editor: Katherine V. Forrest
Cover Designer: Stephanie Solomon-Lopez

ISBN 10: 1-59493-158-5
ISBN 13:978-1-59493-158-1

To Jo Atkinson, with thanks.

Acknowledgment

I set out to write this novel during National Novel Writing Month (NaNoWriMo), November 2008. My goal was to get 70,000 words on paper in just thirty days, which translated to roughly 2,500 a day. Piece of cake.

Except that I hit the wall at 48,000 around November 20th and spent the next six weeks rewriting those words so I could comfortably proceed. That left me barely a month before deadline—here's where I have to pause and thank Karen, Ann and Steph for allowing me to rudely ignore them on my visit to the Pacific Northwest so I could write—and in a state of mild panic. When the due date came, I wasn't quite ready to let it go, but I figured I could stew on it a bit more while it was in the editor's hands for the first pass and make my tweaks later. That's when I learned that Katherine V. Forrest was slated to edit the book. One does not turn in a book that needs tweaks to the esteemed Ms. Forrest. So this one was a bit late.

It's impossible to overstate what Katherine brings to the editing process. She approaches each manuscript as both the reader's advocate and the writer's champion. You have her to thank for the visuals and for the crisp delineation of what might otherwise have been a confusing ensemble.

Thanks also to Jenny for her technical help, to Karen for her meticulous proofread, and to all the folks at Bella for their commitment to putting out great books.

About the Author

KG MacGregor was born in 1955 into a military family in Wilmington, North Carolina.

Following her graduation from Appalachian State University, she worked briefly in elementary education, but returned to earn a doctoral degree in journalism and mass communications from the University of North Carolina at Chapel Hill. Her love of both writing and math led to a second career in market research, where she consulted with clients in the publishing, television and travel industries.

The discovery of lesbian fan fiction prompted her to try her own hand at romantic storytelling in 2002 with a story called *Shaken*. In 2005, MacGregor signed with Bella Books, which published Goldie Award finalist *Just This Once*. Her sixth Bella novel, *Out of Love*, won the 2007 Lambda Literary Award for Women's Romance, and the 2008 Goldie Award in Lesbian Romance. In 2008, she proudly announced the return of the Shaken Series with its first installment, *Without Warning*.

To KG, there is no better praise for her work than hearing she has created characters her readers want to know and have as friends. Please visit her at www.kgmacgregor.com.

Chapter 1

One look and Kelly Ridenour was in love.

At over a thousand feet long and thirteen stories high, the *Emerald Duchess* was the largest ship in the Emerald Cruise Line's fleet. It gleamed against the sparkling Biscayne Bay, a waft of silver smoke streaming from its towering stacks and dissipating into the bright Miami sky.

Yvonne Mooney snapped a photo from the taxi as it crested the bridge leading to the cruise terminal. "There she is—our home away from home for the next twelve days."

A finger in the air, Kelly counted the rows of windows to the ninth deck, which was one of three decks lined with balconies. Her stateroom was in that row, somewhere aft, three levels from the top. "You might have to drag me off that ship when we get back. January in Rochester sucks."

"That's why this was the perfect Christmas present for Steph and me to give each other."

"And me to give myself."

Yvonne crouched to keep the ship in her viewfinder, snapping off another photo as the taxi circled the port. "Now I just have to get Steph off her Blackberry for a few hours, and we'll actually have a vacation."

Kelly chuckled at the image. "You probably should have kidnapped her and made her come down early to go diving with us." The last time she had gotten together with Yvonne and her partner was over dinner at a local Irish pub. Steph, a real estate agent, had spent most of the evening texting a title company to finalize plans for a closing.

"Probably not a good idea. Steph's not into all the water stuff. I bet she spends the whole twelve days on this cruise with her nose in a book."

Kelly marveled at how Yvonne and Steph had endured for eighteen years despite having so little in common. They even looked like total opposites—Yvonne tall and athletic with short spiked hair, and Steph petite with long tight curls that seemed to have a life of their own.

"At least we'll all be warm for a while," Yvonne added. "Steph reminds me every winter that it hardly ever snowed where she grew up in Memphis."

"It's amazing you got her to move to Rochester."

"That's nothing. Natalie moved all the way from Mississippi just to be near us. All she cared about was getting out of Pascagoula."

Natalie Chatham, whom Kelly hadn't yet met, was Steph and Yvonne's longtime friend from college. She had decided at the last minute to come along on the cruise, and accepted Kelly's offer to share a cabin. "I can't wait to meet her."

"Just don't expect her to get in the water. She's a bigger princess than Steph."

"I'm telling your girlfriend you called her a princess."

"She won't care. Both of them would consider it a compliment. And when it comes to being prissy, neither of them holds a candle to Didi or Pamela. You aren't going to believe those two."

Kelly snickered to herself as the cab entered the line to the luggage drop-off. She happened to like prissy ladies. She just didn't want to be one. "What time are the others getting here?"

"Their plane is supposed to land at two fifteen, but who knows if they'll be on time? Steph called while you were in the shower this morning and said Rochester got five inches of snow last night."

"Now aren't you glad we came down early?" In their three extra days, they had managed a deep sea fishing trip and a dive class at John Pennekamp State Park, where Yvonne had picked up her resort dive certificate. Kelly had gotten her PADI Divemaster certificate thirteen years ago when she was in the navy and stationed at Key West. "At least the two of us will be on that ship when she pulls out."

Yvonne stowed her camera in its bag. "We're not due to leave until five o'clock, but that storm socked the whole northeast. I wouldn't be surprised if they held us in port for the late arrivals."

"I may not care if we sit in port the whole time. That ship's a beauty."

"Except if we sit in port, they won't open the casinos. We have to be in international waters for that."

Kelly's jaw dropped in disbelief. "Do you mean to tell me you'd rather sit in a dark smoky room with a bunch of machines than out on a sunny deck watching women walk by in bikinis?"

Yvonne cocked her head to the side. "Now that you put it that way..."

The taxi came to a stop at the luggage drop, where the ship's porters hurried to remove their suitcases from the trunk. Yvonne had already tagged her two bags with the color-coded labels from the cruise line so they could be delivered to their stateroom.

Kelly intercepted her duffel, which didn't have a tag. "I can carry this one."

"You ought to send it up with the baggage handlers," Yvonne said, gesturing toward the clusters of passengers making their way to the terminal. "We could be in line for an hour or more."

"Mine's not that heavy. I didn't pack much."

"How can you go on a cruise for twelve days with just one bag? Oh, wait. I know. You didn't have Steph Sizemore helping you pack and making sure you had three changes of clothes for every day."

"Precisely," Kelly said. "I learned in the navy how to pack light and wash out my own clothes."

Yvonne eyed Kelly's bag and the backpack she had slung over her shoulder. "Didn't you pack some dress clothes for dinner?"

"I have a few things. I promise not to embarrass anyone."

"Oh, I won't be embarrassed. But given the size of that bag, if I see you in more than three different outfits I'm going to be impressed."

At the entrance to the terminal they showed their passports and boarding documents, and followed the mob up the escalator to check-in. True to Yvonne's prediction, the line snaked through the terminal, several hundred passengers deep. Most seemed to be couples, tired husbands in khakis and polo shirts, laden with shoulder bags, and wives in the first of their colorful vacation attire. It was no surprise that several children were in tow, as this was their holiday break from school.

A cheery woman in a tropical skirt and blouse greeted them. "It isn't as bad as it looks. We have over thirty people working registration. You'll be on board sipping a rum runner in thirty minutes."

Kelly dropped her bag and kicked it gently forward in line. "Tell me again who all these people are. There are six of us, right?"

"Right. That's you, me, Steph, Natalie... Steph and Natalie have been best friends since college. They're like soul mates."

"Don't you ever get jealous?"

"No way. Natalie does all the things with Steph that would drive me insane. You know those people who shop until they drop?"

Kelly nodded.

"Well, I shop only until I feel like killing somebody. But those two could go for days without coming up for air. And they trade recipes and pore over all those interior design magazines."

"I like those magazines too." She shrugged at Yvonne's incredulous look. "When I worked with my dad, we used to do a lot of remodels. I like to see what other people are doing."

"That'll give you and Natalie lots to talk about. She bought a house last year that needs a lot of work."

"She'd better be careful. Once I get started, I go crazy with ideas." With a sudden burst, they wound around the ropes and moved up another twenty feet. "So it's you, me, Steph and Natalie. Who are the other two?"

"Didi Caviness and Pamela somebody...I don't remember her last name. Didi and Natalie own what most people consider the nicest women's clothing store in Rochester. Of course, I'm no expert on that. I'm just repeating what Steph said."

"And Pamela's her girlfriend?"

"Yeah, her new girlfriend. They've been together about six months. Before that, Didi and Natalie were together for six years, but they split up a couple of years ago."

"I take it they're still friends as well as business partners, or they wouldn't be cruising together."

"They got along better than ever after they broke up—until Pamela came along. Natalie was hoping she and Didi would get back together, but I'm not so sure that's because she's still in love with her. I think it's because Pamela lives in Manhattan and wants them to move the shop there. Didi's really hot for that idea, but Natalie isn't."

Kelly groaned. "Dyke drama. Let's hope everyone behaves for the next twelve days."

"They haven't killed each other yet."

"That's a pretty good sign, I guess."

Yvonne chuckled as they moved up in the line again. "It's a great sign if you ask me. I probably would have killed Didi myself if she hadn't been Natalie's girlfriend."

5

"What? Is she bad news?"

"Not really. Most of the time she's nice, and she's fun to have around. But she's a real clothes horse. I bet she brings twice as much stuff as any of us, and she'll be immaculate whether she's at a formal dinner or sitting on a barstool by the pool. She always looks good, and she knows it. Her problem is she can't turn off her fashion critique and sometimes that gets old."

"Sometimes?" Kelly looked down at her attire, a white cotton shirt with the sleeves rolled up, olive green, knee-length baggy shorts and Birkenstocks. "I bet she has a field day with me. I should have worn one of my old navy uniforms. At least my shorts matched my shirt."

Yvonne laughed and looked her up and down. "I think you look fine. This is supposed to be a freaking cruise, not a fashion show. Just don't wear a silver watch with gold earrings like Steph did the last time we all went out together. I thought we'd never hear the end of it."

Kelly tugged at her ears, which she had never had pierced. "No danger there. Do you think she'd like to see my tattoo?"

"You have a tattoo?"

She tugged her collar back and leaned forward to show a small black and yellow design at the top of her shoulder blade.

"Aw, man. You'll have to show that to Steph. I've been trying for years to talk her into letting me get one."

"This one's a Sea Bee. Our whole unit got drunk one night in Key West, and we all woke up decorated. Thank God I had the good sense to pick a little one."

They finally reached the front of the line, parting briefly as they checked in at separate stations. Kelly strode to the far left counter and came face to face with the reservation clerk, a young woman of Asian descent wearing a form-fitting dark uniform.

"Welcome to the *Emerald Duchess*..."

Kelly noted the familiar hesitation as the clerk—Kim from Taiwan, according to her nametag—waited for her to introduce herself.

"Hi, I'm Kelly Ridenour...Kelly Ann Ridenour." Her plain

clothing, short hair and lack of makeup or jewelry often kept strangers guessing as to her gender, especially since her voice was deeper than that of most women.

"Is this your first cruise, Miss Ridenour?"

"First one with Emerald. I took a couple of short ones back when I was stationed at Key West. I'm looking forward to the eastern islands." She handed over her documents and waited while the woman completed her check-in.

"This is our most popular itinerary. And we've put in a special request for perfect weather just for you."

"That's great." So was Kim's smile, now that Kelly had a chance to study it. "I bet you enjoy sending people off on their dream vacation."

"Especially since I'll be coming along too." She handed over a business card. "If there's anything you need on board, don't hesitate to call me at Guest Services."

"Will do," Kelly answered, wondering if "anything" included dinner companionship. She stepped toward the gangway and waited for Yvonne. "That man who checked you in…did he give you his business card?"

Yvonne stowed her paperwork and draped her camera bag over her shoulder. "Yeah, and he even said I could call him on board if I needed anything."

"Damn! I was hoping my lady was flirting with me." As they entered the ship's majestic atrium, still decorated with a towering Christmas tree, Kelly drew a deep, satisfied breath. Kim or no Kim, this was going to be the best vacation of her life.

Yvonne grabbed her elbow and pointed to the balcony two decks above. "I'm going to drop my stuff off in the room and see if their plane's in. Then we should meet up there and watch for them to come aboard."

Kelly grinned. "I'll be there, and I'll have a rum runner in each hand."

Natalie pressed her forehead against the window of the plane so she could follow the south Florida coastline directly below.

She hoped her last-minute agreement to come along on this trip wasn't a colossal mistake. When Steph and Yvonne had first floated the idea for a twelve-day cruise to the eastern Caribbean, it sounded like fun, but the more she thought about it, the more she worried whether she could put up with lovebirds Didi and Pamela for that long. In the end, her decision to buck up and make the trip was more a matter of choosing to be miserable with friends in the tropics instead of miserable alone at home in the snow.

Not that she didn't like Pamela Roche just fine. The youthful New York designer knew she was stepping into an awkward situation with an ex-lover when she had started dating Didi, but she had been nothing but sweet and friendly to Natalie during her frequent visits to their shop. That didn't change the fact that Natalie still had feelings for Didi, feelings that were trampled every time she saw the two of them fawning over each other, as they were doing right now up in the first-class cabin.

"What are you thinking about?" Steph asked, hooking her arm through Natalie's. Ever the good sport, she had traded her aisle seat for the center so she and Natalie could sit together.

Natalie sighed. "I'm starting to wonder if this was a good idea."

"Of course it is. Only an idiot would choose snow in Rochester over warm sand in Barbados." She tightened her grip as though sensing Natalie needed a boost. "Yvonne and I were thrilled when you said you'd come. You and I are going to hit every store in the Caribbean, and who knows? You might just get lucky with someone on the cruise."

"You mean if she's rich and gorgeous and wants to worship the ground I walk on?"

If seeing Didi and Pamela as a loving couple wasn't bad enough, there was also the matter of Didi's near-constant badgering of Natalie to sell her half of the store so Didi could move it to New York. Natalie had always known it was Didi's dream to hit the big time as a Manhattan fashion maven, and Natalie might have supported it as a life partner, but she wasn't ready to see Didi walk out of her life for good. Eight years ago when they first became lovers, she had invested her entire savings in Didi's dream, to say nothing of her sweat equity. Now that it was successful, she wanted to celebrate the triumph with Didi and know their financial future was secure.

"Please tell me Kelly isn't twenty-eight-years old," she said, an allusion to Pamela and the fourteen-year age difference between her and Didi.

"She looks like she's more our age. She's been working for the city a couple of years and before that lived in Buffalo."

"How did you guys meet her?"

"Kelly hurt her knee or something and came into Yvonne's clinic for physical therapy. They hit it off and started hanging out." Steph looked at the book bag at her feet. "If you get bored I'll lend you some of my lesbian books. Nothing beats a hot, steamy romance."

"Oh, please," Natalie interjected, shaking her head in the direction of the forward cabin. "It's bad enough I have to put up with those two."

Steph lifted out of her seat to look at Didi and Pamela. "How did they manage to end up in first class? I thought we all booked at the same time."

"Didi called back and upgraded with her frequent flyer miles," Natalie answered. "She said she wasn't going to ruin her vacation by traveling cattle-class. I hope we don't have to put up with that princess routine the whole time we're here. I get my fill of that at work every day." In fact, she hoped to avoid the lovebirds as much as possible, though she wouldn't mind a few chances to get off with Didi on her own. Who knows? She might even be able to talk some sense into her.

Steph stretched across her lap to peer outside as the plane banked over the coast and bounced through one of the billowy white clouds that dotted the sky above Miami. "Are we there yet?"

"Any minute." She patted Steph's back affectionately.

Steph and Yvonne were her dearest friends in the world, the

9

ones who had practically saved her life by encouraging her to move from Pascagoula to Rochester twelve years ago. Mississippi was no place for lesbians, they said, something they all knew from their college years at Ole Miss. Thank goodness for Yvonne's softball scholarship and her eventual return home to Rochester, where Steph and Natalie had followed and made a new life. Other than the fact that people commented on her southern drawl every single day, she felt perfectly at home in Upstate New York.

As the plane touched down, Natalie checked her watch and noted they were forty minutes late, but still had plenty of time to get to the ship. Not bad, considering their earlier doubts they would get out of Rochester this morning in the snow.

Didi and Pamela were waiting in the lounge as they exited the jet bridge. Both were dressed to the nines in smart wool slacks and sweaters, with tasteful jewelry, and what Natalie thought was a tad too much makeup. Pamela's outfit was cut for a girlish figure—low waist and clingy top—which seemed to accentuate the age difference between her and Didi. Either that, or Natalie was just bitter about her ex seeing a much younger woman.

"We had the most marvelous shrimp in lobster sauce," Didi exclaimed. "Did you guys get something good in the back?"

"Very funny. We split a granola bar and washed it down with a bottle of water." Steph reached out and mussed Didi's perfect hair. "And by the way, I intend to eat whatever I want for the next twelve days and I don't want to hear any shit from anyone. I've been eating lettuce for a whole month so I could splurge."

"I think you look terrific," Natalie said, remembering how Didi used to jealously whine in private when she gave compliments to others. Steph had worked hard to avoid extra calories all through Thanksgiving and Christmas so she could enjoy the ship's bountiful cuisine without guilt, and she deserved heaps of praise. "In fact, you've never looked better."

They trudged with the crowd to baggage claim, arriving just as the carousel started to churn. Bags belonging to cruise passengers were already tagged for delivery to their stateroom. All they had to do was pick them up and place them on the luggage cart next to the cruise line representative.

Natalie spotted her brown tweed Hartmann bag and wormed her way closer to the belt. Just as she reached for the grip, Didi's hand came out of nowhere and snatched it away. "This one's mine, Nat. I figured you'd bring yours too, so I tied a ribbon on the handle."

Glumly, she stepped back. Matching luggage had seemed like a good idea three years ago when they were a couple. Now it was just another caustic reminder of a relationship gone sour.

"Here's yours, Natalie," Pamela called cheerfully. "I'll get it for you." She tugged it off the conveyor and set it beside Didi's.

"Thank you." It was impossible not to like Pamela, but equally impossible to feel good about Didi having someone so nice for a girlfriend. "I have one more if you see it, a matching grip."

"So does Didi. And she brought her big garment bag too."

Of course she did. Didi never went anywhere without half her wardrobe. Natalie decided to step back and let Pamela retrieve the bags. She bit her tongue to keep from congratulating Didi for finding someone who would help her in her golden years. "We deserve to celebrate these next twelve days, Didi. Our holiday season was off the charts."

"It was a good year," Didi said. "Could have been even better on Eighth Avenue."

Natalie sighed. "Give it a rest, okay? Let's just call a truce and quit talking about this while we're here."

"Under one condition," Didi said, swinging around to look her in the eye. "You promise we'll talk seriously about it when we get home. And I don't mean just me asking you again and you saying no. I mean we sit down and talk about what it's going to take for you to say yes. I'm prepared to make you a generous offer for your half of the business, but I can't do that if you won't listen at all."

As far as Natalie was concerned, a truly generous offer would have to include Didi ditching Pamela and coming back to her. Whatever their differences, they could start fresh and work things out. Once they got their relationship back on track,

Natalie might even consider moving their shop to New York. "We'll talk about it."

"You promise?"

"I said we'd talk about it," she said tersely, feeling instantly guilty for her tone. "I promise we'll sit down together when we get back to Rochester. Let's just have fun with our friends while we're here." She reached down for her bag.

"That one's mine."

"No, it isn't. Yours has the—" She peered closely at the tags and compared cabin numbers. "I'll be damned," she muttered under her breath. It wasn't enough that they were cruising together. Didi and Pamela were in the adjacent stateroom.

Chapter 2

Kelly nodded approvingly as she entered the stateroom, which was neatly appointed with built-in modules in rich cherry laminate. Immediately to her right was a small bathroom with a toilet compartment and a shower stall. The twin beds, separated by a nightstand, were decorated with cheery aqua spreads that matched the drapes leading out to the balcony. A small couch and coffee table lined the wall between the beds and the sliding glass door. On the opposite wall alongside the closet were a vanity, a column of drawers, and a desk with a small television mounted above.

It was hardly spacious, but it was more room than the navy had allotted four crewmen in its barracks at Key West. She unzipped her duffel bag and removed her toiletry bag, which she placed on a shelf beneath the sink. Chuckling to herself, she wet her hand and flattened the cowlick above her brow.

Next she laid out her clothes methodically, sorting underwear and pajamas from beachwear and exercise gear. Then she pulled out three crisp white shirts, which she had neatly wrapped in a plastic laundry bag to prevent creasing. The last few items—khaki chinos, denim carpenter pants, two pairs of dress slacks, a black dinner jacket and a black silk vest—had been similarly stored, and emerged wrinkle-free.

She stowed her things in the large bottom drawer, leaving the top three empty. She figured her roommate—Natalie—would appreciate the extra space, as well as the convenience of not having to bend over in tight quarters. Natalie could have her choice of beds too.

Her last act, the one she had looked forward to most, was to remove her watch and place it on the vanity. Time wasn't going to rule her for the next twelve days.

After checking to make sure she had her key card, which was also her ID to charge purchases on the ship and to get back on the ship when in port, she headed down two flights to the Internet café that surrounded the grand atrium. Yvonne was already poised on the rail of the balcony so she could watch the new arrivals as they came aboard.

"Did their plane get in okay?"

"Yeah, I just talked to Steph. They landed about an hour ago and were getting off the bus out front. They should be coming through any minute."

Kelly looked down as two women entered. "Now there's an odd couple if I ever saw one." One had bright red hair and was bubbling with excitement and awe. The other, plump with brown hair, was considerably younger and more reserved. She was laden with carry-on baggage, including an enormous camera bag with a familiar book sticking out the top. "Didn't I see that book on your kitchen counter the last time I was over?"

Yvonne squinted to get a look. "I think Steph has that one. It's one of those lesbian erotica anthologies."

14

"So it's a safe bet those two are part of our family."

"I'd say so. They're an odd pair."

Kelly's jaw dropped when a shapely woman with long blond hair entered. "Please tell me that's Natalie."

Yvonne snorted. "Not quite."

A second woman, elegant and forty-ish, Kelly guessed, with short hair stylishly coiffed and shining with blond highlights, emerged through the doorway to stand with her.

"The younger one is Pamela, and the one who looks like she's waiting for someone to carry her up the stairs on a throne is Didi."

"I have to admit, they make a striking couple," Kelly said as the two women stepped onto an elevator and disappeared from view.

"If you make a pass at Pamela, Didi will be the one doing all the striking."

She chuckled. "I consider myself warned."

"There's your roommate." Yvonne waved in vain trying to draw the attention of two women who had just entered the atrium.

Kelly's eyes went first to Steph, then to a tall woman with short black hair. "Natalie looks like a runner."

"That isn't Natalie," Yvonne said as a man appeared and took the tall woman's arm. "Natalie has on the beige sweater."

Kelly shifted her focus to a slender woman with thick brown hair that fell to her shoulders and framed her face. From two levels up, Natalie appeared to be quite attractive, but not as remarkable as either Pamela or Didi. She might have been prettier if not for what looked like a scowl. "Is she always so happy?"

"To tell you the truth, she's been pretty cranky lately over this business with Didi. Let's hope this trip doesn't make it worse."

"I wonder why she decided to come."

Yvonne shrugged. "She and Didi still work together every day, so I guess she thought she could manage a vacation. Besides, she and Steph are best buds. I'm surprised you didn't end up rooming with me."

From the slump of her shoulders, Natalie looked tired on top of cranky. She also looked like someone who needed all the friends she could get, something Kelly understood. If she could help get Natalie's mind off her troubles and return home to Rochester with a new friend, that would make this vacation all the more memorable.

"I'm going to run down and meet Steph in our stateroom. Why don't you head out to the deck for a drink and we'll bring Natalie out so you can meet each other."

"Okay, but try not to get distracted by your girlfriend and forget about me."

Natalie frowned as she walked past Didi and Pamela's stateroom. Over a thousand cabins on this bucket and she had to draw the one next door.

Her mood, which had been dour since rising at four a.m. to five inches of snow, got a lift when she entered the stateroom. The designers had struck the perfect chord for efficiency and comfort, throwing in a cheery décor to boot. She crossed the room to the sliding glass door and stepped onto the balcony, which gave her an expansive view of the towering hotels of Miami Beach.

"Gorgeous, isn't it?" To her left, Didi and Pamela were standing at the rail.

A wave of nostalgia enveloped her as she nodded silently. Though she had seen Didi and Pamela together many times, she was more jealous than ever to know they were here for a romantic getaway, while she would be the odd one out for the entire trip. Steph had promised to keep her company, since Yvonne wanted to play in the casino and go diving with her new buddy, but hanging out with a friend didn't measure up to watching the Caribbean moon on the water with a lover.

Shaking the thought from her head, she went back inside, noticing for the first time a watch on the vanity. That meant her roommate had already been to the cabin.

She opened the closet and studied the dark suit, white shirts, black dress shoes and sneakers. No skirts or dresses. No pumps.

No brightly colored tropical shirts. "Great. I'm rooming with a funeral director."

Unable to resist, she went through the drawers until she found the rest of her roommate's things—cargo shorts, more button-up shirts, tank tops in several colors and a pair of board shorts like a teenage boy might wear. Not much variety...no flair at all.

In the bathroom, she found what looked like a man's shaving kit. Awash in guilt for her nosy actions, she nonetheless peered inside. There was only a razor, sunscreen, baby shampoo and dental care items. No makeup of any kind. No face cream. No moisturizer. How did any woman live without moisturizer?

A knock at the door startled her, causing her to drop the bag. Quickly, she picked it up and stowed it back on the shelf.

Steph was at the door. "You like your stateroom?"

"It's nice. Where are you?"

"We're below you, but we don't have a balcony, just a big window."

"Then you're welcome to come up and use ours, if you don't mind being next door to Pamela and Diva."

"You mean Didi."

"Whatever."

Steph laughed with conspiratorial mischief. "Maybe you and your roommate will hit it off and you can keep them up nights with your moaning."

Natalie shuddered and opened the closet door to show Steph the plain attire. "I don't think so. Something tells me she isn't my type."

"That's how Yvonne's closet would look if I didn't buy her what I wanted her to wear." She closed the closet and opened the door to the hallway. "Let's go up and see everybody. Yvonne said we were all meeting on the pool deck for drinks. It's time to get this party going."

"You're absolutely right," she said with growing resolve. She started out the door, but abruptly turned back and removed her watch, which she set beside the other on the vanity.

Steph was gasping for breath as they reached Deck 11 via the carpeted stairs. "I can't believe how out-of-shape I am."

"You can use this vacation to get back into an exercise routine."

"Why would I want to do that? When I'm not eating I plan to sit in a deck chair and read...and I might take the elevator from now on."

"Silly. It was just two flights."

"There's Yvonne at the rail."

Natalie spotted the familiar face, but couldn't make out the woman behind her. All she could see were long legs clad in dark green cargo shorts and sandals.

Yvonne waved and nudged the woman with her elbow.

The woman straightened up and smiled in their direction, her appearance nearly stopping Natalie in her tracks. She was tall and slim, with dark brown hair no longer than an inch *anywhere on her head*, and her white shirt hung open over a black tank top. "Are you sure that's a woman?" she asked Steph, trying not to move her lips as she fixed a smile on her face.

"Be nice." Steph slipped her arm around Yvonne's waist and turned to make the introductions.

Natalie didn't wait. "You must be Kelly."

"Guilty," she said, proffering her hand, her crystal blue eyes fixed firmly onto Natalie's. "And that makes you Natalie. I'm glad you decided to come along."

"Yes...yes, thank you," Natalie stammered. "I appreciate your offer to share a cabin."

"It's not much, but I think we'll have plenty of room. Besides, I can't imagine we'll be staying in when there's so much to do on the ship."

Natalie was rapidly planning all the things she would do to keep busy. Hanging out with Didi and Pamela didn't seem like such a bad idea after all. "And so many ports. I bet we hardly see each other."

"Except we'll be like the cows that come back to the barn every night for dinner."

A delightful visual, Natalie thought.

A waiter stopped to offer frozen drinks in commemorative glasses.

"This round's on me," Kelly said cheerfully. "I recommend the rum runner. That's the red one."

Natalie plucked one from the tray and raised it in a toast. "To good times."

"And new friends," Kelly replied.

Kelly tucked in her shirttail and zipped her chinos, which hung loosely on her waist. The pants were holdovers from when a knee injury had forced her to take a break from running. She had gained eight pounds in twelve weeks, but had lost it quickly when she returned to her exercise routine.

Giving up on her cowlick, she stepped out onto the balcony to wait for Natalie, who was dressing for dinner in the bathroom. How she managed to get organized in that tiny space was a mystery, but Kelly appreciated that not everyone had jettisoned modesty issues as she had after four years in the navy.

Natalie was an interesting sort, much prettier up close than she had appeared from the balcony over the atrium. Her hair was smooth and shiny, a reddish brown that set off gorgeous green eyes. Though Kelly wasn't usually big on girls in makeup, Natalie wore just the right amount, highlighting her natural features instead of redrawing them. She had a generally trim figure, but on closer inspection, curvaceous hips and high, round breasts. Not that Kelly noticed.

They were off to an awkward start, it seemed. After their meeting by the pool, Natalie had clung to Steph as if they hadn't already spent the whole day together. Even during the lifeboat drill, she made small talk with her ex rather than taking the opportunity to get acquainted. It was hard not to wonder if she found something about Kelly off-putting...which had to be her appearance, since there was nothing else.

It was a common reaction, one Kelly had accepted years ago as a consequence of her choice to buck the norm and be comfortable in her own skin. Even as a child she had resisted her family's efforts to dress her like other girls, going so far as to cut her own hair. The latter earned her punishment, which she had gladly endured to preserve her self-image. Still, reactions of people like Kim at check-in and Natalie always stung a bit at first.

Natalie emerged from the bathroom in crisp linen pants and a sleeveless top. She tied a long-sleeved knit top around her shoulders and stepped into a pair of sandals. Her feet matched her hands, long and graceful, with bright red polish on the nails. "Are you ready?"

"Sure. You look very nice."

Their eyes met briefly before Natalie looked about for her purse. "Thank you. I brought things I could mix and match so I wouldn't have to wear exactly the same thing twice."

"I'm sure we'll all be wearing the same things," Kelly answered, thinking she would have to wash clothes every four days or go naked. "And even when I put on something different, it'll probably look a lot like what I had on the day before."

"I think Didi and Pamela brought enough to change five times a day without wearing the same thing twice. I can't imagine where they put it all."

"I saw Pamela out on the balcony. I didn't realize they were right next door."

Natalie huffed. "It's one of those cosmic jokes God likes to play on Natalie Chatham."

"If it's any consolation, I don't snore, take up a lot of space, leave my stuff sitting out or hog the bathroom. In fact, I'm a lot like a cocker spaniel, except I don't get my ears wet when I drink." She appreciated the small smile the witticism earned her.

"I will try not to do those things either...except when it comes to taking up a lot of space. I've used every empty drawer and hanger, and my stuff is all over the bathroom."

"It's all right with me." She held the door for Natalie to walk into the hallway. She followed single-file down the narrow corridor to the mid-ship stairwell, where they descended to the main dining room on Deck 5. The others were already seated at a round table by the window.

As they walked through the dining room, they passed the odd pair Kelly had seen earlier. Kelly nodded a greeting to the younger woman, and noticed her red-haired companion beaming at Natalie, who walked past oblivious.

"Sorry we're late," Natalie said, reaching for the chair next to Steph.

Kelly glanced out the window, where the sky was ablaze from the setting sun. Natalie's view was partially blocked by the drapes. "Sit here, Natalie. The view's better."

Natalie smiled shyly and took the offered seat.

"Nice pants," Didi said, eyeing her chinos. "Thirty-two long?"

"Thirty-one regular," she cracked, not missing Didi's condescension over her wearing men's pants. "Don't start with me on fashion. Everything I know, I learned in the navy."

"Oh, how interesting!" Pamela said. "Were you on a ship like this one?"

"I didn't spend much time at sea, and never on a lady like this…ship, I mean. I was stationed at the air base in Key West for most of my tour."

"What did you do?" Steph and Yvonne poked each other in the ribs after they asked the same question at once.

"I was in the Sea Bees, the construction arm. Mostly I helped put up buildings on base. And I had a six-month tour in Dubai working on an airstrip."

Natalie looked at her with curiosity. "It must have been disappointing to join the navy and spend the whole time working on something that didn't have anything to do with the ocean."

Kelly shook her linen napkin and draped it across her lap as she scooted forward in the chair. Her head twisted from side to side as she addressed everyone at the table. Only Didi seemed indifferent to her response. "Not at all. I'd just finished my associate degree in construction engineering and it seemed like a good fit. I might have made a career out of it if my dad hadn't

21

gotten sick. I came home to help run his company—he was a general contractor—but then he died a few years ago and I sold out my half to my brother and moved to Rochester."

"Now there's a novel idea," Didi said. "Selling half of a business to a partner."

Natalie shook her finger across the table. "You promised to park it."

Didi threw up her hands. "Sorry."

Kelly recalled what Yvonne had told her about Didi wanting to buy Natalie's half of the business, and she regretted her choice of words. "This weather really takes me back to those years in Key West. It sure was hot in the summer, but I didn't miss that snow at all come January."

Didi groaned and related the mess they'd had this morning getting out of Rochester. As she spoke, Kelly chuckled to herself to realize she and Pamela had changed clothes for the sail-away party and again for dinner.

Through dinner, the six women chatted amiably about their plans, not only for the ship, but in the various ports. Kelly was glad to hear that Yvonne was up for pretty much anything in the water. Steph said she might consider snorkeling from the beach, but not from a boat. Didi, Pamela and Natalie wanted nothing to do with the water, other than to lie beside it in the sun.

"Would you like to try my crème brûlée?" she asked Natalie, who was picking over her chocolate torte. "You don't seem too happy with yours, and this is way too much for me."

"Are you sure you don't mind?"

Kelly pushed the dish toward her. "Help yourself."

Natalie's face lit up as she took a taste. "This is way better than what I ordered."

"Finish it." Kelly poured Natalie another cup of decaffeinated coffee from the decanter and watched as she added cream and artificial sweetener. It pleased her to make Natalie happy. "Does anyone have plans for tonight? I think there's a magician performing at eight o'clock."

"I think I'm going to hit the casino," Yvonne said. "I don't know how the rest of you are even awake."

"Steph and I are going to the shopping gallery to look at swimsuits," Natalie said.

Didi pushed back and waited for Pamela to stand and take her hand. "We're going back to our cabin for a private party."

Kelly noticed from the corner of her eye that Natalie's lips had tightened. "As your nearest neighbor, all I can say is I hope you're serious about the private part."

The indignant look on Didi's face was priceless, but it was nothing compared to the satisfied smirk on Natalie's.

Chapter 3

Natalie snaked a hand out from underneath the comforter to scratch her nose, and was jarred at the unfamiliar feel of her bed. Rolling onto her back, she oriented herself to her unusual surroundings—a twin bed in a stateroom aboard the *Emerald Duchess*. Either the sea had calmed from the small swells that had rocked her to sleep last night, or she had grown used to the steady sway.

She sat up and blinked to adjust to the darkness, as the cabin's only light crept in from around the edges of the blackout curtain. Her roommate was gone. Surprising, since Kelly had tiptoed into the room after midnight the night before, and the digital clock now read ten after seven. If that was her idea of sharing a stateroom, Natalie was all for it.

In all honesty, she couldn't complain about Kelly. However, her secret fantasy of having a fling with her cabinmate just to show Didi she could was now officially kaput, since she wasn't attracted to that type of woman at all. Furthermore, Didi knew that and would see right through it. Still, Kelly seemed very nice, and her unusual background would make for interesting conversation during the times they might find themselves alone in the cabin.

She swung her feet out of her bed and carefully navigated the sitting area to peek outside. The sun was already up, highlighting a clear blue sky and relatively calm seas. Unable to resist, she cracked the sliding glass door to inhale the warm, humid air. It was bliss.

A pair of complimentary robes hung in the closet, and she wrapped one around her before stepping out onto the balcony. A Caribbean getaway in the middle of winter was a brilliant idea, one she would pencil into her official annual calendar, right alongside year-end inventory, tax time and the spring fashion show in New York. Not that she could afford it every year…but it was nice to dream. If Didi ever got her head on straight and realized what a comfortable life they could have in Rochester, they really could plan trips like this one regularly.

Moving the business to New York could ruin both of them. The Eighth Avenue fashion world was cutthroat. A store that failed to find its niche right out of the gate might fold in only six months and all their money would be lost. Of course, Didi had long since stopped thinking of her being part of a move to Manhattan. Two years, two months…and nine days ago, to be exact. That was the night they had broken up.

At first, Natalie thought their breakup might be a blessing in disguise, just the hiatus their relationship needed. Suddenly they seemed to get along better at work, no longer bickering about every little thing. The down side, as she quickly realized, was that she soon felt detached from her own business, since the glamorous fashion side was Didi's area of expertise, while hers was accounting and management. Without Didi's enthusiastic response to every new shipment and her flamboyant penchant for display, the boxes of stylish trapeze wraps or shirtdresses became merely units, items that were either moved or marked down on a schedule that allowed for a constant influx of fresh merchandise. For all the glamour of that, Natalie figured she might as well have been selling plumbing supplies.

Despite her sinking enthusiasm for the fashion business, she couldn't bear the idea of letting go of her life and going back to square one at age thirty-seven. Only since Pamela had emerged on the scene six months ago had she realized that the idea of starting over with another lover was every bit as daunting as carving out a new career. She wanted her life back the way it was two years ago...or maybe five or six...whenever it was she and Didi had last enjoyed one another.

She settled into the deck chair and arranged the robe to allow her legs to catch the morning sun. But no matter how much she tried to relax, it was impossible to escape the debacle her life had become, especially with the fresh memory of Didi and Pamela carrying on with their grunting and moaning last night. At these prices, a little more soundproofing would have been nice.

The sliding glass door opened and Kelly's red face appeared. "Sleep well?"

"Must have. I don't remember a thing."

Kelly's absence this morning was instantly explained as she emerged in jogging shorts, a tank top and sneakers, and balancing two cups of coffee as she closed the door behind her. "You take cream and that blue stuff, right?"

"You brought me coffee! Aren't you sweet?"

"It wasn't any trouble. I always load up on caffeine after I run, and I noticed you got coffee last night with dessert."

"I love it, especially first thing in the morning." She savored her first sip. "I hate exercise at any time, but I can't believe you'd actually get up on the first morning of vacation and hit the treadmill." It was hard not to stare at the vivid muscles in Kelly's legs and shoulders. Natalie would have bet that tank top hid a six-pack. It wasn't exactly a womanly body, but it wasn't unattractive either.

"I enjoy it. I run about three or four miles every morning, sometimes longer on the weekends. I don't mind doing the weights, but I hate treadmills. Lucky for me, they have a running track on the Promenade Deck. I lost count after fifteen laps."

Natalie shook her head in wonder. "Why am I not surprised? They have everything on this ship. Steph and I even found a movie theater last night."

"Good. Maybe we'll all see a movie this week." Kelly tipped her head back and drained her coffee. "You want me to fetch another cuppa joe before I hop in the shower?"

"No, thank you. This was great, though."

"What are you up to today?" The itinerary had them at sea all day en route to San Juan.

"I sort of agreed to go with Didi and Pamela to the spa for a— I can't believe I'm saying this—bikini wax. I made Steph promise to go with me, and if she doesn't show, I'm out of there."

Kelly laughed. "Yeah, I can see how a person might need moral support for something like that. By the way, about that so-called private party of theirs...that's why I left the room and stayed out so late."

"I heard it when I came in. Hell, the whole ship probably heard it. They sounded like a cat and dog tied together," she said, unable to hide her disdain.

"If you ask me, I think it was all for show."

"Why do you say that?"

"I don't know. It just sounded sort of fake, like it was louder than it needed to be."

Natalie felt her face burning at the idea Didi might have staged that just to humiliate her. If so, it signaled a raising of the stakes, since up to now Didi had been a lot of things— critical, condescending, demanding—but she had never been intentionally cruel.

Kelly strolled around the shaded part of the pool deck in search of a vacant chaise lounge. Unlike most passengers, she wasn't interested in getting a tan. During her years in Key West, she had seen hundreds of women who looked old beyond their years due to sun exposure. Besides, if she sat out in her cargo shorts and tank top, she would look silly when she wore something with different lines.

A woman was gathering her belongings from a deck chair as she walked by and Kelly grabbed the vacant seat. She was excited to see the face beside her, the young woman she had seen with the redhead. "Hi, I recognize you from dinner last night." She put out her hand. "Kelly Ridenour."

"G'day, mate. Jo Atkinson."

"An Aussie! What part?"

"Brisbane. You know it?"

"No, but it's on my wish list. You're a long way from home."

Jo nodded and set aside her book. "I came along with my big sister. She wanted a last hurrah before she turned fifty."

Sisters...that explained their vibe, Kelly thought. "I see you're reading the same book as one of the women in our group. She reads those all the time, and I think even her partner sneaks one every now and then." That was her way of laying her lesbian cards on the table.

Jo grinned knowingly. "I brought a whole suitcase full. I'm addicted to romance."

"So where's your girl?"

"No girl for me. My sister Julie gets them all."

"Your sister's a lesbian too?"

"That's right. There's something to that genetic business after all."

Kelly watched from behind her sunglasses as Natalie appeared on deck and spread her towel on a chair near the pool. Staring raptly as Natalie then removed her wrap to reveal a blue two-piece bathing suit, Kelly lost track of what Jo was saying. "What was that?"

"I said the pretty girls always get the pretty girls." Jo took a swig of frozen lemonade through a curly straw. "See for yourself."

In the moment she had turned away, the red-haired sister had zoomed in and taken the open chair next to Natalie.

"Julie's never met a stranger. I tell you, she could give flirting lessons to anyone."

"So she doesn't have a girlfriend either?"

"She has dozens."

"Dozens?" Suddenly alarmed that Natalie might let herself get swept up by some Aussie nymphomaniac on the make, Kelly had the silly urge to run and whisper a word of warning in her ear. Common sense prevailed and she chided herself for her overreaction. If Natalie wanted to make friends with a pretty lady on board, she had every right to do so. "So how come you don't have a girl? Surely Julie leaves a few here and there."

Jo shrugged. "There's one I like, but I don't know if she likes me. Well...I guess she does, just maybe not the same way. She probably just thinks of me as her friend." The lack of confidence was evident from her dismal look.

"Or maybe she's wondering why you don't ask her out."

"Because I'm a chicken." She picked up her book. "I live in these."

Julie suddenly appeared in front of them and snatched up her sister's drink for a hefty swig. "It's bloody boiling out there."

Jo made the introductions. "Should I point out that your ten minutes in the sun was nine minutes too long?"

"I know, but she was cute." She looked at Kelly and tilted her head in Natalie's direction. "Don't you think she's cute?"

"I think she's..." She spun around to look again at Natalie again as Steph took the empty seat beside her. "I think she's very cute."

"Is this the life or what?" Steph asked as she scribbled her signature for her Bloody Mary. Her swimsuit was one piece in a green and yellow floral design. "Yvonne signed on at the Internet café and read that Rochester got four more inches of snow last night."

Natalie clinked her glass of orange juice to Steph's. "I was sitting out on the balcony this morning thinking I'd like to do this every year."

"We could, you know. You can sell out to Didi, and all of us could cruise until your money runs out."

"Very funny."

"Seriously, Nat. I don't know why you don't just move on. You don't even like what you're doing anymore at the store. Let her have it and find something else."

"Like what? I gave up a great job and put everything I had into the store."

"But it was always Didi's store, especially once it started turning a profit. Before that, she needed your investment. Now that you're paid up and splitting the profits, she has both the cash and the cachet."

"And I'm nothing. Is that what you're saying? After eight years of working my ass off?"

"You're not nothing. I think you proved to everyone that you know how to make a business successful. But now you're unhappy at the store, so why stay there? You could probably go back to Kodak if you wanted to, or even start a business of your own."

"I could be happy again at the store. I like what I'm doing. I just don't like the way things are with Didi...and Pamela."

Steph leaned back and pulled a bright yellow visor low on her brow. "I hate to be the one to tell you this, but that particular ship has sailed. Besides, you were feeling perfectly fine about everything after you guys broke up until Pamela came on the scene. That's just normal jealousy. It'll pass."

Natalie had tried over and over to tell herself the same thing. If she really stopped to think about it, she would have to admit that moving into her own house in Corn Hill, a fixer-upper Victorian that Steph had helped her find, had been a refreshing change from the doldrums her life with Didi had become. At first, she had harbored hope of meeting someone new, someone who didn't feel the need to critique her every move or choice, as Didi had since practically the moment they met. But after a few months had passed, she realized she was lonely and nostalgic for their familiar companionship, if not for their intimacy. They started spending more time together away from work, having dinner and going shopping together, and Natalie had even started trying on the notion of them getting back together. Then suddenly there was Pamela and her ambivalence turned into the jealousy Steph had just described.

"How's your roomie?"

The question broke Natalie's train of thought and she automatically looked across the deck to where she had seen Kelly chatting with the young Australian woman, the sister of that pretty redhead who had stopped by to introduce herself. "She's fine…nice enough. She brought me coffee this morning."

"Oh, really?" Steph straightened up and shifted toward her with interest.

She waved at Kelly, who was looking in their direction. "No big deal. Apparently, she runs laps around the Promenade Deck first thing in the morning, and she grabbed an extra cup when she got hers." Natalie didn't volunteer that Kelly had prepared it just the way she liked it.

"Yvonne likes her a lot. So do I. There's something about her I can't quite put my finger on, but I bet she'd be fun to hang out with."

"What do you mean something about her?"

"I don't know. She's just sort of out there, like 'what you see is exactly what you get.' No pretense, no trying to please anybody. I liked how she came back at Didi about her pants, like she didn't give a flip about what Didi thought."

"But seriously, what kind of woman wears men's pants?"

"You tell me. Is it boxers or briefs?"

Natalie felt her face redden. "I wouldn't have any idea, and I don't aim to find out."

Steph shrugged. "I think she's kind of sexy…in a raw, animalistic way."

"Since when? She practically looks like a man. And she makes no attempt at all to make people think otherwise. At least she could wear earrings or something so you don't have to look twice to figure out what she is. I half expected to find aftershave in her toiletry bag."

"You went through her toiletry bag?"

Now she knew she was blushing. Her habit of saying exactly what she was thinking had been her downfall for as long as she could remember. "I couldn't help it. I had to know how a woman could pack all her cosmetics in one little bag."

"I think that's part of her appeal. Yvonne's like that too. It took me ten years to convince her that it was just fine for a physical therapist to wear fingernail polish once in a while."

"But no one's going to look at Yvonne and think she's a man. She has a stylish haircut, and she's not afraid to put a little color on her eyes. And she doesn't buy her clothes in the men's department."

Steph shook her head dismissively. "Listen to yourself. You sound like Didi."

"I do not!"

"Do too. What difference does it make what somebody looks like if she's happy with herself? I'd like to be happy about this spare tire around my gut. Life would be so much easier if I just accepted it and bought bigger clothes."

"Quiet. Here she comes."

Kelly stepped in front of them, blocking the sun from Natalie's face as she tipped her sunglasses onto her forehead and smiled. "This weather really sucks, doesn't it?"

Steph and Natalie laughed and nodded in agreement.

"Be careful not to get burned. With that breeze off the ocean, you might not realize how hot it is out here."

"We won't be out here much longer," Steph said. "Did Yvonne tell you we're meeting for lunch at the terrace buffet?"

Kelly nodded. "I'll be there." She looked directly at Natalie and smiled again before dropping her shades and sauntering off.

Steph rumbled a knowing chuckle. "Did you see that look? She was flirting with you."

"She was not." Natalie had gotten the same impression, if

only for a second or two.

"Was too."

"Well, that's just too bad. She's not my type."

Chapter 4

Kelly strolled through the terrace in search of familiar faces. Finally, she spotted Steph and Yvonne, already eating at a large table just barely out of the sun. She hated to admit that it mattered, but she was glad to see Yvonne dressed in casual shorts and a T-shirt. At least she wasn't the only one in the group who wasn't a fashion plate. "Where is everyone?"

"Natalie is trying to decide what she wants," Yvonne said, her plate piled high with chicken strips, veggies, bread and dessert.

"I told her to do what I did and get some of everything," Steph added. Her platter was overflowing with numerous bite-sized samples.

Unaccustomed to a heavy midday meal, Kelly opted for the salad buffet, where Natalie was poring over the selection. Before she realized it, she caught herself studying Natalie—again. She had covered her swimsuit with shorts and a wrap, but that didn't hide her womanly figure. Very nice legs for someone who claimed to be exercise-averse. The other thing she had noticed was her hands, long and graceful with short polished nails. Lesbian hands for sure.

All morning Kelly had felt bad about bringing up Didi and Pamela's noisy night. Natalie was clearly annoyed by the news, and that made perfect sense. No one wanted to hear about her ex making love with someone else. Unfortunately, there was probably no way to apologize without making it worse.

She stepped up behind Natalie as she was reaching to serve herself. "I wouldn't if I were you," she said, placing her hand gently on Natalie's forearm.

"It's Waldorf salad. That's my favorite."

"I know, but it's…" She lowered her voice so the staff wouldn't overhear. "Anything with mayo is risky, especially on a buffet line, because it sits out for so long."

Natalie's face fell to a disappointed frown.

"Trust me on this. The last thing you want on a cruise ship is to get sick."

"You have a point." She eyed the sesame-noodle salad on Kelly's plate. "Where did you get that?"

Kelly walked with her around the display, pointing out some of the unusual dishes. "I don't eat out a lot, but when I do, I tend to choose things I'll never fix at home."

"Do you cook?"

"Does using a microwave count?"

Natalie looked at her incredulously. "Under no circumstances."

"Then I'd have to say no." She topped off her plate with cantaloupe and pineapple slices, and turned toward the table. "My domestic skill set runs more along home renovations."

"That could come in handy, but I can't believe someone who runs every day isn't more careful about what she puts in her body."

Kelly wasn't sure how to reply. She doubted Natalie really

cared that her evening meals usually consisted of pasta with sauce from a jar and a cold beer or two, which gave her energy for her morning run. "What can I say? A girl has to have a vice or two, don't you think?"

"At least."

She was disappointed when they reached the table and Natalie chose a seat on the far side.

Natalie addressed Steph. "Did you see they're having an art auction? I was thinking of going up there later and looking over what they have."

Yvonne nodded vigorously. "The gallery's right next to the casino. Believe me, there are some serious art buyers on board. They were out this morning snapping pictures on their iPhones."

"Were they getting a signal?" Steph asked. It was obvious she was interested in more than the art.

"No, honey. No one gets a signal out here."

"Your Blackberry doesn't work on the ship?" Natalie asked.

"No," she said glumly.

"Which means she can't work," Yvonne said, poking her partner in the ribs. "I love cruising!"

"That's big talk from you. You're already turning me into a casino widow."

Yvonne grinned and batted her eyes innocently. "I have a system for beating the house...I guess that would be beating the ship. I started with a hundred bucks and played for almost an hour. I made about thirty bucks, so I put the first hundred back in my pocket and played with just the thirty. Now I'm up to sixty-five."

"You'll pay for your trip if you keep that up," Natalie said.

"Don't encourage her," Steph said. "I realized this morning that if she's going to live in the casino, my six books aren't going to last me for twelve days."

Remembering what Jo had said about her suitcase full of books, Kelly spoke up. "Hey, I talked to somebody this morning who says she's addicted to reading those romance books you like.

Maybe she'll swap you a few."

"Was that the girl you were talking to on the pool deck?" Steph asked.

"Yeah, her name's Jo. She's from Australia. And that redhead with her is her sister, Julie."

"I saw her. She's a hottie. I think she hit on Natalie."

Natalie appeared to choke on her drink. "She did not. She just came over and said hello."

"I loved her accent. Didn't you find her attractive?"

Kelly waited raptly for Natalie's response to Steph's obvious goading. Julie had certainly seemed interested, but had given no clue as to whether or not it was reciprocated.

"She was okay, but I could hardly understand a word she said."

Yvonne laughed heartily. "I bet. It hasn't been all that long since you couldn't understand New Yorkers."

"Now don't you start making fun of the way I talk." Natalie tossed a grape at Yvonne. "I'll have you know I now talk faster than anybody in Pascagoula and they can't understand me anymore."

Didi and Pamela arrived and took the last two chairs. Their plates were piled high with Waldorf salad.

Kelly glanced at Natalie and found her looking back, a hint of a smile on her face. "That looks delicious."

"I hope I like it," Didi said. "It's tricky to get a good Waldorf salad outside of…well, the Waldorf."

Natalie rolled her eyes at that, and Kelly shot her a wink.

"Did you guys hear the screaming this morning when Steph and Natalie got their bikini wax?" Didi asked. "I know, you probably thought it was the ship's horn."

Steph covered her face with her hands. "I thought I was going to pass out."

"You got a wax?" Yvonne's face lit up with obvious excitement.

"Just around the edges."

"Pamela and I got the French, which, as you may know is *almost everything*."

Kelly glanced at Natalie for her reaction. She wasn't happy.

"And what about you, Nat?" Didi asked teasingly. "Where did you stop?"

"None of your business." Her voice had an edge that said she wasn't playing.

"Oh, come on. You can tell us. We won't tell a soul. Where did you stop?"

"Who says I stopped?"

"These are very nice," Natalie said as she perused the stack of paintings. "I wish I could afford something. My house needs some color."

"Your house needs more than that," Steph said. "Like a whole new kitchen...bathrooms...to say nothing of closets. Didn't Victorian people have any clothes?"

"Listen to you. You talked me into buying that house in the first place. Now you're telling me everything that's wrong with it." Natalie was only yanking Steph's chain. She had known full well the house needed lots of work, and at first she had looked forward to doing it. Then as the situation at work deteriorated, she had lost interest in the project. In fact, she had lost interest in pretty much everything.

Even the idea of a Caribbean cruise over New Year's had failed to excite her at first—until Steph said that Didi and Pamela were coming along. She couldn't bear to think her best friends would be out there sailing through the islands with her ex and her new lover. That was wrong. Breaking up and finding a new girlfriend was one thing, but Didi wasn't getting custody of her friends.

"Something eating you, Nat?"

Only two people called her Nat—Steph and Didi.

When she didn't answer, Steph pulled her by the hand into the corner. "Didi got under your skin at lunch, didn't she?"

Natalie sighed and set her jaw in frustration. "How can she tease me about something so personal with Pamela sitting right there? It's like she doesn't have respect for either one of us."

"You know Didi. Nothing is ever off-limits. She never, ever pulls a punch, and she just doesn't see that it bothers people."

"That's because whoever programmed her left out the sensitivity chip."

"So would you mind telling me why you're still so concerned about what she thinks? I don't understand why anyone would want to be with someone who thinks of herself first every single minute, whose first words are always something about how that color you're wearing isn't flattering to your hair, or that your shoes went out of style six years ago."

"That's not how it felt to me. She always helped me feel good about myself. When I walked out the door with her approval, I knew I looked like a million bucks. I felt glamorous and sophisticated. Take my word for it—I never got anything like that in Mississippi."

"Except from Theresa."

The parallel between Didi and Natalie's first lover was inescapable. Theresa Payne had been a graduate student at Ole Miss, and had swept Natalie off her feet with her beauty and class. "I can't help it, Steph. That's just the kind of woman I'm attracted to. And I've got a lot invested with Didi already."

"Are you telling me your type of woman is somebody who puts you down all the time?"

"Of course not. That's how Didi is with everybody. She's not trying to be mean."

"You want to know the truth? If it weren't for you, there's no way Yvonne and I would have Didi for a friend. We barely made it through that first year you guys were together."

Natalie's relationship with Didi was complicated, but love was love and she couldn't simply will it away. "Let me ask you something, Steph. Are you going to love Yvonne for the rest of your life?"

"What kind of question is that?"

"Just answer it."

"Okay, the answer is yes."

"What if something happens and you don't want to be

together anymore? Will you stop loving her?"

Steph gave her a puzzled look. "I can't imagine not loving her."

"Exactly. Some people you love for life. You can't help yourself, and no matter what happens you're always going to feel that way."

"Are you telling me that you're never going to get over Didi?"

"I don't know, but I know I'm not going to stop loving her." She looked around to make sure no one could hear them. "I hate to see her making a fool of herself with Pamela. What twenty-eight-year-old wants somebody fourteen years older than her? How's she going to feel in a few years when Didi starts going through the change just as Pamela's hitting her stride? I'm telling you, this whole thing's going to pass, and when it does, Didi's going to be hurt."

Steph shook her head. "I'd worry about Didi if I thought she was head over heels with Pamela. But we both know better. Pamela's just a trophy, and if Didi gets hurt, it's her own fault."

"I don't care whose fault it is. I don't want to see her get humiliated. We were this close"—she held her index finger and thumb only millimeters apart—"to getting back together when Pamela started coming into the store twice a week. The next thing I knew, Didi was going to New York every weekend. How do I know Pamela isn't just trying to get control of the store? That could happen if I sold Didi my half."

"But it isn't your job to save Didi from herself. You have to look after Natalie, because no one else is doing that."

Natalie looked up to see Didi and Pamela heading their way in the art gallery. "Speak of the devil."

"You said it, not me."

"Hello, ladies," Didi said, looking around the gallery. "Where's your roommate, Nat? Don't tell me. She's down below working on the engines."

"Very funny," Natalie said, mentally correcting her earlier defense of Didi. She could be mean sometimes. "I'll have you

40

know Kelly's very nice."

"I don't know about nice, but she certainly looks strong." Didi mockingly flexed her bicep.

"I kind of like that look on her," Pamela said. "It doesn't work for everyone, but Kelly carries it off pretty well. She's not bulked up or anything, just defined."

"I suppose," Didi conceded, shrugging.

Natalie was momentarily shocked at Didi's acquiescence. She rarely budged from her opinions, especially when it came to how someone looked.

Pamela went on, "I might talk to her and see if there's something she thinks I ought to be doing for my upper arms."

"I'm sure she'd be glad to show you her workout," Natalie said. "As I said, she's very nice." She glared at Didi before spinning and walking away.

Kelly gazed out from her balcony at an island in the distance. She couldn't have asked for a more beautiful day, a more comfortable stateroom or a more relaxing atmosphere. If anything was lacking so far on the cruise, it was companionship. She had hoped to feel more a part of the group than she did, but it was apparent the other women already had their preferred alliances. In particular, Natalie seemed attached at the hip to her friend Steph, which left little opportunity for getting to know the only other single person in their group. At least she could count on Yvonne, but she had no interest at all in the casino. It was going to take a concerted effort to break into the circle.

The sliding glass door onto Didi and Pamela's balcony *thunked* as if it were thrown open.

"Come out here and get some air," Pamela shouted. "Maybe that'll help."

"Oh, God," Didi said. "I'm going to be so sick."

Kelly heard an agonizing moan as Didi went back inside.

"Hurry up in there. I've got to go too," Pamela said.

The Waldorf salad? Kelly went to the rail and leaned out to find Pamela drawing deep breaths of ocean air. "Are you guys okay?"

"No. Something wretched just came out of nowhere and hit both of us at the same time."

"What?"

"You name it. Vomiting...diarrhea. Didi says she's sweating like a whore in church."

Almost four hours had passed since lunch, plenty of time for tainted mayonnaise to work its way into their digestive tracts. "It's probably just a bacterial infection from something you ate. Is anyone else sick?"

"Not that I know of." Pamela clutched her abdomen and grimaced. "Hurry up!" She ran inside and Didi appeared at the rail.

"I was just telling Pamela that it sounds like you guys might have a bacterial infection. You should probably just stay in your cabin for a day or two. It'll pass."

"Believe me, it's already passing."

"Do you want me to call the ship's doctor? I bet they have something to make you feel better."

"The person I'm going to call is my travel agent. I want my money back." She doubled over and yelled back into the room. "It's my turn again."

Pamela reappeared, looking green around the gills. "I think we need some medicine."

Kelly quickly paged through the ship's directory, located the number for medical services and placed a call. "They're sending someone up, and said for you to stay put. I guess they're worried about you being contagious." It was possible they both had picked up a bug—stomach maladies were common on cruise ships because people didn't always wash their hands—but smart money was on the Waldorf salad, especially if no one else in their group turned up sick.

From inside the stateroom, she heard steady retching next door, interspersed with occasional groans and angry outbursts.

Natalie burst through the doorway, her face a mask of worry. "What's going on next door? I just saw the nurse coming out of there."

Kelly jumped up and put her finger to her lips. "Are you feeling okay?"

"I'm fine. Why?"

"I think it was the Waldorf salad. Didi and Pamela are both sick."

A loud groan next door was followed by a curse word and another retching sound.

"Are they going to be okay?"

"I'm sure they'll be fine in a few hours. They're both pretty miserable right now." She led Natalie onto the deck and leaned over. "Pamela?"

The younger woman emerged onto the balcony. "We're confined to quarters for seventy-two hours. That's three whole days!"

"You're going to miss San Juan!" Natalie wailed.

"And St. Thomas and Tortola," Pamela added. "But they gave us each a voucher for a future cruise at half price."

"Which we'll use next year if we live," Didi said miserably from the doorway.

"What will you do about meals?"

"They're going to bring us room service, but I told her I'd kill anybody that showed up at our door with food tonight."

The two of them jammed the doorway as they raced one another to the bathroom.

"Poor things," Natalie said. "They're going to go stir-crazy."

"No kidding. We probably should be careful about being out on the balcony when they're out there. If it turns out they're contagious, we could get sick too." Kelly lowered her voice. "But I think it was probably the mayo."

"Then I have you to thank for saving me from myself."

Kelly gave her a sheepish look. "I feel a little guilty for not saying something when they showed up with their lunch."

"Don't worry about it. For what it's worth, Didi wouldn't have listened. In fact, she probably would have gone back for more just to emphasize the point."

"Say, I was looking in the daily guide and saw the new James

Bond movie is playing tonight at the theater. It starts right after dinner. You think anyone would want to go?"

"That actually sounds pretty good. You want me to call Steph?"

"Sure. It would be fun for all of us to do something together." And even better if Didi and Pamela were confined to quarters, she thought. Maybe Natalie would loosen up a little.

Chapter 5

On her second morning aboard ship, Natalie knew immediately where she was when she awoke. Her biggest clue was Kelly standing at the foot of her bed, coffee in hand, flushed and sweaty from her run.

"We're in San Juan. It's gorgeous out there."

Natalie sat up and stretched, trying not to think what her hair must look like. "You brought me coffee again. I'm going to have to figure out how I can pay you back for this."

"No need. It's really no trouble at all. I thought about letting you sleep, but I have a feeling the captain's going to break in any minute and announce that the gangway's open."

She swung her feet out of bed and reached for her robe. "I don't know what's happening today. I was supposed to go shopping with Didi and Pamela, but they can't leave the ship. I don't want to go by myself."

"Do you like to ride? Bikes, I mean. I'm signed up for a bike tour. We're supposed to go about ten miles on some tropical road where we can look at the scenery, and then we end up on a beach to swim for a couple of hours." Kelly had set down the coffee and was loading fruit and bread into her backpack.

"I don't think I'm in shape for something like that."

"I bet you are. The brochure said it was a leisurely ride."

Though it sounded interesting, Natalie didn't want to make a fool of herself by getting winded after the first half mile. Then Kelly would feel obligated to hang back and ride slowly with her, when someone in such great shape might otherwise be leading the pack. "I think I'd better pass...unless they have those little sidecars where one person does all the work and the other one sits on her tail like a slug."

She went out onto the balcony with her coffee and was taken aback to see another massive cruise ship docked alongside theirs.

Kelly stepped out behind her. "Those guys pulled in while I was out running this morning."

"That ship is enormous."

"We're actually bigger than they are. You'll be able to see that when you get off." She sat in the deck chair and propped her feet on the rail. "If you want to do something else today, I'll cancel my bike tour. I toured a couple of these islands when I was stationed at Key West, so it isn't like I'd be missing something I hadn't seen before."

She was tempted by the kind offer, but seriously doubted Kelly would enjoy the sort of sightseeing and shopping she had in mind. "I couldn't let you do that. I'm sure I can tag along with Steph and Yvonne. Lord knows they're used to having me as their shadow by now. I've been following them around for almost twenty years."

"I can tell you guys have known each other a long time. You and Steph especially."

46

"We all met at Ole Miss when I was a sophomore. Steph's from Memphis, and Yvonne was there from Rochester on a softball scholarship because they hired her high school coach." As she spoke, she realized she hadn't told her getting-to-know-each-other story to anyone in several years. She and Didi had enjoyed a vibrant social life, but Natalie had never felt particularly close to anyone other than Steph and Yvonne, certainly not close enough to share the details about her struggles to fit in back in Mississippi and the rift she had caused with her family when she left home for good.

"I wouldn't have pegged you for a softball groupie."

"Believe me, I wasn't. But I went to the games with Steph because Yvonne was her"—she used her fingers to make air quotes—"'best friend.' I was a clueless idiot back then. They had to hit me over the head before I realized that meant they were sleeping together."

Kelly chuckled. "I think all of us went through a clueless phase. Thank God I figured it out before I joined the navy or I would have been like a kid in a candy store. Half the women on my base were lesbians, but at least I knew enough to lay low and not get caught."

"That must have been tricky."

"It was, but we had our little underground. Everybody knew who was gay, but as long as you didn't hit on somebody who wasn't, they left you alone."

The captain's voice blared over the loudspeaker with the official welcome to Puerto Rico.

Kelly finished her coffee and stretched. "I suppose I should get my shower so I can go off and get hot and sweaty again. You need the bathroom?"

"No, go ahead." When Kelly disappeared inside, she entertained the idea of taking her up on the offer of a bike tour after all. Steph and Yvonne would probably appreciate a day on their own for a change. But again she imagined herself huffing and puffing along the road, her legs crying out in agony. Not only would that be embarrassing, it probably wouldn't be much fun for either of them. She had given up active pastimes when she met Didi, whose idea of recreation was flicking her wrist when she presented her credit card.

No sooner had Didi entered her thoughts than the sliding door opened on the balcony beside her. The deep groan told her it had been a miserable night.

"Hey, over there," she called.

"At least you didn't say good morning. I might have had to kill you."

"Are you guys still sick?" She went to the rail and peeked around the divider.

"I think the worst is over. Pamela drank a whole pitcher of orange juice by herself while I was in the shower. Selfish bitch."

Natalie smiled to herself, thinking Didi was back to normal. "What are you two going to do today?"

"We're going to stay in and fight over the bathroom. What other choice do we have?"

"Who are you talking to?" Pamela asked as she came out on the balcony.

"Natalie...though why she's here on the ship when she's free to leave and wander through beautiful San Juan is beyond me."

It was hard not to feel sorry for the two of them. Not only were they recovering from a horrid bout of vomiting and diarrhea, they were probably on each other's last nerve from being stuck in their tiny stateroom for the last eighteen hours. And that was only going to get worse. "I guess I'll go out on my own. Do you want me to pick up something for you?"

"You mean something like a T-shirt that says 'My friends went to San Juan and all I got was food poisoning'?"

"I'm really sorry you're going to miss the island. Maybe you can come back when you use your half-off cruise voucher."

"They probably only give those to people they think are going to die."

Natalie chuckled, appreciating Didi's macabre sense of humor. "No, yours is half off, so they're giving you a fifty-fifty chance. I'll look for something nice. You want me to ask Steph to lend you any of her books when she finishes?"

"They're supposed to bring us some movies today for the DVD player," Pamela said. "I'm going back to bed."

"Where will you go, Nat?"

"Walk around the city, I guess. Kelly invited me to come along on a bike tour, but I didn't think I could keep up with her."

"A bike with Spike?"

"Behave yourself. I'll have you know Kelly's very nice"—she lowered her voice dramatically—"though I don't get that look of hers at all."

Didi shuddered visibly. "You can say that again. What self-respecting lesbian goes for that?"

"I told Steph you might as well be with a man," she whispered, and they both snickered.

"Hey, do you remember that time we both got the stomach flu?"

Natalie nodded grimly. "At least we had two bathrooms."

Didi checked over her shoulder to see that Pamela was out of earshot. "What I remember most about that was how you went up and down the stairs waiting on me, and you were just as sick as I was."

"That's because listening to you complain so much was worse than being sick."

"I know, but Pamela's useless. All she thinks about is her own misery."

To say that Didi was high-maintenance was an understatement, but Natalie hadn't minded all that much. Didi had spoiled her in other ways, buying her expensive jewelry and beautiful clothes. "I'd help if I could, but there's a note on your door that says you have the plague."

"Figures. Look, if they have to bury us at sea, have them put me in that cranberry Halston dress. I'd hate not having a chance to wear it."

"Forget it. I'm keeping that dress for myself. Besides, they'll probably have to burn you with the bedclothes." It felt good to laugh with Didi. They didn't have much time alone anymore to

49

really talk.

"Have fun today, Nat. If you want to talk later, just knock on the wall and I'll come out."

"Feel better. I'm really sorry you can't come." A small part of her felt guilty for not passing on Kelly's warning about the Waldorf salad, and she compounded that by wishing Pamela had been the only one who had gotten sick. Then she and Didi could have had the day together in San Juan.

Kelly descended the stairs behind Natalie toward Deck 2, where throngs of passengers lined up to exit the ship. She was mesmerized by the sway of her hips and disappointed when they reached the bottom step. "Last chance to come along on the bike tour."

"Thanks, but I think walking through Old San Juan is more my speed."

"Give yourself plenty of time at the fort. That's the most interesting part if you ask me." She wasn't sure what to make of the fact that Natalie had declined her offer to cancel her ride and join her for a walking tour, only to accept the same invitation from Steph and Yvonne. Ostensibly, she didn't want to ask Kelly to give up her plans, but Kelly guessed it was more than that.

For whatever reason, Natalie seemed to be keeping her distance, especially when the others were around. She was friendly enough when they were alone in their stateroom, but clearly preferred the company of her close friends. Some people were like that, Kelly thought. Perhaps she was shy, or took a long time to loosen up around new people. At least they got along well enough to pass the time.

Steph and Yvonne were waiting on the dock. "Are you coming with us?" Steph asked.

"I have a bike tour," she answered. *And I wasn't invited.*

"We should have done that," Yvonne said. "A little exercise would have been nice."

"Walking is exercise," Natalie said. "Besides, Steph and I would never be able to keep up with you and Kelly."

At the end of the dock, a woman stood holding a sign for the bike tour. From the looks of things, the small bus was almost full.

"Here's my ride," Kelly said. "You guys have a good time."

She was looking forward to her bike tour, but couldn't shake her feeling of disappointment at going off on her own. The whole idea of this cruise had been to make new friends but it was clear she wasn't fitting in with the others, at least not with anyone other than Yvonne. And while she hated to admit it, that familiar desolate feeling from junior high, when she was on the outside of the popular girls' clique looking in, was inescapable. It was ironic that the navy had been the only place where she felt she really belonged, and she had lived the whole time under the radar of "Don't Ask, Don't Tell."

"Hey, mate."

She looked up to see Jo clearing the seat beside her. Like Kelly, she was dressed casually in shorts, a T-shirt and sneakers. "Hey. You by yourself?"

"Oh, yeah. Riding a bicycle isn't exactly Julie's idea of a good time. Shopping and sightseeing. That's all she cares about."

"Sounds familiar. That's what my roommate's doing too."

"That's the pretty girl with the dark brown hair. Natalie... right?"

"Yeah."

"Not your girlfriend?"

"No, I just met her a couple of days ago. Friend of a friend. She came along at the last minute."

"That's good. I think Julie's hot for her. Said she hoped to hook up with her today in town."

Kelly got a sinking feeling in the pit of her stomach. "Hmmm." She hadn't meant to say that aloud.

"She's not moving in on your sweetie, is she?"

"Oh, no! Of course not. It's just that..." Just that what? "Natalie's sort of hung up on somebody else, I think."

"That won't stop Julie. She's one of those 'love the one you're with' types."

"Hmmm."

"What is it, mate? You're having me on, aren't you?"

"What do you mean?"

"You're sweet on her."

Kelly had to think about it. "Maybe a little."

"So how come you're here and she's not?"

"I asked her to come, but she turned me down. I get the feeling I'm not her type."

"What's her type?"

Kelly made a face. "Probably somebody like Julie."

Jo nodded. "Just like I told you yesterday. The pretty girls get all the diamonds. The rest of us get the shaft."

In her gut, she knew Jo was right, at least as far as Natalie was concerned. She finally put her finger on what she had been feeling, that she was outside Natalie's clique because she didn't have the stylish, feminine look of the others. Even Yvonne, who was athletic like she was, came dressed for dinner in her silk blouse and scarf, with a small bit of jewelry and makeup. She herself didn't have that in her. She was who she was, no more, no less. She liked the way she looked, with the possible exception of her cowlick.

The bus came to a stop at a hut where rows of bicycles, identical except for the color and crossbar, sat gleaming in the sun. Kelly strapped on her backpack and waited in a line of about twenty before picking out a blue bike. As she fell in behind Jo she noted that not all of the bikers were athletic types, which reinforced her wish that Natalie had come along.

"I'd like to get the diamond just once, Jo. You know what I mean?"

"So would I, mate, but I won't ever get up the nerve."

"Tell me about your girl."

"Sarah." Jo's face took on a dreamy look. "She works at her mum's bakery. I go in there practically every day and get a ginger biscuit." She patted her round stomach. "As you can probably tell."

"She's a pretty girl?"

52

"Gorgeous. Long blond hair and blue eyes that could slay you from across the room."

That's exactly what Kelly thought about Natalie's green eyes. "What is she like?"

"She's got a crazy sense of humor. She teases me about everything…not mean or anything. Just silly. And I love it when she smiles."

They started along a trail of tightly-packed dirt and shells that was lined with mangroves. On one side was a lush green hillside, on the other the aquamarine water of the Caribbean.

"Sounds like she might be interested in you too."

That prompted a blush. "I wish. But I'm too chicken to find out." They stopped at an opening in the mangroves that afforded a view of the ocean and Jo began taking photos. "I'm afraid I'll mess things up, you know?"

"You mean if you ask her out and she says no, then you won't be friends anymore?"

"Right, like it might be awkward."

"Does she go for girls?"

"I think so…maybe. I never see her talk to guys like that. She's just all business with them."

They started pedaling again, this time in single file. As she rode along, Kelly thought about her interactions with her intriguing roommate. Their deepest conversation so far was this morning, when Natalie had alluded to her confusion about coming out, but offered scant details. What they needed was more time alone, time in their stateroom or sightseeing. Or maybe a stroll on the Promenade Deck. The trick was separating her from her friends. Maybe after dinner they could—

"Whoa!" The column of bikes had stopped and she had to veer suddenly to keep from ramming Jo. Her front tire hit a football-sized rock and twisted sideways, and the next thing she knew, she was airborne. "Son of a—"

"You all right, mate?" Jo was at her side at once.

She was lucky to have landed in the tall grass that lined the road. "Yeah, I think so. Just brain-damaged."

"How's your bike?"

She inspected it, and was relieved to find it still in one piece. "Good to go."

"That's a relief. Except we're done going. We're at the beach."

Indeed, before them was a crystal blue lagoon.

They turned in their wheels to their guide, who supervised a small crew that was loading the bikes onto a truck for delivery back to the starting point. Their bus was parked in a shaded area where several vendors had spread out their wares on blankets and straw mats.

Kelly unzipped her backpack and followed Jo to a concession stand. "Buy you a beer?"

"Don't drink…unless you count lemonade."

She put her hand on Jo's as she reached for her wallet. "It's on me. One lemonade, one Medalla," she said, smiling to remember the last time she had enjoyed Puerto Rican beer. It was in the navy with Sandra, on one of their weekend passes from the base.

Jo went ahead to stake out a couple of chairs under an umbrella. Kelly soon followed and handed her the cold drink.

"I was thinking some more about your question…about what Sarah's like? I left off the thing I like most."

"What's that?"

"She always treats me special when I come in. Like she'll save back something if it's the last one and she knows I like it. Or if it's crowded, she'll have mine ready when I get up to the counter. It makes me feel good."

"What do you do special for her?"

She shrugged. "Whatever I can. Like she'll get busy and I'll go around and pick up plates and napkins."

"You ever show up at closing and walk her home?"

"Now that would be like asking her out. I told you, I'm too chicken for that."

"Why? It's just a walk home." Kelly chided herself. Here she was giving advice on picking up girls, and she hadn't had a date since moving to Rochester two years ago.

"Maybe one of these days." Jo stretched out in the chair. "Wake me up when the bus is pulling out. Or when the sun hits my feet."

"You got it. I'm going to go check out the souvenirs." Kelly grabbed her wallet and walked back to the shaded area, where she was instantly accosted by several brightly clad women shouting all at once for her to buy their pretty trinkets. She didn't need anything, and no one back in New York was expecting a gift, but she wanted to support the local economy.

"This look good on you," a woman said, holding up a black coral choker with a carved sea turtle.

Not bad, she thought. A simple necklace she could wear to dress up her beach clothes. It might even look good with the white shirt and black suit she had brought along for formal night. "How much?"

"Twenty dollar."

She held it up for inspection. It wasn't elaborately made, but it should hold together for the next two weeks. "Did you make it?"

The girl nodded. "Fifteen...twelve."

"Fifteen is fine. It's a fair price."

She dropped it into her backpack and studied the other items on display. Nothing fancy...nothing on these tables that might make a nice gift for someone like Natalie, who had impeccable taste when it came to jewelry. Her earrings, bracelets and necklaces seemed to match perfectly and complement whatever she chose to wear.

At the end of the row, a thin, dark-skinned man stared out at the lagoon. "You enjoy our pretty beach?" he asked, his accented English easily understood.

"Very much." She looked out across the water again, remembering the things she had enjoyed about Key West. "It's beautiful."

"Take it with you." He reached for a woven bag and pulled out several small watercolors. "I paint them every hour. This is your hour, the water as you see it."

"Wow." She knew she had squandered her bargaining position, but he had brilliantly captured the color of the water in the afternoon light. "Ten dollars, right?"

"Fifty."

She smiled to herself and opened her wallet. Natalie would love it.

Chapter 6

Natalie pushed her shopping bags through the X-ray machine on the ship and walked around to pick them up from the other side. For once, shopping had been an afterthought, a last-minute frenzy through the vendors at the entrance to the dock, all because she had offered to pick up something for Didi.

Her day in Old San Juan had been fascinating, especially the fort Kelly had mentioned, where Julie had joined their group. The two of them peeled off after lunch, and while that gave them a chance to get to know each other, the best part for Natalie was knowing she was freeing Steph and Yvonne for some private time. Though they hadn't made her feel unwelcome, it was obvious they were looking forward to enjoying their afternoon on their own.

Almost as soon as they parted, Natalie had second thoughts, as Julie turned out to be possibly the biggest flirt she had ever met. The Aussie made no secret of her interest in anything Natalie put on the table, so much that Natalie found herself steering topics away from the personal and back to the quaint characteristics of Old San Juan.

"There's a show tonight," Julie said invitingly, hooking her arm through Natalie's as they started up the stairs.

"Steph mentioned that this morning," she lied. "We planned to go right after dinner and get good seats. Why don't you and your sister join us?"

Julie's disappointment that it wouldn't be a solo date was obvious, but she agreed. "This is my deck," she said after two flights. She planted a kiss on Natalie's cheek. "Thank you for a lovely afternoon. Maybe we'll do this again tomorrow in St. Thomas."

Natalie smiled wanly and nodded. She had never been good at fending off suitors, a trait she associated with her Southern upbringing where the polite thing was to accept all invitations graciously. That had generally led to more dead-end dates than she wanted, since she usually formed her opinion of a woman within the first few minutes, an hour at the most. Julie was pretty, interesting and sweet, but prompted no spark at all. And while Natalie had given herself tacit permission to have a meaningless fling aboard ship—especially one that had the potential to make Didi jealous—she wasn't the sort to go through the motions when it came to sex. Either she was swept up in the heat, unable to rein in her passion after sharing a fiery kiss, or she couldn't be bothered.

She was pleased to find Kelly already back in their stateroom. All morning she had felt guilty for turning down the offer to share the day, though she had rationalized that it would have meant asking Kelly to give up her active plans in favor of a lazy stroll around town. "How was your bike ride?"

"You would have loved it, but I won't rub it in, especially since you obviously had a good time yourself." She gestured to the shopping bags. "I saw the vendors packing up and figured you bought them all out."

Natalie spread her bags out on her bed. "I bought a few gifts to take to the girls at the store. Then I found something I thought looked like you, so I bought it."

Kelly's eyebrows lifted in surprise. "Something that looked like me? I'm almost afraid to ask."

She found the right bag and reached inside. "You don't have to wear it. Well, maybe you do, just to humor me for a night or two."

Kelly's eyes lit up at the black coral necklace with the carved dolphin. "Oh, wow! I love it."

Natalie beamed, pleased with herself for finding just the right statement for Kelly, eye-catching without being too prissy. The trinket had cost her only twelve dollars, the bargain of the day considering the smile it had produced. "Let me put it on you." She looped it around Kelly's neck and fastened it in the back. Then she situated the dolphin so that it rested in the hollow of her throat. "It's definitely you."

Kelly whirled around to check her look in the mirror. "It's perfect. Thank you."

"Am I forgiven for not coming along?"

"Absolutely."

Natalie was delighted at Kelly's reaction, a beautiful smile that boasted perfect white teeth and tiny dimples on both cheeks. She hadn't noticed those before. "I promise I won't go looking for matching earrings and make you wear those too."

"Thank you, because I'd really hate to hurt your feelings." Kelly reached into her backpack and produced a small canvas. "I got you something too. It's a painting of what you missed today."

"Oh, my goodness. It's beautiful."

Kelly nodded vigorously. "So was the lagoon. I really wish you'd been there."

She was touched by Kelly's thoughtfulness. "Now I'm sorry I didn't go with you."

"You can make up for it if you come snorkeling with me tomorrow in St. Thomas."

"Me jumping off a boat? That'll be the day."

"You don't swim?" Kelly flopped on the small couch and crossed her feet on the coffee table.

"I know how, but I haven't been swimming in years. Lake Erie just doesn't hold all that much appeal."

"You can't compare the Caribbean to Lake Erie. The water here is spectacular. Bright coral and a thousand different species of fish. Even a shark if you're lucky."

"If I'm lucky? Now I know I'm not going." In fact, she had been tempted to do something out of the ordinary, but only barely. Making a fool of herself on a bike was one thing, but in water over her head?

"Don't say no yet. Just think about it."

The idea was growing on her, but she would have to get up her nerve. "Have you heard anything from next door?"

"They're out on the balcony."

Natalie took her other gifts outside and leaned around the divider. Didi and Pamela sat in deck chairs, both of them looking bored and miserable. "How are you feeling, ladies?"

"Suicidal," Didi said. "The stomach thing is over, but they still won't let us leave our stateroom. By the way, I had to swear we'd had no contact with anyone so don't get caught leaning over or they'll lock you up too."

"I brought you these." She had picked up two pairs of earrings, long dangly shells decorated with brightly colored coral beads. "You can fight over who gets what."

Didi rolled her eyes. "Just what we need—something else to fight over."

"Thank you, Natalie," Pamela said graciously. "I apologize for Didi's lack of manners."

"What'd I do?"

Natalie chuckled to herself, remembering what a grouch Didi could be, especially when she was sick. Despite her feelings for Didi, she was happy to let Pamela deal with her in this state.

Kelly fingered the dolphin pendant as they entered the dining room. The turtle necklace she had bought for herself, almost identical to this one, was tucked away in a corner of her drawer, destined as a gift for someone in the city planning office. The dolphin trinket wasn't an extravagant gesture, but it was a welcome sign that Natalie liked her...or at least that she didn't dislike her. Up until now, it had been hard to tell.

She gave a small wave to Jo as they walked past the table, and was surprised when Natalie abruptly stopped.

"Hello, you must be Jo. I hear you did the bike tour today too."

Kelly was taken aback, since she hadn't told Natalie about her bike ride at all.

"And I bet you're Natalie. Julie's been talking about you nonstop."

That explained it...much to Kelly's chagrin, since Jo had described her sister as being on the prowl. From the smile on Natalie's face, she was probably happy to be pursued.

Jo frowned and pointed at her necklace. "I thought you—"

"Isn't this great? Natalie picked it up for me." She shot Jo a wink as they continued on to their table.

Kelly gallantly held the chair for Natalie to sit as she greeted the others.

"Another night without Didi and Pamela," Yvonne said, elbowing Steph. "You could have gotten away with wearing that turquoise pantsuit Didi hates so much."

"And I could have worn my carpenter pants," Kelly added with a chuckle.

"I've seen those," Steph said. "They're *real* carpenter pants. I can just picture a hammer hanging off the back, paint smears on the knees..."

"What exactly do you do?" Natalie asked.

"I'm a building inspector for the City of Rochester. I check to make sure everything has been done to code, and then I issue a certificate of occupancy."

"That's when I saw Kelly the first time," Steph explained. "I didn't know who she was though until Yvonne asked her to dinner. You know that condo project over by the river that I sell every now and then? I had to wait on one of them while Kelly issued the CO."

"Did you learn about construction in the navy?" Yvonne asked.

Kelly was pleased that the conversation had moved away from fashion—one of her least favorite topics—and onto her job, which she was more than happy to talk about. "Actually, my dad was a general contractor. My brother and I grew up in the business and we learned all the trades."

"What do you mean by all the trades?"

"The usual construction jobs...carpentry, plumbing, roofing, drywall."

Yvonne elbowed Steph. "Too bad she didn't blow out her knee back when we were remodeling the kitchen."

"Hey!" Natalie's face lit up. "You're just the person I need to talk to about my house. Steph made me buy a Victorian in Corn Hill, but it needs a lot of work."

"I love those old houses. How many rooms?"

"Three bedrooms upstairs, but only one bath."

"So you want to add a bathroom?"

"What I really want"—she looked at the others—"Sorry, guys. Talk amongst yourselves."

"I want to hear this too," Yvonne said. "I can't believe we're finally having a dinner together where the main topic is something besides what everyone in the room is wearing."

Natalie shifted in her seat to talk directly to Kelly. "I want to enlarge the master bedroom and add a bath. I don't care if I lose a bedroom. And then I want a half bath downstairs off the kitchen, and all-new cabinets and counters."

"So you're probably looking at replumbing the whole house. And if you're taking out interior walls, you might as well rewire it too."

Throughout dinner, she laid out in detail the typical steps in such a renovation. Natalie had obviously given her remodeling ideas a great deal of thought, and peppered her with questions about materials and costs. Their conversation continued as they made their way to the theater for the evening variety show.

"What really matters is what you're planning to do with your house in the long run. Everything you put into a remodel affects the resale value, but if you plan to live there, you give more weight to things you want to enjoy every day."

Natalie's face fell suddenly, her enthusiasm giving way to doubt. "I really don't know what my plans are. I might live there for forty years, or I might sell it next year and move to Manhattan."

Kelly picked up a trace of resignation in her tone, and figured it all had to do with Natalie's uncertainty about Didi. "Which one of those would make you happier?"

Absently following Steph to take a seat in the middle of the row, Natalie lowered her voice and answered pensively, "What good is a house if I have to live there by myself?"

"That depends on what you make it." Kelly sat next to her, resisting the urge to give her thigh a reassuring pat. "A home can be a lot more than a house, but it won't be worth much if you have to sacrifice what your heart really wants."

Natalie took her applause cues from those seated around her. Distracted by Kelly's pointed question on what would make her happy, she was glad when the show ended, and eager for an active diversion. She needed to clear her head of the gloomy thoughts, especially her doubts about a future with Didi. Otherwise, her dour mood would keep her awake all night.

"Anyone up for a drink?" Kelly asked.

She almost declined when the others called it a night, but the idea of returning to the stateroom still dwelling on her uncertainty seemed like a recipe for depression. She followed Kelly to the dark observation lounge on the upper deck, where they settled into a comfortable booth and ordered drinks, a German beer for Kelly and a glass of red wine for herself.

Kelly raised her drink in a toast. "Here's to new friendships. I can't tell you how glad I am to meet a group of women from Rochester who aren't hanging out at the bars or the ball fields."

"I was lucky when I moved to New York. Steph and Yvonne had lots of friends, and they accepted me right away—even though they all said I talked funny."

"Your accent isn't all that pronounced, and besides, I like it. My chief petty officer was from Alabama and I could have listened to her chew my ass out all day."

Natalie recalled how Didi had mocked her for laughs when they first met. It had taken getting angry about it to finally get her to stop. "I've lost a lot of it in the last twelve years, but whenever I go back to Pascagoula for a visit it gets me drawling again."

"How often do you go back?"

"Every couple of years. I used to go back every Christmas, but when Didi and I got together she wanted me to spend the holidays with her. Now I have an excuse because it's the busiest time of the year."

"Didi wouldn't go with you?"

"Oh, Lord, no! In the first place, she never had any desire to see Mississippi, but that was fine by me. My family would have done an intervention if I'd come home with a woman."

"They don't know you're a lesbian?"

"They probably do, but they don't want to see it or hear about it. That's why I left in the first place, so I could have a life."

"Sounds like 'Don't ask, don't tell' in the navy."

"Whenever I went home I had to pretend I lived in a total vacuum. No life at all." She couldn't keep the bitterness from her voice. "Both of my sisters are perfect, you see. Republican husbands and so many children I've lost track of their names. I just have to plaster a smile on my face and tell them no, I'm not dating anyone, and I have no particular desire to get married or have children. Then they look at each other and shake their heads, like they've lost all hope. I just keep telling myself their opinion of me doesn't matter."

Kelly nodded, as if in agreement with every word. "That's all you can do with anybody. The only thing that matters is what you think of yourself."

The waiter interrupted to check on them and Kelly ordered another round.

It had taken Natalie the last twenty years to feel good about herself, and much of that she owed to Didi's guidance on how to make herself more attractive. Steph had characterized the constant critique as a putdown, but Natalie couldn't dispute that she generally looked better when she took Didi's advice. It was amazing how her confidence grew when she knew she looked good. Even her sisters had remarked on her new appearance, though they couldn't understand why it mattered if she wasn't interested in a man. She asked Kelly, "Do you see a lot of your family?"

Kelly shook her head. "Not much anymore. My brother and I didn't really get along growing up. He was Mike, Jr., the chip off the old block. I tried to compete with him for Dad's attention as a kid, but it didn't really matter what I did. He was always Dad's favorite, hands down."

"What about your mother?"

"She went into a coma when I was six and died a few months later without ever waking up. Dad always said she had a reaction to some medicine she was taking, but my grandmother said she took too much because she was trying to kill herself."

Natalie was mesmerized by both the story and Kelly's somber face. "That's terrible."

"I don't know which is sadder—the fact that she might have died so young by accident, or that her life was so miserable she didn't want to live anymore. I try not to think about it too much."

"That's so sad." No matter how much distance she felt from her own family, Natalie doubted her life had been as painful as Kelly's. "And it must have been hard on your father to raise two children on his own."

"He was pretty wrapped up in his business. That's why I started working there, so I could be with him more. Then he had a stroke while I was in the navy and asked me to come home and help Mike out. I worked the business with my brother until he died."

It was no wonder Kelly looked and dressed the way she did, Natalie thought, considering she had grown up without a mother figure, competing for her father's affections by trying to emulate her big brother. She leaned back and sipped her wine, now intent on learning as much as she could about Kelly, who was fast becoming someone she wanted for a friend. "What brought you to Rochester?"

"It was time to part company with Mike. He'd been cutting corners on some of his projects for years, and I knew that would catch up with him eventually. I just hope he sells out to somebody else before he gets caught and ruins the family name."

"How did your father feel about you being a lesbian?"

"We didn't talk about it much, but he knew. I didn't date a lot…just hung out at the pool hall like a baby dyke."

Kelly grinned at that last bit, flashing the dimples Natalie had noticed earlier. Her features seemed softer in the dim light, distinctly feminine. Natalie was willing to bet the older butch lesbians thought Kelly was a prize. "I bet you had a lot of girlfriends."

"Believe it or not, only one, and that was when I joined the navy. I met Sandra on the base at Key West and we were together for a couple of years, but we had to be really careful about people finding out. She got shipped out to Guam just before my tour was up. I asked about getting stationed over there if I re-enlisted, but they planned to send me to Jacksonville."

"That's awful. You and Sandra must have been devastated."

Kelly tipped her bottle upward and drained the last of her beer. "It was hard at first, but I sort of expected it. She wanted a career in the navy and I was already getting noise about coming back to Buffalo."

Natalie nodded in commiseration. "Still…I remember how lost I felt after I graduated from Ole Miss and went back to Pascagoula. I missed Steph and Yvonne so much I thought I'd die. I went up there to visit every chance I got."

"I'm sure it felt good to follow your heart on that one." Kelly waved toward the waiter and gestured for another round, their third. "So what does your heart want to do now?"

Natalie was determined not to let the question unsettle her as it had at dinner. "I don't have a clue. It feels like it changes from one day to the next."

"You still have feelings for Didi, right?"

"Please tell me it isn't that obvious."

Kelly shook her head. "It isn't. I just got that impression from Yvonne when she was giving me the lowdown on how you all knew each other."

"Didi and I were together for six years, but to be honest, the last three or four were just sort of blah. Work took over everything and we got so we went home at night to different parts of the house. I'll spare you the ugly details, but we finally split up a couple of years ago." She shuddered at the memory, and took another drink of wine. "Once we got away from each other, we started being friends again. I thought we might work it all out, but then she met Pamela and that was it."

"Do you still love her?"

"Apparently." She remembered her conversation with Steph, but doubted she could articulate complicated feelings tonight, as she noticed for the first time the alcohol's effects. "I like being with somebody who makes me feel good about myself."

"Didi does that?"

"She helps me feel pretty."

"I have news for you, Natalie Chatham." Kelly's dimples appeared as a smile crept across her face. "You can feel pretty without Didi's help."

Her lips turned up in a smile. "I think I might be a little drunk."

Kelly chuckled. "That's okay. Someone else is driving." She pushed her beer aside and stood. "Maybe we should call it a night while we still have our sea legs."

Natalie hooked her hand into Kelly's elbow as they walked

back to their stateroom. She was comfortable with Kelly, far more than she would have expected. It was probably the wine. "I want to make Didi jealous," she blurted.

Kelly patted her hand. "Considering she's in quarantine and you're out having a good time, I bet she probably already is."

"No, I mean jealous of me being with somebody else. I bet Julie would help me."

"Julie from Australia?"

Natalie nodded seriously. "She likes me. I can tell."

"You want to have an affair with her?"

"Not a real one. Just a pretend one." Her words were slurring. "So Didi will see what she's missing."

"I get it." Kelly chuckled. "Except I don't think Julie has pretending in mind."

Natalie scowled. A real affair was out of the question. She didn't feel attracted to Julie that way. Heck, she thought, she felt more for Kelly than for Julie.

Chapter 7

Kelly set the coffee on the nightstand and debated the merits of waking her roommate. If the low, steady snore was any indication, Natalie had enjoyed the Sleep of the Dead. However, they were sailing into St. Thomas one hour from now and Kelly remembered from a cruise video that it was a particularly beautiful entry, one she wanted Natalie to see.

Their long talk last night in the lounge had Kelly feeling they were firmly on the path toward friendship, though she didn't discount the impact three glasses of wine might have had on loosening Natalie's tongue. It had certainly brought out her southern drawl. What Kelly appreciated most was how they had talked not of trivialities but of the pivotal events that had shaped their lives. That was a foundation for understanding each other.

After hearing how Natalie felt marginalized by her family, it was easy to see why she craved validation, even in the form of critical judgment from someone like Didi.

She thought back to the embarkation only three days ago, when she and Yvonne had leaned over the atrium to watch the others arrive on board. Pamela was the one who had stood out that day, her long blond hair and youthful figure prominently setting her apart from the others. After their up-close meeting Pamela no longer held that appeal. In the first place, a woman looked different when she was on someone else's arm, and while Didi seemed fairly nonchalant about their relationship, it was obvious to Kelly that Pamela was devoted to her.

In the second place, it was Natalie who commanded her attention now. There was something about her beauty that was natural and classic, and that persisted each morning even as she crawled out of bed with her face puffy and hair askew. Those unguarded moments cast her in a light far different from the one to which she seemed to aspire, the flawless look that only fashion and makeup could render on anyone. Natalie's was an everyday beauty, pure and artful, one that suited her years.

Kelly gently shook her shoulder. "Natalie…coffee…buttery croissants."

A small smile played across Natalie's lips, but her eyes remained closed.

"Scrambled eggs…ripe, red tomatoes…more coffee."

"I don't smell any of those things."

"No, but if you get up and get dressed, we'll go get them. And we can watch the ship sail into port. It's beautiful…mountains all around the harbor."

Natalie opened one eye. "I'm afraid to sit up. My head might crack open."

"And just think. Today's New Year's Eve. You'll have to do it all over again tonight."

She frowned. "I seriously doubt I could. I've never been much of a drinker."

"Then you probably aren't up on all the new scientific studies.

I've read that riding on a catamaran sailboat cures a hangover."

"Mmmm. You read that, did you?" She sat up and pushed her hair from her face. "Not as bad as I thought it would be."

Kelly caught herself staring at a bare shoulder as Natalie's pajama top fell to one side. "Uh, here you go." She handed her the Styrofoam cup. "The nectar of life."

"Bless you."

She waited on the balcony while Natalie showered and dressed. They made it to the terrace buffet just as the ship entered the port.

"This is lovely," Natalie said as she took a table near the rail and gazed out onto the towering green hills that encircled the St. Thomas harbor. "I'm glad you got me up to see it."

"The snorkel site is out there on one of those islands," Kelly said, pointing behind the ship. "If you don't have plans already, you really ought to think about coming out for the ride. The water is clear all the way to the bottom. I bet you'd be able to see the fish without even getting wet."

"Isn't Yvonne going?"

"Yes, and she said Steph was thinking about coming out too."

"Steph snorkeling? She's pulling your leg."

"I don't know about snorkeling, but she was going to come along for the ride."

Natalie cocked her head to the side as she thought about it. "I'm tempted, but I already told Julie I'd think about doing one of those carriage tours."

The mention of Julie's name ratcheted up Kelly's motivation to change her mind. "I've read that St. Thomas and St. John have the clearest water of all the islands...and lots of species on the coral."

"Hmmm. I can't think on an empty stomach. Shall I go get breakfast while you keep our table?"

"Sure."

No sooner had Natalie left than Yvonne took her place. She was dressed already for the boat outing, her swimsuit peeking out from underneath her tank top. "How's it going, Kelly?"

"Couldn't be better. I'm working on Natalie to get her to ride out with us on the catamaran today. Is Steph going?"

"She hasn't decided, but I bet she will if Natalie does. How are you two getting along?"

"Better than I thought we would at first," she said, checking over her shoulder to make sure Natalie wasn't within earshot. "But not as much as I'd like to."

"It might be too late for that. Steph talked with Didi on the phone last night, and it's finally hit her that she might be too old for Pamela. Apparently she said something about getting back home and sorting things out with Natalie." Yvonne lowered her voice. "Who happens to be coming up behind you."

Kelly absorbed the news with a wave of disappointment, though she couldn't help but be glad for Natalie, since getting back with Didi was what she ultimately wanted. Love was complicated, full of compromises and bargains. Once a couple invested six years together like those two had, it was probably easier to go back to the familiar with lessons learned than to start from scratch with someone new, especially when the friendship remained intact.

Besides, she admitted to herself, it was silly to think Natalie would go for someone the total opposite of what she was used to.

"Do you think I still have time to get a ticket on the catamaran?" Natalie asked.

Kelly leapt eagerly from her seat before she could change her mind. "I'll go down to the excursion desk right now."

"Get Steph's too," Yvonne called.

Even though her mood had been dampened by Yvonne's news, Kelly was still excited at the prospect of spending the morning with Natalie out on the water. Finally they were all doing something together. She didn't have many sophisticated friends like these. When the cruise was over and they returned to Rochester, she wanted to be part of this circle, and especially a friend and confidante of Natalie's.

"Hey, mate. Where you headed today?" Jo appeared out of nowhere, dressed like Kelly in sandals and cargo shorts but with a T-shirt instead of a tank top.

"Snorkeling. You?"

Jo rolled her eyes. "I promised Julie I'd do a carriage ride with her if she couldn't find someone else to go. She's been calling your friend Natalie ever since she got up, but nobody answers."

"Natalie's coming with me," Kelly said proudly. "Oh, and by the way..." She fingered the dolphin hanging around her neck. "Thanks for catching on about the necklace. I didn't tell her about the other one."

"So you and Natalie...?"

"Just friends. I like her, but what was it you said, that bit about pretty girls?"

"Pretty girls only like pretty girls."

"Right. But at least she's mine today. Sorry about your sister." She grinned. "Well, not really."

"Look at all those stores, Steph," Natalie said wistfully as they walked to the end of the dock to board the catamaran. "We could be shopping."

"This will be way better," Kelly said. "I promise you'll have a good time."

Natalie took her hand as she climbed aboard the gently rocking vessel. The benches on the main level were filling up, so she followed Kelly upstairs to the sun deck. Yvonne and Steph were right behind. "I'll never forgive you if you let me fall off."

"You'll be fine."

The catamaran soon pulled away from the dock on a wide circle around the ship.

"There's Didi out on her balcony," Kelly said as she stood to wave.

Natalie waved too, and grinned broadly when Didi finally noticed them and waved back. Pamela was nowhere in sight, a likely sign they were avoiding each other after being cooped up together for two solid days. She had no idea what Pamela was like under duress, but Didi would drive anyone crazy in a situation like that. "Just in case I haven't told you lately, thank you for not letting me eat the Waldorf salad," she whispered.

"I'm glad you listened. Otherwise I'd be out here by myself and it's way more fun with you."

Yvonne and Steph had moved to the other side of the deck and were staring off at the islands in the distance. Once again, Natalie acknowledged a small wave of guilt that she always seemed to take away their private time and vowed to be more conscious of her imposition. Abruptly, they got up and gathered their things.

"Steph can't deal with the sun," Yvonne shouted above the roar of the flapping sail. "We're going to find a space down below."

Natalie turned back to see the wind blowing Kelly's fine hair off her forehead, revealing the surprisingly delicate face she had noticed last night. Her eyebrows were perfectly arched, as if sculpted by a cosmetologist, and her lips were full and soft-looking. There was no mistaking she was a woman, even with her trim, muscular physique and boyish board shorts.

"There's a turtle!" Kelly said suddenly, pointing to a ripple in the water. The round shell was clearly visible from their perch. "Damn! I didn't bring my camera."

"I have mine."

"I meant my underwater camera. I could have dived down and gotten pictures of the coral so you could see what you're missing. Maybe I'd have seen another turtle up close."

"I thought snorkeling was swimming around on top of the water."

"It is, but if you let the air out of your vest you can dive too, as long as you remember to hold your breath." She pointed over the side again. "See those dark places we pass over? That's either seaweed or coral. That's where all the fish are."

"I bet it's beautiful."

"Sure you don't want to come? I'll get you a mask and fins."

Natalie shook her head vehemently. "I'll enjoy it vicariously through you."

The catamaran coasted to a halt and a crewman tossed over the anchor. Then he dived off the side.

"What's he doing?"

"Setting the anchor so we don't drift."

Another crewman called everyone to the back of the boat for instruction.

"You don't have to come since you're not going in," Kelly said.

Natalie watched from behind her sunglasses as Kelly stripped down to her shorts and sports bra, showing off the muscles in her upper back. She felt a strange sense of loss as Kelly started down the stairs. A part of her—an extremely small part—wished she had come prepared to get into the water. Her logical side, however, was content to stay on the sun deck and watch.

When the instruction was complete, Kelly waved up at her and pulled her snorkel apparatus into place. Holding onto her mask with both hands, she stepped off the side and disappeared into a cloud of bubbles.

Natalie held her breath until she saw her emerge and swim off with Yvonne in the direction of the darker water. Periodically, they would vanish, only to reappear a few feet away. It was impossible not to envy their fun.

Her thoughts went back to Didi, who must have been astounded to see her sailing off, especially if Didi had assumed she was heading out to go snorkeling. Too bad Julie hadn't come along. That might have made Didi jealous, while her being with Kelly probably wouldn't.

Not that Kelly didn't have plenty of nice things to offer someone. She was attractive in a number of ways Natalie had noticed only in the last day or two. It wasn't just her fit body and decidedly feminine face. It was also her quick smile and dimples, and that she was always so attentive, holding chairs and opening doors. Natalie enjoyed the special treatment. She had never gotten that before, not from Didi or anyone else. It was nice to have someone fussing over her for a change, especially after she had done all the fussing with both Theresa and Didi.

Swimmers began returning to the boat, where a crewman helped them aboard and divested them of their rented gear.

Natalie scanned the surface for Kelly, finally spotting her swimming slowly toward the boat like a child who didn't want to leave the water until she had done one last lap. She waited eagerly for her to board and climb the stairs to the sun deck. Soon they were underway, headed back to the ship.

"How was it?"

"Fabulous. The sun really lights up the coral. We were so lucky to get out here on a day like this."

"Did you see any fish?"

"Only a couple of million or so. Little blue and yellow parrotfish and"—she held her hands apart—"a grouper this big." She wrapped her arms around her midsection. "It feels cold once you get out of the water."

Natalie had already noticed Kelly's erect nipples straining against her sports bra. Furthermore, she observed that her breasts appeared larger than they had under her tank top. Not endowed, by any means, but definitely feminine. And while her legs were muscled, they were sleek like a woman's, not bulky like a man's. When she bent over to dry her legs, it was impossible not to see that her butt was tight and round, accentuated by the cling of her wet shorts.

"Did you see anything nice from here?"

Natalie's face went instantly hot. "I was looking at...you mean...?"

Kelly spun back around and leaned over the side. "Look. That's either a stingray or another turtle. I can't tell from here."

"I saw several schools of fish," Natalie lied, realizing she had watched Kelly the whole time.

"You really ought to come with me next time. It's amazing how beautiful it is under there." She wrapped the towel around her shoulders and stretched her legs in the sun. "I'll swim with you the whole time."

"That sounds like fun for one of us."

"I'd love it. Half the fun is talking afterward about what you saw together."

Though she doubted she would actually get up the nerve to do it, she smiled to imagine how surprised her friends would be, especially Didi. In fact, the notion of shocking Didi held a lot of appeal. "You better be careful what you ask for. If I come snorkeling with you, I might expect you to come shopping with me."

Kelly made an X with her index fingers, as though warding off a vampire. "I bet I'm way more afraid of shopping than you are of snorkeling."

"It'll be great fun. You can wait in the fitting room while I bring you all the pretty sundresses to try on. Then we go looking for a matching purse and—"

"Oh, no, you don't. There are few things more hideous than me in a sundress. I'd rather wear a clown suit." Her voice took on a hint of agitation, as if she'd had this conversation before.

"I'm sorry. I was just playing."

Kelly looked away sheepishly. "Yeah, I know. I overreacted." She scrunched her nose and stared off into the distance. "When I was growing up, my aunts told my father he needed to get married again to a woman who could dress me up right. I heard that over and over until I was sick of it."

"Oh, Kelly." Natalie felt a wave of shame for being part of something so hurtful. "I wouldn't change anything about you. Please don't think I'm like them."

"I know you're not. It just called up those old memories for a second there. The day I left the navy was the last day I let someone else tell me how to dress."

"I bet you looked great in your uniform."

"As a matter of fact, I cut quite a handsome figure, if I do say so myself. Maybe I'll show you a picture one of these days."

Natalie breathed an inward sigh of relief that Kelly had forgiven her for the callous remark. The catamaran pulled into the dock, which was lined with over a hundred shops catering to the cruise ships.

"I won't make you go with me but I don't think I can resist all those shops. They're calling my name."

"And I hear a shower calling mine."

"So I guess I'll see you back on the ship."

Kelly caught her arm as she started down the stairs. "Thanks for coming out with us. I hope you had a good time."

"I had fun watching you guys have fun."

"And you'll think about getting wet next time?"

"I'll think about it."

In the fitting room, Natalie twisted from side to side to study her reflection and smiled with satisfaction at her find, a dark green silk dress that tapered from her hip to just above her knee. With its plunging neckline, she appeared taller and slimmer, a look that would most certainly win Didi's approval. Not that Didi would see this dress tonight. She and Pamela were quarantined for one more day, so they would miss the first of three formal nights at dinner.

She took her new dress to the sales counter. As she signed her credit card slip, Steph entered the store sporting a new straw hat with a hot pink sash.

"Did you have fun on the catamaran?"

Natalie grinned. "Kelly was right. It's beautiful out there. How did you like it?"

"I liked the ride. I discovered I had a signal on my phone and caught up with my office while they were in the water."

"You're an incurable workaholic."

"Houses don't sell themselves. It looked like you and Kelly were having a good time. You like her?"

"She's nice. How well do you know her?"

"We've had her over for dinner a couple of times. She and Yvonne work out together at the gym sometimes. Other than that, not much."

"I'm afraid I hurt her feelings today." As they returned to the ship she related the conversation about Kelly trying on a dress. "She said she was okay about it, but I still felt bad."

"I wouldn't worry about her. She's pretty easygoing."

"Sometimes I think I've been around Didi too much. I just look at somebody and blurt out whatever's in my head."

"Nobody's as bad about that as Didi. Yvonne tunes her out completely, and I always tell her I dress this way just to piss her off. That usually shuts her up."

Natalie laughed. "I'll have to remember that. Shutting her up was a skill I never mastered."

They reached the ship's gangway where a long line of passengers waited to run their purchases through the X-ray machine.

"You know, Natalie...I haven't made it much of a secret that Yvonne and I were glad to see you and Didi split up, because you're a lot nicer person than she is. I always hated the way she put you down all the time."

Natalie couldn't help feeling defensive, not only of Didi, but of her choice to stay with her all those years and to win her back if she could. "I've already explained that a million times. I never felt like she was putting me down. I always knew I looked good if I had her seal of approval, and that was a feeling I enjoyed."

Steph bobbed her head from side to side thoughtfully. "I guess. Phyllis saw it that way too. She says she learned a lot from Didi and it helped her make a good impression with her banking clients." Phyllis Linder had been part of their group for a while before taking a job in Ithaca.

"Didi doesn't do it to be mean. Once I understood that, it was easy to accept her advice."

Steph passed her shopping bag through the X-ray machine and picked it up on the other side. "I wonder how Kelly feels about being on the receiving end."

"If her reaction today was any indication, it probably annoys her more than she lets on. But I love her attitude. She dishes it right back. She's definitely somebody who likes who she is, and too bad if other people don't."

Steph looked around to make sure no one was within earshot. "So...could you see yourself going out with somebody like Kelly?"

"Oh, no." Natalie shook her head adamantly. "She's not my type."

"I forgot. You don't like nice people." She dodged a playful smack from Natalie. "I still think you're missing something. Kelly's hot. I know she's not what you're used to, but I just love the way she carries herself, all laid back and self-confident. I can't believe you don't find that appealing."

Natalie shrugged. "I'll admit she's grown on me. Have you noticed her eyebrows? They're perfect. I'd give anything to have eyebrows like that."

"You can have the eyebrows. I want her legs. They're like a gazelle's."

"And she has the cutest dimples. What's funny is that one minute she looks all strong and tough. Then she smiles and looks like a little girl." They started up the stairs to their staterooms.

"So you actually do like her," Steph said. "That's good, because I was beginning to think there was something wrong with your head."

Natalie stopped in her tracks, realizing too late that Steph had led her by the nose through the whole conversation.

Chapter 8

Kelly checked her look in the full-length mirror on the back of the door, adjusting the dolphin necklace so it hung perfectly in the open neck of her stiff white shirt. It looked good with her black suit and polished shoes. Complemented...that's the word Natalie would use.

She sat on the couch to wait, smiling at the thought of her roommate who had been in the bathroom for over an hour getting ready for the formal dinner. It was beyond her what women did for that long, but she had little doubt Natalie would emerge looking like a million dollars, showing off whatever she had been hiding in that shopping bag.

The door finally opened. "Can you help me with this zipper?"

She leapt to her feet and crossed the room, getting her first look at a gorgeous green cocktail dress and the woman in it. "Wow."

Natalie met her eyes in the bathroom mirror and smiled demurely as she pulled her hair off her neck. "I think I have a thread caught in it."

Kelly's fingers shook as she grasped the tab and eyed the expanse of skin between Natalie's neck and the base of her spine. With a gentle tug, she reluctantly guided the zipper to the top. "Mark my word, you will be the most beautiful woman in the room tonight."

"Especially with Didi and Pamela stuck in their room." She fluffed her hair around the top of her shoulders before turning abruptly. "I'm sorry. That was rude. What I should have said was thank you."

"You're welcome." Kelly watched mesmerized as Natalie turned back and applied her lipstick. "I'll try not to stare."

"I'm sure everyone will look nice tonight." She touched the dolphin necklace and stepped back to take in Kelly's suit. "I'm glad you like this black coral. It really complements your outfit."

Kelly stood perfectly still as Natalie brushed the lint from her shoulders.

"This is a very nice suit."

"Thank you. Believe it or not, I actually bought it in the women's department," she added.

Natalie smiled and fingered the lapel. "I know. I can tell by the cut. Men's jackets don't taper at the waist."

A small detail Kelly had never noticed. "I have a vest that goes with it, but I thought that was overkill. Besides, I plan to wear it without the jacket on our next formal night."

"I'm sure that will look just as nice."

She held the door and walked behind Natalie down the narrow corridor, unable to take her eyes off her swaying hips. The dress fit her like a very tight glove.

It took them a moment to realize the reason for the line outside the dining room. "They're taking photos in front of the

Christmas tree," Kelly said, thinking she would love a picture with Natalie. "You really should get one in that dress. It will help you remember where you were on New Year's Eve."

"We should wait until we can get one with all six of us. Wouldn't that be a nice memento?"

Yes, but not the one Kelly wanted most. She followed Natalie out of line and directly into the dining room. Yvonne and Steph were already waiting, and gushed with praise for Natalie's new dress. Natalie returned the gesture, complimenting Steph's lavender silk brocade dress and Yvonne's embroidered tunic.

Over dinner, they talked about their plans for Tortola, the next day's port. Yvonne and Kelly had signed up for a wreck dive. Steph and Natalie planned to tour the Baths at nearby Virgin Gorda.

"Anyone feeling brave tonight?" Yvonne asked as the waiter cleared their dessert plates. "After the show tonight, there's a party in the Tropical Nightclub. I wouldn't mind ringing in the New Year out on the dance floor."

"That's my girl," Steph said with a grin. "Out and proud."

"I think it'll be cool," Yvonne said. "There were two guys doing the jitterbug in the lounge last night and people were cheering them on."

Kelly studied Natalie's reaction, which was less than enthusiastic. It was hard to know if she was averse to the idea of dancing in general, or upset that she wasn't with Didi. She waited for Natalie to make the call.

"I wish Didi and Pamela weren't stuck in their room," Natalie finally said. "It would be more fun if all of us could be there."

"I have an idea." Kelly picked up the wine list. "Maybe we can go to the show, dance awhile and then get a bottle of champagne and meet them out on the balcony. That way we can ring in the New Year together."

"That's a wonderful idea." Natalie looked to the others for support. "You guys?"

Steph chuckled. "I feel sorry for them, but not that sorry."

Yvonne jabbed her with an elbow. "Same here. Clearly, Kelly's a better person than we are."

"That's because Kelly doesn't know Didi as well as we do," Steph chimed in.

"Fine," Natalie said, setting her jaw firmly. "Kelly and I will go by ourselves."

Natalie could feel Steph's eyes on her as she applauded the singers' final bow. Without looking, she leaned sideways and said, "If you're thinking about giving me grief, don't."

"I can't believe you're going to pass up a New Year's Eve dance to sit out on the balcony and listen to Didi grumble about what a miserable time she's having. We both know she wouldn't do that for you."

"She has a right to complain, Steph. They've been stuck in their cabin for three days. And it's New Year's Eve. I think they'll appreciate the fact that not everyone has forgotten about them." She didn't add that it was hard to forget them when she could hear them yelling at each other through the wall, nor that she had picked up a hint or two that the bloom was coming off the rose for Didi. If Natalie's instincts were right, it was a perfect time to remind Didi that she was still interested. "Besides, it wasn't my idea. It was Kelly's."

Kelly had jumped up as soon as the show ended to order a bucket of ice and champagne for their stateroom and was steadily making her way back to their table in the theater.

"She's just trying to do whatever she thinks you'll like…in case you haven't noticed."

Natalie looked at her with indignation. "Noticed what?"

"That Kelly is hanging on your every word…that she watches for a chance to wait on you. Don't even try to tell me you aren't enjoying it."

She glanced sideways to gauge Kelly's proximity. "That's just silly. If she were interested in me, why would she suggest a party with Didi?"

"You got me there, but I know what I see."

Natalie wasn't sure if she liked that idea or not. On the one hand, she *had* noticed the attention, and she couldn't help but be flattered by it. On the other, she was more focused than ever on winning Didi back, and things could get sticky if Kelly made an unwelcome overture. "I think you're imagining things. We're just getting to know each other as friends. And whether you choose to believe me or not, Kelly isn't my type. Besides, I happen to be interested in someone else."

"Right…Didi." Steph snorted. "If you ask me, you'd be better off with Kelly."

"I didn't ask you." That came out sharper than she had intended, so to keep things light, she stuck out her tongue.

"Better not do that with your roommate. She'll think you're making a pass at her."

Natalie kicked at Steph's foot as Kelly arrived. "Behave yourself."

"I ordered the champagne. They'll deliver it in about ten minutes."

"We should go."

"Kelly, if they drive you nuts, come on up to the Tropicana," Yvonne said. "I'll let you dance with my girlfriend."

"Good deal."

When they reached the hallway outside their stateroom, Natalie stopped, thinking she should put Steph's conjectures to rest. "You don't have to miss the party upstairs for this, Kelly. For all I know, Didi and Pamela are asleep already. And even if they aren't, they might have plans of their own." In which case, Natalie planned to guzzle the entire bottle of champagne and pass out on her bed.

Kelly slid her key card into the door and held it while Natalie passed through. "If this doesn't work out, maybe we could both go to the party."

"I should probably warn you that if I drink champagne, there's a possibility I'll get drunk again tonight."

"All the more reason for me to stick around," Kelly said. "Someone has to keep you from falling over the rail."

Now that Steph's impressions of Kelly's interest were

top-of-mind, it was impossible not to read more into what might otherwise have been friendly support. As much as Natalie appreciated the attention, she didn't want to encourage anything when there was no chance she would reciprocate. "It's really nice of you to do this, but I feel bad about dragging you into this dyke drama. You probably think I have no morals when it comes to getting between Didi and Pamela, and you might be right."

Kelly pushed her hands into her pockets and rocked forward on her toes. "People can't help how they feel. If she's right for you, I hope it works out."

"I just don't think we're finished. We hit a few bumps in the road, and instead of dealing with them we split up because it was easy. It was okay at first, but I think all we really needed was a break from each other. Then Pamela came along and I think Didi's enamored right now with the idea of having a younger woman on her arm, but once she gets it out of her system she'll realize what we had was the real thing."

"Sometimes it takes getting hit over the head to realize what you want."

"I guess." She stepped outside onto the balcony, satisfied she had put the issue of Kelly's attraction to rest with her talk of Didi.

Over her shoulder, Kelly was holding the door as their cabin steward set up the ice bucket with a bottle of champagne. Moments later she came outside and shut the door behind her.

"It's warm out here," Natalie said. "Perfect for a balcony party."

"We should let the bubbly chill a while, don't you think?"

"Maybe I ought to call next door and tell them we're out here."

Kelly caught her elbow and spoke in a voice that seemed unusually loud. "Why don't we wait a few minutes? It's only a little after eleven."

"If I know Didi, she'll be asleep by two minutes after midnight, if she isn't already." She flung open the sliding glass door and reached for the phone.

"Seriously, Natalie." Her voice rose even louder. "Let's sit outside and talk for a little while first. I really wanted to ask you—"

"Why are you shouting?" That's when she heard it, the steady, panting grunt of heated sex emanating from the other side of the wall. Didi's moan was unmistakable, and Natalie felt a wave of nausea.

Natalie had said barely a word since bolting from their stateroom and settling at a small table in the shadows on the deserted pool deck. Kelly followed quietly and then went back to their room for the champagne and bucket.

"This is the last of it," she said, pouring into Natalie's flute. "Save a sip for midnight."

"We should drink to Plexiglas, because if it weren't for that, I would have thrown myself over this balcony by now."

"Does it hurt that much?"

Natalie sighed heavily. "Not really. But there's nothing quite as humiliating as hearing the person you're in love with having sex with someone else."

"Try having your watch stop so that you accidentally go into the barracks shower during the designated men's hour."

"Did you really do that?"

"I sure did. I got catcalls everywhere I went for a week."

Natalie chuckled. "That would have been humiliating."

"Yeah, and the second time it happened, they all accused me of needing attention."

"The second time?"

"It was a cheap watch." That earned her a belly laugh. "Speaking of watches, I wonder what time it is."

Natalie squinted. "The clock over the bar says about five minutes till. We can go back to the room if you want. I can pretty much guarantee you Didi's sound asleep by now."

"I'm comfortable right here if you are."

"I wouldn't exactly call it comfortable."

"Tell me what you're feeling."

"I just had it all fixed in my head that Didi might be coming to her senses. She said something yesterday about the old days, and how nice it was for her when we were together. Pamela isn't going be there for her the way I was, and Didi knows it."

What Kelly couldn't understand was why Natalie wanted to be with someone who needed someone there for her, but didn't feel the need to be there for Natalie. "Was she there for you too?"

"More or less...probably less. But I had that good solid southern upbringing where I was trained to take care of a husband, so I just adapted and took care of her."

"And what was Didi trained for?"

"What really drives her is making something of herself. She grew up in New Jersey, and her family didn't have much. It always hurt her pride that the other girls looked down on her, and I think that's why she's so focused on hitting the big time in New York. She wants to go back and rub all their noses in it."

If there was one thing Kelly understood, it was having the other girls look down on her. "That explains a lot about her."

"I know. People who don't know her well think she's an asshole most of the time, but I see her as a little girl getting picked on and fighting back."

Kelly almost chuckled at hearing Natalie call Didi an asshole. If the accompanying drawl was any indication, the champagne had taken over her tongue. "So...how come you two broke up?"

Natalie looked away. "It's a very embarrassing story, which I don't ever plan to tell. I hope she doesn't either."

"Sorry, I didn't mean to be nosy. I retract my question."

"It's okay. Let's just say it wasn't the sort of thing people would normally break up over, but it was symptomatic of all the things that were wrong with us. We weren't being—I wasn't being honest about my feelings, and I got caught."

Whatever it was, Natalie was clearly shouldering the blame. "Sometimes when we put a little distance between us and our mistakes, we realize they weren't so terrible after all."

"It's a mistake I won't ever make again."

Kelly was itching to know what had happened, but didn't want to pry more than she already had. Instead she checked the clock again and pulled Natalie to her feet. "We have about one minute left. What would you like to throw away from this past year?"

"You mean something besides tonight?"

"Was tonight really the worst thing about last year?"

"Not by itself." She squinted thoughtfully. "I want to throw away all this aggravation."

Kelly nodded. "Sounds like a good choice."

"And you?"

"I'm throwing away all those nights and weekends I sat at home alone. I want to go into the New Year with friends, with people I care about."

The ship's horn suddenly sounded a long blast.

"Happy New Year, Natalie." She clinked their glasses together.

"I hope you'll count me as one of your friends."

"I already do."

Natalie sealed it for certain by planting a kiss on her cheek.

Chapter 9

Kelly twitched her nose at the familiar aroma. Coffee. She opened her eyes to see Natalie sitting across from her, a Styrofoam cup in hand.

"I finally woke up before you did. And since you said you weren't running today, I thought it might be my only chance to return the favor."

She pushed up in bed and rubbed her eyes with the heels of her hands. The back of her head throbbed. "I should know better than to drink champagne. Even one glass gives me a headache."

"I'll get you some aspirin."

"That's okay, this is my penance." She took the coffee and smiled. "Coffee helps, though. Are we in port?"

"Not yet. You want to sit outside and watch us dock?"

Kelly stumbled straight from her bed to the balcony without changing from the flannel shorts and tight white tank top she slept in. Mornings with Natalie had become her favorite part of the trip.

"Isn't this weather gorgeous?" Natalie remarked as she sank into a deck chair, her mood surprisingly cheerful after last night's misfortune.

"Fantastic. We're not even halfway through the cruise and I'm already dreading going home to Rochester."

"I would think your kind of work would slow down in the winter."

"Some parts of it hit a lag, like laying foundations and putting on roofs. But it's a big season for interior remodels and that's harder to keep up with because people do a lot of their own work, and some of it is pretty shoddy. That keeps me busy because I have to keep going back to the same places over and over."

"I really would like it if you'd come over and walk through my house with me. I'll pay you whatever the going rate is for contractor advice. I don't want to take advantage—"

"Hold on there. I thought we agreed last night we were going to be friends when we got back home. I don't charge my friends when I help them out."

Natalie grinned. "You say that now, but you haven't seen my house. Once you realize how much work it needs, you may go looking for new friends."

"Not a chance. It takes me a while to make friends, so once I do I tend to hold onto them."

"I'm the same way, which probably explains why I have trouble letting go of other things too," Natalie said quietly, tilting her head in the direction of the balcony next door. "By the way, thanks for putting up with me last night."

"I didn't consider that 'putting up' with you. I just wish you'd felt more like celebrating."

"I feel better today. I slept on it, and I have an idea."

"An idea?"

Natalie leaned forward with her elbows on her knees and

91

lowered her voice. "When I came on this cruise, I was thinking I might try to give Didi a taste of her own medicine…maybe have a fling with somebody and rub her nose in it for a change. You remember Julie, the redhead from Australia?"

Kelly's stomach dropped and she nodded.

"I thought about hooking up with her, but she was a little too interested."

"Yeah, I remember you said that the other night. So if not Julie…?"

"I was wondering if maybe…you?"

Kelly wasn't sure she was hearing this right. "You want Didi to think we're involved so she'll be jealous?"

Natalie nodded. "It doesn't have to be over the top or anything. Maybe just a little hand touching, a few suggestive looks…pay me compliments whenever she's around, that sort of thing. I would never ask you to do something that made you uncomfortable."

Uncomfortable wasn't exactly the word for it. Well…maybe it was. She realized she was actually twisting in her chair with discomfort. "But there wouldn't actually be anything between us."

"Oh, no." Natalie wrung her hands as if nervous. "It's a lot to ask, I know. And I'm not even sure she'd buy it."

"Because you go for women like Didi."

Natalie nodded. She went for femmes. Now she was the one looking uncomfortable. "This was a stupid idea, wasn't it? I shouldn't have—"

"I'll do it." It might be the closest she would ever get to dating a woman like Natalie. "Whatever you want me to do, just say it."

A brilliant smile broke over Natalie's face. "Kelly, you're terrific."

"Not so fast. We have to sell it." Her mind was already racing about the possibilities. "And there's one more thing. I don't want this to turn into a sticky situation later on. I want us to be friends when we get back to Rochester, so whatever we do, let's not piss anybody off."

"We'll make it work. If she goes for it, we'll just act like I told you I was going back to her and you took it well and wanted to be friends anyway. We won't try to make her think we were like…you know, intimate."

Kelly felt her pulse rate pick up. *Intimate with Natalie.* "I guess we should probably start doing more things together. Wouldn't that be a good idea?"

Natalie's eyes got big. "Can we start after you go scuba diving?"

Their laughter broke the tension, and they relaxed as the island of Tortola came into view off the bow.

From behind her sunglasses, Kelly studied Natalie's profile, admittedly excited at this new turn. She was a very pretty woman, one of the prettiest she had ever known personally. The sun brought out the red highlights in her hair and turned her green eyes aqua. Those colors accentuated a smooth, creamy complexion which belied her thirty-seven years. Given Didi's taste for beautiful women, it was easy to see why she had been drawn to Natalie.

"Gorgeous, isn't it?"

"Totally," Kelly said, turning her attention back to the island, where small cottages and majestic terraced homes dotted the hillside. Kelly lifted her sunglasses so Natalie could see her eyes. "You have a beautiful smile, by the way. I like seeing it, and I'm going to make it my personal mission to put one there every chance I get." Her declaration sounded more flirtatious than she had intended, but when Natalie gave her another full-on smile in response, she decided it was a good thing.

The door opened on the balcony next door. "If she says no, I'm jumping off the side," Didi yelled.

"Good morning," Natalie said, leaning over the rail. "Happy New Year."

"It will be if we get out of here. Pamela's on the phone with the nurse and they might spring us in time to get off the ship."

"I take it you're both feeling better."

"Physically, we're fine. But we're cracking up from being inside this pillbox." Didi lowered her voice. "Come closer, Natalie."

Since she was still in her chair, Kelly was out of Didi's line of sight, but could hear her clearly.

"If the nurse says we can leave the ship, will you go somewhere with me? I don't think I'll survive five more hours alone with Pamela. I need a break."

Natalie shook her head and smiled. "I've already made plans with Steph to go over to Virgin Gorda since Kelly's going diving with Yvonne."

Kelly recognized the inflection as Natalie's way of saying she was making her plans based on Kelly's.

"But you two are welcome to join us...provided Pamela still wants to put up with you."

"I guess we could do that. I just need to see some new faces."

"I'm sure she does too."

"Are you implying that I'm difficult?"

Kelly covered her mouth too late to hide a snort.

"Hey!" Didi peeked around the divider. "You better not be laughing at my misery. I'll report you to the nurse. I'll say I saw you throwing up. That'll get you seventy-two hours in lockup."

Kelly raised her coffee cup in a toast. "To your health."

Didi squinted at her. "You're going swimming with the fishes today? Literally, I mean."

"Scuba diving."

"Will you take Pamela?"

"Hush," Natalie said. "She's going to hear you."

It was interesting that Natalie seemed concerned about Pamela's feelings when a fight between Pamela and Didi could have blown things up once and for all. Clearly she was serious about making sure nobody got hurt.

"Are you talking to Natalie?" Pamela emerged on the other side of the divider.

"What did the nurse say?" Didi asked, ignoring her question.

"She's doing rounds. She won't get here for another hour or two."

"Natalie just invited us to come along with her and Steph. Or you can go with Yvonne and Kelly if you want." She leaned around and gave Kelly an exaggerated wink. "You're going out on a boat, right?"

"Yes, but—"

"They're going on a boat ride around the island or something."

"We're full, actually. Yvonne got the last seat, and we're going scuba diving on a shipwreck."

"I could never do something like that," Pamela said. "But it sounds exciting. I hope we get to hear about it at dinner."

Still leaning around the divider and out of Pamela's line of sight, Didi made faces as Pamela talked, eliciting a glare from Natalie.

"Kelly and I are going to breakfast now. Good luck on getting the all clear. Maybe we'll see you down on the dock. If you're not there, we'll see you when we get back. We can all have a drink together while we're pulling out of port."

Kelly gave Didi a mocking wink and followed Natalie inside.

Steph poked Kelly in the chest. "You're the one who talked Yvonne into this, so I'm holding you personally responsible for bringing her back to this dock in one piece and breathing on her own. You got that?"

Kelly nodded emphatically as everyone laughed.

"Fine. Then go have fun."

Yvonne and Kelly hurried along the dock to a waiting dive boat while Natalie and Steph walked toward their ferry.

It hadn't occurred to Natalie that scuba diving was risky. "You're not really worried about them, are you?"

"Oh, no," Steph answered, shaking her head. "In fact, I'm thrilled to see Yvonne out having a good time. She's been so wrapped up with work lately that she hasn't let herself have fun.

95

And it's great she's made a friend who likes to do that kind of stuff."

"I don't know how you two do it," Natalie said. "One of the things that worked so well with Didi was we liked to do the same things."

"Overrated if you ask me," Steph said. "And I hate to point out the obvious, but things didn't exactly work all that well with you and Didi."

"True, but it wasn't because we grew apart." Actually they had, but not because they didn't have things in common.

Steph led the way onto the ferry and slid into a seat on the lower level. Most of the passengers had gone upstairs for the sun and the view. "I like the fact that Yvonne and I have different interests. It gives us more to talk about. I like to hear about her day and she likes to hear about mine. We never seem to get bored with each other."

Natalie thought back to her last few years with Didi. It was true they shared an interest in the store and the fashion industry, but working together all day obviated the need to talk about it at night. "We didn't talk about work at home because we talked about it at work."

"So what did you talk about at home?"

She shrugged. "We liked our own space. She had the bedroom. I had the den."

"That's what I'm talking about. I think your next girlfriend should be totally opposite from Didi," Steph said. "Now let's see…who do we know that doesn't care all that much about fashion? Maybe someone on the athletic side…someone not so fixated on appearances?"

"Not again." Natalie sighed and shook her head. "Kelly isn't my type and that's all there is to it."

"Natalie, I've known you for twenty years and you've only had two relationships that lasted longer than a month. Considering the fact you were only marginally happy in both of them, maybe you ought to think about getting a new type."

She rolled her eyes and blew out a breath of irritation. "A

person can't just decide to be attracted to someone. It's all about the chemistry."

"No, chemistry is about sex appeal. And for me, sex appeal is about a little spark in my brain that says Yvonne Mooney is the sexiest creature on earth, and it has nothing to do with what she looks like or how she dresses. I think she's beautiful inside and out."

"In other words, you think I'm shallow."

"I didn't say that. But I hope if you meet someone really nice, you won't blow her off just because she doesn't look like a fashion model."

Natalie had already conceded that Kelly had her virtues, but the spark she needed to turn that into sexual attraction just wasn't there. It suddenly occurred to her she needed to fill Steph in on her scheme to make Didi jealous so that she and Yvonne wouldn't think it was real. "By the way, if you notice something between Kelly and me, don't jump to any conclusions. I asked her to help me plant a few ideas in Didi's head."

"Excuse me?"

She wouldn't look at Steph directly, but that didn't matter since she could practically feel her look of dismay. "She's going to help me make Didi jealous."

"I can't believe you'd use someone like that," Steph said indignantly.

"It's okay. Kelly doesn't mind, so why should you?"

"Because you've lost your mind."

Natalie sighed. "Look, she's just helping me out. I don't want to go through the rest of my life feeling like I didn't do everything I could for this relationship. I know how you guys feel about Didi, but I love her and I think she loves me too. Kelly understands that and she wants to help."

Steph glared at her with obvious irritation. "I don't like it, Nat. Somebody's going to get hurt with all these games. If you and Didi are so immature that you can't sit down with each other and talk honestly like adults, then either both of you deserve to be alone for the rest of your lives or you belong together in misery."

"Now don't be that way. This is complicated. If Pamela wasn't in the picture, Didi and I could talk about it. But I can't just go marching in there and push Pamela out of the way. Didi has to be the one to do that."

They paused long enough to politely decline drinks from the ferry's steward.

"I'm more worried about Kelly getting hurt," Steph told her. "What if Didi falls for this? She'll make Kelly's life miserable. That isn't fair."

"We already talked about that. We're not going to carry things so far that we won't be able to be friends when it's over. I promised her that."

The ferry docked at Virgin Gorda and they filed off to start their tour of the Baths. Natalie didn't want to belabor her plan, but she wanted Steph's assurance that she wouldn't interfere. The only way to get that was to make concessions.

"Look, Steph. I don't want anyone hurt either, especially Kelly. If this starts to get out of hand, we'll drop it. But please let me have this one last chance."

Steph sighed and rolled her eyes. "All right, but I still think you've lost your mind."

"And make sure you tell Yvonne, okay?"

"I think we'll just eat some Waldorf salad and spend the rest of the trip in our room."

Kelly grasped Yvonne's forearm and pulled her onto the landing. "Was that fantastic, or what?"

Yvonne kicked off her flippers and loosened the straps on her tank so the dive instructor could stow it with the others. "That was freakin' awesome."

"And you're okay, right? I don't want your girlfriend kicking my ass."

"I'm good. You get to live another day. But if you tell her about seeing that shark, you better say I was out of the water already."

"Got it."

They stepped over the scattered gear and made their way to the front of the dive boat where Kelly began to scroll through her digital pictures from the wreck. "Natalie's going to love these."

Yvonne toweled her hair briskly and slid an oversized T-shirt over her swimsuit. "So what's up with you and Natalie?"

Kelly was surprised by the question, and her first thought was to unveil the scheme she and Natalie had concocted to make Didi jealous. On second thought, she decided to leave that to Natalie. "Nada."

"You don't like her?"

"I never said that. I think she's…" Unable to find the perfect word, she simply grunted her approval.

"You think she's…" Yvonne grunted too. "So what are you doing about it?"

Kelly knew she was blushing, but couldn't contain her grin. "I'm not going to do anything. I don't get the feeling that she wants me to. I wish I did."

"Maybe you need to hit her over the head."

"Why? So I can drag her back to my cave? I don't think so."

"You know, I've known Natalie for eighteen years, and in all that time she's only fallen for two women—Theresa and Didi—and both of them were divas. I think she needs something different, whether she realizes it or not."

"The cave thing?"

Yvonne smacked her forearm. "Not that, you idiot. You need to hit her over the head with the fact that you know how to treat a woman. I watched her last night when you guys came to dinner. She actually waited for you to get her chair. Believe me, Didi never did shit like that for her."

"But Natalie must like doing those things too," Kelly replied. "Otherwise, she wouldn't be attracted to women who expect it."

Yvonne shook her head. "I don't think that's it. I think she's attracted to pretty women, but aren't we all? Didi isn't my favorite person in the world but she's damned attractive. I'll give her that."

"I think she's cast a spell over Natalie or something."

Yvonne nodded vigorously. "She can be very charming when she wants to be and make you feel like the most beautiful woman in the room. I think Natalie's basically insecure so she looks for approval from the people she admires."

"That's all fine and good, but where does that leave me? If she doesn't find me attractive, my approval of her isn't going to mean anything. Besides, I don't think she's over Didi."

"That's true, and I'm not so sure Didi's over her. I think she knows full well how Natalie feels about her and she's eating it up. The minute she feels Natalie start to slip away, she'll yank on that leash and pull her back."

That made perfect sense now that Kelly had more of the puzzle pieces. Thinking back on her impressions from their first night at sea, it was no wonder the lovemaking noises from next door had sounded contrived. Didi was goading Natalie, hoping to make her jealous. And after the feverish display last night—which she had probably orchestrated for Natalie's benefit—there she was on the balcony this morning trying to get Natalie to go off alone with her.

If Didi was playing her game too, it meant both of them wanted to get back together, so it was only a matter of time. Kelly wanted to be happy for Natalie but all she felt was frustration, as if she had just barely missed something really special.

Chapter 10

Kelly's bare leg rested against Natalie's as they sat together on the couch in their stateroom. As discreetly as she could, she studied the texture of Natalie's thigh, which showed the first hint of a tan. It was soft and supple, just as she would have predicted for someone so elegant, and Kelly could do little but desire to feel more.

"I can't believe how beautiful that is," Natalie said, peering at the viewfinder of the underwater camera. "Look at all those fish."

"Wait till you see the next one." Kelly shook off her sensual thoughts and advanced the screen.

"Oh, my gosh! Is that what I think it is?"

"It's a reef shark. They're all over the Caribbean. Mostly

harmless, unless you're dangling a bloody foot."

Natalie shook her head in awe. "You can't show this to Steph. She'll have nightmares."

"Yeah, Yvonne said I had to swear she was already out of the water when this one came by."

"Was she?"

Kelly looked about innocently before shaking her head.

"Weren't you scared?"

"Nah, they're just curious. They live around there, so I'm sure they're used to seeing divers come out to the wreck."

"It's so fascinating. If I weren't such a chicken, I'd love to see it for myself."

"You can, you know. You don't even have to dive. You can see a lot of this stuff just snorkeling."

"Right. You want me to jump off a boat into water over my head where there might be a shark waiting to chomp on me because I have a hangnail."

Kelly laughed. "Look, you won't have to jump. You can go into the water like some of the others did on the boat yesterday. You just glide right off the ladder."

"But—"

"And you'll have your vest on, so you can't possibly sink. When you get comfortable with your mask and snorkel, all you do is lie on your belly with your face in the water." Though Natalie was clearly dubious, Kelly knew she was making headway with her sales pitch. "I'll be right there beside you the whole time."

"I remember an old joke…something about how you wouldn't have to swim faster than the shark."

"Right. I only have to swim faster than you." She jabbed her elbow in Natalie's ribs as they laughed. "So how was your tour today?"

"It was fine, I guess. We walked all along the Baths and heard about their history. I would tell you what I learned, but Steph and I talked over most of it."

"I bet you got in trouble for that at school."

"I did. I spent more time out in the hall with my nose against the wall than anyone else in my class."

"If we had been in school together I would have been out there with you. My dad said I used to talk all the time and so fast that no one could understand me."

"Talking too fast was never my problem," Natalie said, emphasizing her Mississippi drawl.

"Did you guys hook up with Didi and Pamela?"

"Never saw them. But I called their room when we got back and didn't get an answer. Either they're out or they killed each other. I'm not sure which one I'd bet on."

"At least they got sprung. It really is too bad they missed three days."

"You can feel sorry for Pamela, but trust me, Didi will get a lot of mileage out of telling the story."

"…so there we were, Pamela on the toilet and me with my head in the sink puking my guts out—"

Yvonne cleared her throat loudly. "We're trying to eat here."

Didi sighed dramatically. "Fine, but if you ever get deathly ill don't come crying to me."

Natalie took pity on her. "What did you two do this afternoon to celebrate your freedom?"

"We got out too late to catch a tour so we took a cab into Road Town and walked around the shops. Pamela found some sandals but I didn't see anything I liked."

"You liked that orange scarf," Pamela interjected.

"But I certainly wasn't going to pay ten dollars for it. If she had come down to five, we would have had a deal." Didi motioned for the waiter to bring her another gin and tonic. "There's a place in Antigua called Heritage Quay that's supposed to have some good duty-free shopping. You with me, Nat?"

"You know, I was thinking I might try something a little more adventurous."

Didi's mouth dropped open in exaggerated shock. "You?"

Natalie tilted her head and scowled. "I never said I was going to dangle a bloody foot in a shark tank." She turned toward Kelly and gave her a wink that Didi couldn't see. "Kelly was showing me the pictures from where they went diving down to a shipwreck and I thought it was interesting."

"I want to see those," Steph said. "Yvonne said it was gorgeous."

Kelly pushed her chair back. "Let me run get my camera. I didn't order an appetizer, so go ahead and start without me."

Didi folded her arms and smirked at Natalie. "So now you're outdoorsy. Does this mean you're going to go get all your hair whacked off?"

"I will if I want to," she answered sharply.

"Girls, girls," Yvonne chided. "Antigua has a really nice beach. We were thinking it might be fun for all of us to go together. We can rent some chairs and umbrellas, and—"

"If we're going to the beach, there will be no umbrella for us," Didi said emphatically. "We have to make up for lost time. I'm not going back to Rochester with my skin lily-white."

Kelly returned as they were starting the first course and passed her camera around.

"I think we've planned a day at the beach," Natalie said. "So we'll have to put off our adventure for another time."

"That sounds like fun. I read in the brochure that Dickenson Bay is supposed to be one of the best beaches in the Caribbean." She leaned in front of Natalie to address Didi. "It'll be great to have you guys join us. You've missed out on too much fun. We'll have to make up for it."

Didi smiled stiffly and nodded.

Pamela was more gracious. "Kelly, it's so nice of you to say that. You've had to listen to so much of our complaining."

Natalie wanted nothing more than to sneer at Didi, but she resisted. There was sweet irony in having Kelly kill her with kindness.

Natalie dipped her toes in the warm, churning water of the spa. "This feels divine."

"Wait till you get all the way in," Steph said. "It feels like you're floating in Jell-O."

She inched into the hot tub and positioned herself so that a jet pounded on her lower back. It was a beautiful night and the winter sky was full of bright stars. "I wish I'd known about this place last night. Kelly and I would have been out here drinking champagne."

"Did you see the look on Didi's face when Kelly made nice with her at dinner? In all the years I've known her, that's the first time I've ever seen her speechless."

"It takes a lot to shut her up, that's for sure. And Kelly was so sweet and innocent about it."

"I like her, Nat. I hope she'll come around when we get back to Rochester…dinners and things. She fits in well with our little group, don't you think?"

"Is this going to turn into the same conversation we've had already?" She lowered her voice, suddenly aware they were shouting over the jets.

"I just can't believe you don't think she's hot. She looks really strong and agile."

"Like Yvonne, which explains why you like that."

"No, Yvonne isn't built like Kelly. She's athletic, but she doesn't have that sleek runner's body."

"But that athletic look isn't my type."

"How do you know? When did you ever date someone like that?"

This was a circular argument. "Never, because that look doesn't appeal to me. I can't just manufacture an opinion like that. It would be like kissing my sister."

Steph scrunched her nose in disgust. "I've met your sisters. Kelly has it all over both of them."

"Bad example. But the point is if I'm going to kiss somebody, there has to be some kind of spark that makes it interesting. I'm not saying"—she looked around to make sure they were alone—"I want to have sex with everyone I kiss, but I want the possibility to be there. To me, a kiss is intimate. I'm not going to share that with someone who doesn't excite me sexually."

"Is it just the way she looks?"

"No…yes. It's hard to explain. The way she looks is the way she is. Everything about her is…" The word "masculine" seemed pejorative in this context. Besides, it was undeniable that Kelly had a distinctly feminine side. "There are things I like in a woman that don't interest Kelly at all, like clothes, hair and makeup… jewelry. There's nothing wrong with that in a friend, but it isn't the kind of woman I want to have a romantic relationship with. It's perfectly fine if some people find that attractive. Kelly obviously accepts who she is, and why shouldn't she? She has a great body and a gorgeous smile. And she couldn't be nicer."

Steph leaned back and rested her arms on the edge of the hot tub. "You're right. I can't see why on earth you'd be attracted to someone like that. Not when you can have pretty women who expect you to drop everything and kowtow to them—like Theresa and Didi."

Natalie was growing frustrated under the scrutiny, and was tempted to pick up and go back to her room. She was tired of defending herself when it came to her choices. "You know, friends are supposed to be supportive. Back when you and Yvonne almost broke up over buying the house, I stood right there with both of you."

"I'm sorry, Nat. I don't mean to sound so snarky, but you're my best friend and I hate to see you pouring yourself into people who don't give it back. It isn't just about Didi, though I told you already I never liked you two together. You always go for women who need to be adored and told how special they are. When are you going to let someone do that for you?"

"Maybe you haven't noticed, but women aren't exactly standing in line in front of me to do that."

"You're the one who hasn't noticed. Kelly's already doing it." She leaned over and put her hand on Natalie's shoulder. "Look, I'm not saying you ought to get involved with her. I just want you to be open to it if it happens. Even if it doesn't work out, at least you'll know what it's like to be on the other end of the giving spectrum."

"I don't want to be on the end of anything. I want a partnership that feels equal."

"Did you ever feel equal to Theresa or Didi?"

She had a point.

"Natalie, you know you have it in you to really love someone with all your heart. Just try doing it with someone who can love you like that too."

Natalie hadn't planned to turn her whole life upside down in the hot tub. This was one soak that left her anything but relaxed.

Chapter 11

With a mighty thrust, Kelly jammed the umbrella into the soft sand. "Think that'll stay?"

"How should I know?" Yvonne said. "You're the construction engineer."

"Smart-ass."

Natalie stood off to the side, her arms loaded with towels and a beach bag. Her sunglasses hid the fact that she was watching Kelly closely, studying the contrast between her and Yvonne that Steph had pointed out. Indeed, Kelly was sleek, almost catlike, with sinewy muscles that wrapped around her legs and shoulders.

It was impossible not to notice Didi and Pamela also, who were spreading a rented woven mat in the sun. Pamela in particular looked great in her bikini, better than Didi, who had no business wearing something that small at forty-two years old.

"Who wants sunscreen?" Kelly asked.

"I wouldn't mind getting a little sun," Natalie said. "Not much, just enough for my legs to look nice without nylons."

Kelly rummaged in her backpack and produced a plastic bottle of oil. "Try some of this. It's got sun block in it but lets you tan."

As she smeared the oil on her legs, she noticed that Kelly was slathering herself with thick white lotion. "Don't you want to get a tan?"

"Nah, I go from white to brick red in about an hour. Then I spend the next two weeks molting."

"Eww, that's gross," Didi said.

Natalie looked at Kelly and rolled her eyes. "This from a woman who told us every detail of her digestive system during dinner." She stretched to cover her upper back with the oil.

"Let me get that," Kelly offered.

She smiled to herself, wondering if Didi had caught the hint of familiarity in Kelly's voice. Kelly had played this beautifully all day, carrying her bags and complimenting her on her outfit. At one point, she was almost certain she had seen Didi scowl.

She turned her back and savored the warm feel of Kelly's hands. Too bad Didi couldn't know what she was feeling, the gentle pressure of the fingertips that slipped underneath her straps and the edges of her suit. She wasn't even aware of her smile until she raised her eyes and met Steph's, which twinkled with mischief. Natalie responded in her usual way—she stuck out her tongue.

"Anyone else?"

"Sure," Steph said, turning her back so Kelly could apply the oil.

"Careful where you put those hands," Yvonne cautioned.

"I was just thinking I'd died and gone to lesbian heaven. Then you had to spoil my fantasy." Kelly grinned and wiped the excess oil onto her neck. "We can rent some Wave Runners over there. Anyone up for that?"

Didi rolled onto her stomach and grinned. "Natalie said she was ready for adventure."

"Not on one of those," she said emphatically. "I was thinking more along the lines of putting my face in the water under extremely controlled circumstances. I didn't say I was giving up living."

"If you'd like to come, you can ride with me and we'll take everything nice and easy," Kelly offered.

"Aw, isn't that sweet?" Didi said sarcastically, prompting a glare from both Natalie and Steph.

Yvonne took some bills out of her wallet. "I'm in, but I'm not taking anything nice and easy. In fact"—she pointed to a buoy well offshore—"I think we should start way down on that end and race to that buoy. You up for that, Grandma?"

Kelly grinned. "Did you just call me Grandma?"

"I do believe I did."

"Let's go. I'm going to smoke your ass."

"In your dreams." They hurried off to the vendor stand and moments later took to the water aboard two of the Wave Runners.

Natalie settled in a lounge chair alongside Steph to watch. "My money's on Kelly."

"She's toast. Yvonne cheats."

Even Didi and Pamela sat up on their blanket to see the race.

Natalie grew concerned as the jet skis scooted farther and farther offshore. "Why do they have to go so far out?"

"They have to get past the swimmers," Steph explained. "Don't worry. They have on ski vests."

Finally they came to rest side by side in the ready position. The course was set to run parallel to shore about two hundred yards out in what looked like choppy water. "There they go!"

Kelly got a slow start, but her water exhaust—the rooster tail, as Steph called it—grew as she caught Yvonne at the halfway point. She then surged ahead before sinking into a trough, which

Yvonne jumped cleanly. But once again, Kelly overtook her and pulled slightly ahead.

Natalie jumped to her feet and cheered, and Steph joined her. Didi yelled for Yvonne, Pamela for Kelly.

In a mad dash for the finish line, Yvonne swerved into Kelly's path, causing her to lurch sideways to avoid a collision. Kelly toppled over a wave and her Wave Runner came to a standstill. She was nowhere in sight.

"Oh, my goodness," Natalie said, running toward the shore.

"It's okay," Steph said.

Yvonne circled the buoy with her fist in the air and doubled back to taunt Kelly just as she surfaced over the chop. Kelly climbed back aboard her jet ski and fell into line behind Yvonne as they snaked a course of jumps, donuts and spins through the waves.

"Everybody's okay, right?" Didi asked nonchalantly.

"They're fine. They're like a couple of children," Steph said.

"Who won?"

Natalie sneered. "The cheater." She settled back in her chair to watch the antics of the two women in the water, laughing when Kelly exacted her revenge on Yvonne by aiming her rooster tail in her face.

Kelly shook her head in disbelief as Didi and Pamela returned to their mat after lunch. She could already see red lines at the edges of their bikini bottoms, but they stubbornly resisted putting on sunblock or moving into the shade.

"I think I'm ready for something a little stronger," Natalie said, interrupting her thoughts. She was holding the tube of sun block Didi had declined to use.

"Good idea." Kelly was more than ready to help Natalie with her lotion again, though the episode with the oil had nearly done her in. Even standing behind her, she had gotten a jolt of desire from lowering the straps of her bathing suit to run her fingers over her naked skin. It might have killed her had Natalie asked her to do the backs of her thighs. "Anyone interested in a walk on the beach?"

"That could be fun," Steph said.

Yvonne gave Steph a poke. "I'm ready for a nap after all that food."

"That sounds even better. Never mind."

"I'll go," Natalie said.

"I want to come too," Didi said, jumping up abruptly.

"Wait, I need you here," Pamela said. "I think I need some of that sunblock on my back. It's starting to burn."

"I think that's smart," Kelly said. "You don't want to be hurting later." She put her hand on Natalie's back and quickened their pace to put distance between them and Didi. "Was that too obvious?"

Natalie snickered and looked over her shoulder. "I don't think so. I think she's catching on, though. She's been watching us all day."

"I hadn't even noticed." Kelly's attention had been riveted all morning to finding opportunities to be close to Natalie. She wasn't going to waste permission, and she couldn't have cared less if Didi was watching them or not. "I'm glad we all came out here. It's turned into a nice day."

"It's fun for all of us to be together. It's almost like being back in Rochester, except without the snow."

"And having to get up for work in the morning."

"And since you mention it, having someone bring me coffee in bed."

"Yeah, I have to admit, it's a little different sharing space with someone," Kelly said.

"I hope I haven't been a bad roommate."

"Not at all. I've enjoyed it." She almost laughed at her lame conversation, like that of a teenager on a first date, shy and vapid.

"I was talking with Steph last night out in the hot tub, and we both said we hoped you'd join our group when we got home. We get together for dinner a couple of times a month or we go to movies, things like that."

They reached the water and waded up to their knees.

"You're going to see a lot of me at your house if you're serious about those renovations." They strolled casually and talked of remodeling until Kelly turned them around and headed back. When they reached the Wave Runners, she stopped. "How about coming for a ride?"

Natalie shook her head adamantly. "I've seen you in action. Lord only knows where the nearest chiropractor is."

"I won't go that fast with you. I promise. You told Didi you were going to do something adventurous."

"You can't let me fall off. I'd panic and drown both of us."

"Not a chance." She returned to the rental hut and collected another key and two ski vests. "What's your favorite color?"

"Green."

"The color of your eyes." Kelly grinned, recognizing that she was still in full-flirt mode even though Didi was nowhere to be seen.

"Or we could take the blue one that matches yours."

"Nope. We're taking green." Kelly pushed the small craft into waist-deep water and climbed aboard. "You always get on one of these from the back. Just grab my shoulders—" Her words trailed off as she felt Natalie's arms encircle her waist and her body press against her back. "You catch on fast."

"Not really. I started thinking about whether or not there were any sharks swimming around my legs, and I had an overpowering urge to get out of the water."

"There weren't." She pulled gently on the throttle and started forward. "The guy in the vendor hut told me about a sandbar. It's about half a mile down the beach, but not too far out. I'm not going to go very fast, but we'll still have some bumps. Just hold on and you'll be fine."

Telling Natalie to hold on was unnecessary, since her hands were clasped tightly in Kelly's lap. As their Wave Runner rounded a bend, they lost sight of the beach where their friends were, and bounced along in the steady chop for ten minutes before running aground on a high shelf of sand.

"How did you know it was right here?"

"The guy said to go out about three hundred yards parallel to the coast until we passed the blue house with the widow's walk." Kelly pointed to the shore.

"Look at these. They're beautiful," Natalie said excitedly as she sloshed through the ankle-deep water and picked up a colorful conch shell.

"Not only that, they're alive."

"Shells?"

"Turn it over and look inside." She smiled at the look of wonder on Natalie's face. "We used to pick these up off Key West all the time. In fact, they call Key West the Conch Republic."

"I'd love to have one of these to take home, minus the critter, of course."

"You definitely don't want the critter. They don't smell so good when they die in there." Kelly climbed back onto the Wave Runner and scooted forward. "I bet you can find a shell like that in Nassau."

Natalie poked her in the ribs as she settled in. "What do you know about shopping?"

"I saw it once in the movies." When she felt Natalie's arms go around her waist again, she realized that two things had her giddy—the fact that she and Natalie were off on their own, and that Natalie finally trusted her. She wanted to make the feeling last as long as she could. "We'll take it nice and easy on the way back."

A motorboat passed towing a parasail, and she felt Natalie shudder. "There isn't enough money in the world to get me on something like that."

"I did it once down in Cozumel. It's kind of a rush, but once you've done it, the thrill is gone." She eyed a series of waves headed their way from the motorboat's wake. "Hold on. We're going to rock a little."

Natalie's grip tightened as they rode out the gentle swells.

Steering only with her throttle hand, Kelly dropped her other hand and intertwined her fingers with Natalie's. She savored the sensation for as long as she reasonably could, and couldn't resist giving a light squeeze before grasping the handlebar again.

Too bad there weren't any more boats headed their way.

Natalie trudged through the sand toward their group while Kelly returned the Wave Runner key and their vests to the vendor. She needed the few moments to collect her thoughts on what had just happened. It was only a small, protective caress when the motorboat had passed, so benign that Kelly probably hadn't even realized she was doing it. The fact that they had been well away from shore—and Didi's line of sight—made it clear that Kelly's gesture had nothing to do with their scheme. For that matter, neither did Natalie's response.

"How was it?" Steph asked.

"I hate to admit it, but it was a lot more fun than I thought it would be," Natalie said as she reached for a towel.

"You should have seen Didi. She got up and started pacing the minute you two disappeared around the bend. She came back over here twice to ask Yvonne how far you were going and if it was dangerous out there. Then she started on Kelly for taking you so far out and probably scaring you half to death."

That Didi was suddenly worried about her was proof positive their plan was working. It would have been understandable had they gone parasailing or scuba diving, but a simple ride on a Wave Runner was no cause for concern. No, she wasn't concerned. She was jealous.

Natalie scanned the beach, locating Pamela at the refreshment hut and Didi by the shore where she appeared to be collecting shells. It was interesting that Didi had been frantic about her well-being while she was gone, but not enough to express her relief when she returned. Instead, she was behaving with her usual nonchalance, never overtly showing that she cared. Natalie chuckled to herself, thinking if she had gone out there wearing the wrong swimsuit she would have heard about it the second she returned.

Kelly hummed to herself as she ambled down the hallway

toward her stateroom juggling two ice lattes she had picked up at the coffee shop in the atrium. The day at the beach couldn't have gone much better, though she could have done without Didi's persistent efforts to get Natalie to commit to shopping with her in Barbados and St. Lucia. Natalie had resisted the efforts to nail down her plans, but it was plain the idea was appealing. Kelly had hoped for more time together, even if it was orchestrated to make Didi jealous.

She found Natalie out on the balcony, fresh from her shower, but still in her robe.

"Here's your latte. I ran into Steph. They're going to order room service tonight. So I guess it's just us and the girls next door for dinner," she said, her lack of enthusiasm obvious.

Natalie chuckled. "Do I detect exuberance in your voice?"

Kelly laughed aloud. "Oops." She slumped into the other deck chair and propped her feet high on the rail. "I'm sure it will be fine. I was just thinking about what to wear."

"Don't worry about it. Just be yourself." Natalie got up to peek around the corner of the balcony divider to make sure they were alone. "I think we got to Didi today."

"Yeah, she seemed kind of peeved, like we'd gone off without her permission or something." Kelly was still reveling in the fact that their closest contact—when Natalie held her hand on the Wave Runner—had happened well outside of Didi's line of sight. "Didi or not, I had fun out there. I'm glad you went with me."

"I wouldn't have missed it for anything. I've never done anything like that before. Where I come from, it wouldn't have been considered ladylike."

"Believe me, Natalie. Everything about you is ladylike."

"You say the sweetest things. If the women back in Rochester had any idea what they were missing, you'd have a line out the door."

She met Natalie's eyes and gave her a small smile. "I save my best for ladies who interest me."

The awkward silence that followed seemed to last for hours, as Natalie merely looked away and sipped her coffee. For once,

Kelly welcomed the sound of the sliding glass door on the next balcony.

"Hey, girls," Natalie called. "Steph and Yvonne are ordering room service. It's just the four of us for dinner."

"Did you bring any aloe?" Didi asked gruffly, peering around the divider to show off her bright red face. "I can barely move. We're both burnt to a crisp."

"Oh, my goodness." Natalie stared slack-jawed.

"I'm sure it isn't as bad as it looks. It should turn into a tan overnight, at least for me. Pamela has bright red stripes on her thighs that look like they're going to blister."

Natalie located a tube of lotion in the stateroom and passed it around the divider. "Poor Pamela. I hope this makes her feel better. Kelly and I were thinking we might go up to that bistro by the observation lounge. It has a nice romantic atmosphere and such a lovely view."

Kelly's ears went up at Natalie's dreamy tone. Not that she minded the idea of a romantic dinner one bit.

"Peachy," Didi hissed as she turned on her heels and disappeared back inside.

Natalie made a sheepish face. "I think I pissed her off."

"And you didn't even try."

She chuckled and shook her head. "You must think Didi's truly awful, and that I'm totally insane for wanting her back."

"I don't really know her all that well." That sounded better than saying she hadn't yet discovered anything that made up for the dour mood and relentless criticism. So far, her favorite thing about Didi had been the retching sounds from beyond the walls as she puked up her guts. It was impossible to imagine someone as easygoing as Natalie had been charmed into a relationship with Didi that lasted six days, let alone six years.

"It took a long time for Steph and Yvonne to warm up to her, but they eventually did. She really can be a very sweet person."

Kelly didn't want to disagree since it was obvious Natalie cared about her, but she couldn't hide her skepticism. "She doesn't really give that sweetness off to me. I guess that's why it feels like I don't know her very well."

They finished their coffee as the ship turned toward the sunset.

"I thought maybe I'd come snorkeling with you tomorrow," Natalie said out of the blue. "If that's all right?"

"Are you kidding me? I'd love it."

"It'll be perfect. If today was any indication, you-know-who will go nuts."

Kelly felt her insides deflate. Natalie's sudden interest in snorkeling had nothing to do with her.

Natalie paused to admire in the mirror the light brown tone of her arms and chest against the lacy white top Didi had given her for Christmas two years ago, just before they split up. Another two or three days of sun would deepen her tan and make her the envy of everyone in the store once they returned to Rochester.

She smiled again to think of Kelly's "ladylike" compliment, and wished Didi had been there to hear it. It was rare to get compliments in Didi's presence, since Didi usually commanded most of the attention. That other bit—ladies that interested her—had taken her off guard momentarily. She hadn't minded the idea that Kelly thought she was interesting...which is what she must have meant by her remark. It was highly unlikely she had meant *interested in*, because Kelly understood how she felt about Didi.

As frivolous and petty as it seemed, she relished all the details Steph had shared about Didi's frantic concern at the beach. It was amazing how well her plan was working. She never would have guessed being with Kelly—of all people—would have tweaked that green-eyed monster, but she was beginning to think Steph was right after all. There were plenty of things about Kelly that were appealing, and Didi obviously saw them too.

As she rummaged through the closet for her shoes, her musings were interrupted by the sudden halt of the shower.

"Hey, Natalie."

The bathroom door cracked a bit, just enough for Natalie to

see Kelly standing with her back to the door in her underpants—they were purple briefs, low-slung and rectangular shaped, showing the bottom third of her butt cheeks—as she slipped a gray tank top over her head. "Uh, I'm right here by the door."

Kelly's head jutted through the opening, along with a bare leg. "Maybe you should check again with Didi. If we're going to the bistro we may need a reservation and I should probably dress up a little."

"You could always wear your black pants again…maybe with the vest this time." She turned away from the eyeful in the bathroom and dialed Didi's room. "Hey, there." She explained her reason for calling. "You're kidding. Is it that bad?"

By now, Kelly was standing behind her, rolling up the sleeves on a white button-down-collared shirt that hung to the top of her thighs.

Natalie replaced the phone. "They're burnt to a crisp. Didi's eyes are swelling shut and Pamela has little blisters on her shoulders and legs. The nurse is on the way."

"Are they going to be all right?"

"I think so. Didi has a flair for the dramatic."

"No!" Kelly's dimple twitched.

"I can see you trying not to laugh. You should be ashamed of yourself." She knew her own mouth was turned up at the corners. "And as soon as I stop laughing, I'm going to tell on you."

Kelly was smiling now, showing off, not only her dimples, but her bright white, perfect teeth. "You think I should wear the vest with this?"

"You know what I really think? We should go eat a juicy hamburger in the pub and see if we can find a movie or something. Wouldn't that be more fun?" She owed Kelly a good time, considering her help with the Didi situation. Besides, she loved a cheeseburger just as much as the next person, but Didi had always given her a hard time about enjoying junk food. Now she had an excuse to actually enjoy one.

Chapter 12

Didi glared through her swollen eyes at Natalie, who hung over the balcony rail sipping her morning coffee. "Saying 'I told you so' is not helpful. You could show a little more sympathy."

Natalie bit her tongue to keep from expressing her sorrow that Didi had chosen to ignore their warnings. "I'm very sorry it hurts. How is Pamela feeling?"

"Probably worse than I do, but don't tell her I said that. At least she has medicine to put on her arms and legs. I can't use it on my face." She held out her hand for Natalie's cup and took a sip. "I guess shopping is out for us today. What are you going to do?"

She couldn't wait to see the look on Didi's face. "I've decided to go snorkeling with Kelly. We had such a good time the other day on the catamaran and then again yesterday on the Wave Runner. I had no idea water sports were so much fun."

"You've got to be kidding. You hate showers because you get water in your eyes."

"I'll be wearing a mask. And Kelly promised to hold my hand."

"Isn't that sweet?" Didi proclaimed, heavy on the sarcasm. She peeked around the divider to make certain Kelly wasn't on the balcony. "Does she run around without her shirt on?"

Natalie bristled. "Now you cut that out. She's very nice, and she's been very concerned about your sunburn." *Despite giggling.*

Didi sighed, clearly admonished. "Just promise me you aren't going to start wearing board shorts."

"As you well know, that is not a fashion statement I'm inclined to make. But why should I care if it's what Kelly likes? And why should you?"

"Because it offends my poor eyes," Didi wailed dramatically. "Seriously, Natalie. I've seen the"—she made finger quotes in the air—"'androgynous look' on the runways, and it can be sort of hot on the right person. But that's one of those high-fashion looks that doesn't translate to the real world and even if it did, Kelly's not pulling it off. It only works if the women are women."

In the ten years they had known one another, Natalie had heard literally thousands of fashion critiques from Didi on people they ran into, but rarely one tinged with such personal venom. "That's silly. Kelly's definitely a woman. I can vouch for her personally."

The look on Didi's face was one of pure shock, and Natalie realized she had stepped over the line she and Kelly had agreed to about what impressions to leave. The decent thing to do was to clarify what she meant, that her quiet, serious talks with Kelly had revealed a feminine side, though one that was edgier than any she had known. But there was a distinct advantage to playing her cards close to her vest, namely, that Didi's jealousy had visibly escalated.

"Is there something going on with you and Kelly?"

"If there is, it's my business."

"Natalie, come on. You can't seriously find someone like that appealing." She looked over her shoulder to see where Pamela was. "A woman like you deserves better than that, not some butch trying to make a statement about how she is what she is. And just in case you've forgotten that you have a business to run, keep in mind that she's exactly what turns people off about lesbians. They want to see people like us, not people like that."

By the time Didi finished, she was practically spitting her words. It was well beyond her usual criticism, so vicious that Natalie sprang angrily to Kelly's defense. "You don't know the first thing about Kelly and who she is. It just so happens she's one of the nicest people I've ever met, and you should keep in mind that not everybody in this world judges people by how they look."

"Maybe not, but that's how they judge them first, whether they admit it or not. Be honest. What did you think the first time you saw her? That she was nice? Or that she looked like a teenage boy? You even said being with her would be like being with a man."

She could feel her ears burning. "What difference does it make? What matters is that I know her now, and so do you. She's never been anything but nice to you, so stop being an ass and show her a little respect."

Didi let out a heavy sigh in her usual dramatic style. "She's perfectly nice, and I'm sure if I knew her a little better the other things wouldn't bother me so much. I just don't want to see you getting all swept up in that just because you're feeling lonely. I'm always right here, and you can join us for anything. Believe me"—she checked again over her shoulder—"there's a lot to be said for young and sexy, but once you've said it, there's not much else to talk about, if you get my drift."

Natalie rolled her eyes, though secretly celebrating the fact that Didi was voicing exactly what she felt—that being able to talk about things and enjoy each other's company was a better foundation for a relationship than sex. Now she just needed for Didi to turn those thoughts into actions. "Look, we can go shopping tomorrow in St. Lucia."

"All of us?"

She shrugged. It wasn't her place to suggest the two of them go off alone. Kelly would do whatever she wanted, but Pamela was Didi's responsibility. "Whoever wants to go. They're having another formal night in the dining room and I wouldn't mind having something new to wear."

"Now you're talking. That's the Natalie I know and love."

A warm feeling enveloped her as Didi shot her a smile. "You should put some ice on your eyes today so the swelling will go down. You want me to fix you a cloth?"

"Oh, you're so sweet. Lord knows no one else cares enough about me to do that."

She went back inside to raid the ice bucket and found Kelly sitting on the couch—very close to the sliding glass door—going through the daily newsletter that detailed the ship's activities.

"How are Didi and Pamela?" Kelly asked, with not even a hint she had overheard the balcony conversation.

"They're better. Didi still has a little swelling around her eyes. I was just getting her some ice. They won't be going ashore today so I was thinking I might go with you if it's not too late."

"You mean out on the boat, like you did the other day?"

"I was actually thinking I might give it a try, if you still feel like helping me and all."

Kelly shot up off the couch. "Are you kidding? I'll go down to the excursion desk and get your ticket now."

Natalie packed the remnants of the previous night's ice into a cloth and took it back outside. "Here's a pack for your eyes. You should lie down and rest with this on."

Below their balcony, crewmen were scurrying onto the dock at Barbados to secure the massive ropes to giant cleats along the dock. The gangway would go down soon to allow them ashore.

"You're an angel, Nat."

An angel on a mission, she thought…a mission to make Didi jealous enough to come back to her. "Kelly just went to get our

123

snorkeling tickets. I'm so excited."

"You're really going through with that?"

"Of course. I'll tell you all about it at dinner. You and Pamela feel better, okay?"

"You better not drown. I'll be really mad at you!"

When they stepped onto the boat, Kelly saw a familiar face and waved. "There's Jo."

"I wonder where Julie is. I haven't seen her around in the last couple of days."

"She must have gotten the message that you weren't interested."

"I guess," Natalie said sheepishly. "She was nice, but not really my type. Sort of...not really pushy, just kind of obvious about what she wanted. I guess I prefer a little more subtlety, if you know what I mean."

Kelly chuckled to herself, thinking back on her conversation with Yvonne. "So you don't really go for that being clubbed over the head and dragged back to the cave?"

"Not usually."

They took a seat on a cool plastic bench near the bar where a young woman was serving juice and cookies as they ferried out to the snorkel site. As usual, Kelly wore her board shorts and a sports bra, with a sun-blocking long-sleeved shirt on top. Natalie was dressed casually also, tan shorts and a loose cotton polo shirt over her swimsuit, and the sandals she had worn to the beach the day before. Her large beach bag held their towels, sunscreen and Kelly's underwater camera. At their feet were two sets of fins and snorkel masks.

"This is going to be fun, Natalie. I'm really glad you decided to come."

"I promised Didi I wouldn't drown."

"Yeah, that would be a real bummer." She could tell Natalie was nervous. "You want to try on your gear?"

"I guess." She slipped off her shorts and shirt and worked with Kelly to apply sunscreen. Finally she pulled her hair back and secured it with an elastic band. "Okay, I'm ready for this."

Kelly sprayed their masks with defogger and rinsed them in a large garbage can filled with fresh water. Then she walked Natalie through the process of sucking the air out of her mask in order to make a watertight seal around her face. Next she tightened the straps and adjusted the snorkel so that it slid easily into Natalie's mouth. "Of all the things you can do in the water, snorkeling is probably the easiest. Once you put your face in, you forget about everything except what you see."

"And you're sure it doesn't matter that I'm not all that good a swimmer?" she asked, lifting the mask to her forehead.

"Not with this." Kelly lifted an inflatable vest over her head. "Stand up and I'll fix it for you." One of the ties wrapped around the waist and she made quick work of fastening it. The other hung from the back, which meant looping it through Natalie's crotch and snapping it on the hook just below her breasts. She tried not to think about the fact that Natalie might consider it overly familiar for someone to reach between her legs.

"That's awfully loose."

"You don't want it really tight, just enough to keep it on your chest instead of around your neck. But either way, it keeps you afloat." She tugged on the valve and let some of the air out. "In fact, you don't even have to keep it fully inflated. Just a little bit of air is probably enough."

Natalie nodded at a couple who were also getting ready. "Those people over there didn't blow theirs up at all."

"They probably want to dive down into the reef. You can't do that if you have air in your vest. I probably won't blow mine up either."

"Great, the person who's responsible for making sure I don't drown isn't even going to use her life vest and plans to run off and leave me flopping in the water."

"I promise not to leave you, Natalie. If I dive down, I'll still be right in front of you where you can see me. I won't even do that if you don't want me to. Just let me know by holding onto my hand."

125

Natalie's eyes grew wide as the boat drew to a stop, and one by one, the snorkelers jumped off the boat into the clear blue water.

"Come on. We'll go down the ladder." She waited until everyone else had gone before leading Natalie to the ladder, their flippers slapping across the deck. Then she made the final adjustments on their masks and slipped into the water to wait.

For a few seconds, she wondered if Natalie would follow through. Finally she did, cautiously descending the steps and practically gliding into Kelly's arms. "Everything okay?"

Natalie nodded, though the look on her face was pure terror.

"You're doing great. Let's move away from the boat." She swam backward for several feet and towed Natalie along. When the water below turned dark she stopped. "The coral's right under us. Are you ready to put your face in the water?"

Another nod.

"Okay, here we go." Kelly bit into her mouthpiece and lowered her face into the water, shifting so they were side by side with their fingers tightly intertwined. Then she kicked her flippers to send them over the coral, which was swarming with dozens of species of brightly colored fish. With her free hand, she pointed from one sight to another as they floated on the surface.

Again and again, she looked at Natalie's mask for any signs of leakage or distress. None appeared, and when she flashed the A-OK sign, she got one in return.

Kelly kicked harder and steered them into deeper water, where larger fish trolled near the sandy bottom for the occasional morsel. She snapped off a few photos, including one of a sea turtle, about a foot and a half in diameter, as it scuttled away.

Several yards ahead, a larger bank of coral teemed with life. As they neared it, she spotted a conch shell on the bottom. She wriggled her hand free and dove about twelve feet to the spot, where she lifted the shell and turned it over. A lively conch flapped from the folds. She gently replaced it and kicked upward, expelling the air from her lungs as she resurfaced.

126

To her surprise, Natalie had raised her head and removed her snorkel. "This is fantastic!"

"I told you. Did you see the conch?" Natalie began to cough and Kelly swam quickly to her side. "You okay?"

Several coughs later, she regrouped and adjusted her mask. "Let's look some more."

Kelly stuck close by and took more photos as they crisscrossed the reef, lifting her head occasionally to check their position relative to the boat and the other snorkelers. They were well away from the crowd, but close enough to get back easily when it was time to leave.

She felt almost silly for being so happy about swimming around with Natalie and holding her hand. Natalie probably had no idea she was getting such a buzz from it.

A swimmer suddenly appeared below them, gesturing to his camera. He was a crewman taking souvenir pictures he would print and offer for sale before they returned to the dock. Kelly and Natalie waved with their free hand as he took the photo. Then he pointed in the direction of the others and motioned for them to follow.

They kicked along behind until they found themselves among the others, who were looking on as their snorkel guide fed a small reef shark. They floated, mesmerized, for several minutes until the guide surfaced and called them all back to the boat.

"Let's hang back until people are out of the way," Kelly said. She removed her mask and tossed it to a crewman on the deck. "Is that okay?"

Natalie nodded and pushed her mask up too. "I can't wait to tell Didi I actually saw a real live shark. She's going to freak out."

She cringed at hearing Didi's name, but tried to put herself in Natalie's shoes. Natalie wanted to brag to her friends that she had done something thrilling, something they wouldn't have expected. "I got a few pictures you can show her." She nudged Natalie toward the ladder, where the gentle waves rocked it up and down. "Grab the rail and try to sit on the steps. I'll take your fins off."

Kelly scooted up behind to keep her from falling back into the water. When she realized Natalie was struggling to time her upward thrust with the swell of the waves, she placed a palm on her butt to give her a lift. One last wave rolled into them, drawing out the contact, which Kelly didn't mind at all.

Natalie finally spun onto the ladder, kicked off her fins and climbed onto the boat with Kelly following. "That was so amazing. I see now why you love it," she said as she toweled off.

"We were lucky you picked this one. It was a gorgeous reef, and there wasn't a cloud in the sky."

"A shark! I can't believe I'm going to be able to tell people I saw a shark. Do you think we can do this again?"

"I don't see why not. We have...what? Three more ports?" Kelly could not keep from grinning at Natalie's excitement. Everything about their day had been perfect as far as she was concerned. Besides all the things they had seen, Natalie had trusted her at every turn. Not only had she been excited about everything she saw in the water, but now she was also brimming with a newfound confidence and sense of adventure. "St. Lucia tomorrow, then the private island and Nassau. Of all of those, St. Lucia would probably be the best."

Natalie made a face. "I promised Didi I'd go shopping with her in St. Lucia. I can't believe I'm saying this, but I actually don't want to. I bet the devil's sharpening his ice skates."

"You can always cancel out, maybe plan shopping for Nassau. The water won't be as warm there." Kelly was in favor of anything that meant breaking a date with Didi.

"I'm worried I'll hurt her feelings. I haven't done anything with her on this trip except our outing to the beach yesterday." She rubbed her eyes and blinked. "I think I have salt water in my eyes."

"Hold on." She wet a corner of her towel from a jug of fresh water and gave it to Natalie to wipe her face. "You want a beer?"

"Sure."

At the bar, Kelly ran into Jo and chucked her in the shoulder.

"How's it going? Did you see that shark?"

"Hey, mate. That was cool. I took a load of pictures."

"Yeah, me too. I haven't seen you around."

"Nah, I've been up in the library reading mostly. Taking it easy." She tilted her head in Natalie's direction. "You seem to be doing okay."

"Not bad. Just…taking it easy too." She grinned. "What's Julie up to?"

Jo rolled her eyes and smiled. "She got a splinter in her toe."

"Wow, is it serious?"

"The splinter isn't, but I'm not so sure about the nurse. Julie's spending every free minute at the clinic, and they went off today touring some sugar plantation. She said the nurse suggested it because she was so sweet."

Kelly winced.

"Yeah, that was my reaction too. But they're having a good time. That's what we came for."

"I know what you mean. I came to make friends." She picked up her two beer bottles and turned toward Natalie. "I think I'm doing pretty well."

"Good on ya, mate."

She delivered the beer to Natalie and clinked their bottles together. "To a fabulous day."

"Look what I got." She offered a small plastic picture viewer on a key chain. "It turned out great."

Kelly held it up toward the sun and closed one eye as she peered into the viewer to see the photo the crewman had snapped. Even wearing their masks and snorkels, their smiles were evident. And best of all, they were holding hands.

"I got two of them, and a couple of refrigerator magnets. I thought that would be more fun than just pictures."

"These are great." She locked onto Natalie's eyes and held her gaze. She could feel something hokey welling up inside her chest, but she didn't care to stop it. "This has been the best day of all, and that's because I got to share it with you."

"It was my best day too."

As they smiled at one another, Kelly wondered if there was even the slightest chance Natalie had enjoyed it for any of the same reasons she had.

Chapter 13

Fresh from her shower, Natalie smoothed her skin with moisturizing lotion and studied her reflection in the bathroom mirror. Her breasts stood out bright white against her darkening tan. She had never liked them. They were average in size, but on her slender torso were more prominent than she would have liked. Didi always said it "threw off" her look, since most fashion was designed for rail-thin women with no breasts at all.

The rest of her was mostly fine. She secretly liked the curve of her hips, a stark contrast to the shapelessness of the usual runway models. Her fingers followed her eyes to the soft bare skin of her pubis. The waxing technician had left an artistic swirl of dark, trimmed hair, barely an inch across, and in the shape of a flame. No doubt the rest would grow back before anyone had the chance to admire her handiwork, but Natalie was glad to enjoy it herself.

She tucked the towel between her breasts and checked its security. After sharing a cabin with Kelly for the past week, she was perfectly comfortable walking out of the bathroom only partially clad, but had never been one to parade around totally nude, even with Theresa or Didi. She didn't have a body like theirs, petite and perfectly proportioned, and it always made her self-conscious to think her features were under their scrutiny.

"It's all yours," she announced as she exited the bathroom.

Kelly was out on the balcony, apparently talking to Didi or Pamela. Natalie hoped she was telling them what a wonderful time they'd had on their snorkeling trip. If they hadn't still been in port, she would have joined them in her towel just to see the look on Didi's face.

Hurriedly, she dressed in Capri pants, a sleeveless top and sandals, and opened the sliding glass door. "I'm through in the shower."

Kelly spun around and smiled. "I was just telling them how much fun we had, but I saved you all the best parts."

"So you didn't tell them we saw a shark?"

"You saw a what?" Didi practically screamed.

Natalie gushed out the details, making no special effort to exaggerate what a good time they had. Her excitement was genuine, and it was obvious Kelly's was as well. "We thought about going again tomorrow. You want to come?"

"You promised to come shopping with me"—Didi glanced at Pamela—"with us tomorrow. We haven't had a single chance to go."

"Okay, okay." It had been worth a try, but she should have known Didi would protest. What she didn't know was if her objection had more to do with her not going shopping, or with her spending another day with Kelly. Didi's jealousy was probably sufficiently piqued but Natalie didn't want to miss the chance to drive it home one more time. She turned to Kelly, who was heading inside to shower. "Maybe we can do it again in one of the other ports."

"You're turning into a regular Jacques Cousteau," Didi groused.

"It's fun. You should try it. And doing it with Kelly was really nice, because she was right there beside me the whole time, holding my hand. She took care of all the little details so I could just concentrate on feeling safe and seeing everything." Though she had thrown in the part about Kelly just to twist the knife, her words rang absolutely true. Kelly had focused totally on making certain she had a good time, something Natalie wasn't used to at all.

Pamela spoke up for the first time. "Something like that would be a lot of fun with someone who knew what she was doing."

Pleased to see the scowl on Didi's face, Natalie congratulated herself and changed the subject to underscore her nonchalance, asking about their respective sunburns. When the phone rang, she excused herself with one last dig. "I better get that. Kelly's in the shower, and she's liable to run out naked."

Steph was calling to hear about her day and to brag that Yvonne had actually come along on a carriage tour of the city. They agreed to meet for a drink at the poolside bar.

If she had thought about it, she would have suggested meeting in about fifteen minutes instead of right away. The shower was still running and she hated just to dash out without saying anything to Kelly, especially after they'd had such a nice day together. She cracked the bathroom door, allowing the steam to escape. "Kelly?"

"Yeah?"

"Steph called and wanted me to meet her upstairs for a drink." The condensation on the mirror evaporated and Kelly's nude body came into view, every bit as sleek and defined as her outward appearance had implied. The biggest surprise from this angle was her butt—high, firm and *decidedly feminine*. Natalie was glued in place in hopes she might turn.

"Will you come back here before dinner, or do you want to meet in the dining room?"

133

"I, uh…the dining room is fine."

"All right. See you then. Oh, and Natalie?"

"Yes?"

"If it's okay with you, I'd like to come along if you decide to go shopping tomorrow."

"You're kidding."

"No, I want to find a new shirt, something nice for dinner. Is it okay?"

"Of course it is." She closed the door and leaned against it, willing her heartbeat to slow.

Kelly had never been very good at reading women, and Natalie Chatham was no exception. One minute she was warm and almost inviting; the next, distracted and aloof. There was nothing about any of it that seemed intentional, but it was hard not to feel at times invisible, particularly when Didi came into the picture. Still, there were moments when the charade seemed to fade away and Natalie's attention seemed genuine.

A breath of frustration spurted from the corner of her mouth as she dropped her towel and pulled on her briefs. Her plans for the afternoon—relaxing with Natalie and talking more about their excursion—were shot, and while that was no big deal in the grand scheme of things, it was a disheartening confirmation that Natalie wasn't as interested in spending time together as she was.

She had gotten a nice vibe from their outing this morning, especially as they held hands in the water. But when Didi came on the scene, Natalie invited them along on the next excursion as if to underscore that it was the adventure, and not the time with her, that had made it fun and special.

Aware that she had allowed thoughts of Didi to sour her mood, she shook off the exchange on the balcony and tried to focus on something more pleasant, namely, that glorious moment when the boat had rocked as she held Natalie's beautiful rear in the palm of her hand. It was a feeling she would not forget anytime soon. And when she had glanced over her shoulder from the balcony as Natalie popped out of the bathroom wrapped only in a towel, it was almost more than she could stand.

Enough of that. No sense getting worked up over something that was out of her control. Natalie was the one calling all of the shots in this game, and this was about making Didi jealous. Period.

She chose a black ribbed tank top because it let her get away with not wearing a bra. Her cargo shorts would do until dinner, when she would change into chinos and add an over-shirt.

A shudder announced they were pulling out of port, and she grabbed a beer from the minibar and returned to the balcony. By the silence, she surmised that Pamela and Didi had gone back inside.

"Goodbye, Barbados," she murmured softly, committing to memory her wonderful day. When they returned to the dead of winter in Rochester, it was thoughts of holding Natalie's hand in the warm water that would—

The sliding glass door opened forcefully on the balcony next door. "I think you should go," Didi said firmly. "You heard what Natalie said. Kelly showed her how to do everything and stayed right there with her. I bet she'd do that for you too."

"But wouldn't it be more fun if it was all of us?" Pamela asked.

"It might be more fun for all of you, but I have zero interest in flopping around in the water like shark bait just to see a bunch of little fishies eating each other. That's what coffee table books are for."

"Fine. Then we'll go shopping. That could be fun too."

"Are you intentionally trying to make me feel bad, Pamela? I'm trying to give you what you want. I don't want you to miss out on something you want to do just because I'm a stick-in-the-mud. This is a no-brainer. You want to go snorkeling. I don't. So you go, and I'll go shopping with Natalie. What's the big deal?"

Pamela sighed. "Does it occur to you that I might want to be with you, Didi?"

"Jesus, we had three whole days of being locked up together.

Can't we just take a little break?"

Kelly sat perfectly still so as not to give away her presence.

"That's what I thought," Pamela said, her tone giving away hurt feelings. "This isn't about you wanting me to have a good time. It's about you getting away from me."

"I never said that."

"You know what, Didi?" Pamela's voice began to shake. "When we first started dating, a lot of my friends asked me why I'd want to be going out with a woman who was so much older than I was. I told them I was glad to finally find somebody who was mature. I had no idea how wrong I was."

The sliding glass door slammed.

"Shit," Didi muttered. Then, to Kelly's embarrassment, her head appeared around the divider. The swelling in her eyes had lessened, but they were still puffy and red. "You could have cleared your throat or something, you know."

Kelly could feel herself blush. "It all came down pretty fast."

"Most arguments do. Where's Natalie?"

"Off with Steph."

"So what do you think? Am I right? You should ask Pamela at dinner to come snorkeling with you tomorrow, and Natalie and I can go shopping."

Kelly suddenly realized that Didi was definitely up to something, but that Pamela had only half the picture. It wasn't just about ditching Pamela for the day. Didi was jealous, and either wanted Natalie for herself or wanted to keep her from having a good time with someone else. "Actually, I already told Natalie I'd come with her shopping tomorrow. You'll be there too, right?"

Didi squinted, opened her mouth as if to speak, then closed it.

"I was thinking khaki chinos for dinner. That sound okay to you?"

Natalie stared off from the terrace bar as Barbados grew smaller on the horizon. She had told Steph all about the snorkeling trip—the fish, the turtle and the shark—but nothing about her interactions with Kelly. If she closed her eyes, she could still envision the steamy reflection of water cascading over Kelly's sinewy backside.

"Where is your head, Nat?"

She took a sip of her drink, an ice cold beer like the one Kelly had shared with her on the boat. It was probably only the third or fourth beer she had ever drunk, and it went down pretty well. "You remember those little kaleidoscopes we used to have when we were little that you could look through the hole and twist it so it changes shapes and colors?"

"I can't wait to hear where you're going with this." Steph twirled the ice cubes in her Collins.

"That's how I feel right now, like somebody's just twisting me back and forth so that everything looks different."

"What are you looking at that keeps changing?"

"Didi...mostly." Actually, the mostly part belonged to Kelly, but the question of Didi was the one that had to be answered first. "One minute I feel like I have to get her back or I'll just go insane. But then whenever I start to feel like she's within my grasp, I don't want her anymore."

Steph was shaking her head in obvious disapproval.

Natalie continued, "I know you don't want to hear any more about Didi, but I can't just put her out of my head. This is complicated."

"No, it isn't. Whenever you feel like you don't want her anymore, it's because there's a little voice in the back of your head telling you not to go through with it. You need to listen to that voice."

"But why does it keep telling me I do? I've made up my mind a dozen times in the last two years to let it go and get on with my life, and I'll be all right for a few weeks, or even a month or so. Then Didi comes around to talk at work or maybe we just run off to lunch together, and there I am—right back where I started."

"Right back where Didi wants you is more like it. Every time you start to feel okay about moving on, she reels you back in like a big tuna." She gripped both of Natalie's forearms forcefully. "You know what you have to do."

Natalie stared back defiantly.

"You need to sell her your half of the store and let her go. That's the only way she will leave your life."

"I don't want her to leave my life. I told you, I love her and I always will. I know you don't understand that, but I can't help it. I just want to settle things between us once and for all. Either we get back together, or we break up for good."

"You only have control over one of those, Nat."

The way she was feeling right now, walking away from Didi might be the only way to save her sanity. What scared her was thinking about what waited in the wings. When had she started lusting after muscles?

Kelly looked from one face to another as the waiter served their appetizers. The air was thick with tension that emanated from all around the table. Didi and Pamela were still fuming over their fight this afternoon. Even Steph and Natalie were unusually quiet and serious after their long talk over drinks. Only Kelly and Yvonne seemed unaffected, and they tried in vain to lift the group's morale.

"I hear we're going to hit the stores tomorrow and find something nice to wear for formal night," Yvonne said. "I should head to the casino tonight and raise a few bucks."

"Win about seven hundred dollars, honey."

"I probably don't have enough money to buy forgiveness," Didi said, looking sheepishly at Pamela. "Would you consider taking it out in trade?"

From the corner of her eye, Kelly saw Natalie look away, shaking her head almost imperceptibly. Remembering how she had responded to the display on New Year's Eve, she reached beneath the tablecloth and patted her thigh.

Natalie responded with a small squeeze and cleared her throat. "I think we'll all have a great time tomorrow. Even Kelly's going to come along. Let's show her how the pros shop."

"There's no way I'm going to be able to keep up with all of you."

"You won't have to. Just follow the trail of frazzled sales clerks and we'll be at the other end."

"What will you be looking for, Spike?" Didi asked.

Kelly noted the biting tone and nickname, but refused to rise to the bait. "Nothing in particular. I just thought I'd go along to help Natalie with her packages."

Didi's eyes flashed with jealousy.

"But you never know," Kelly continued. "We might pass a tuxedo shop. That would be pretty hard to resist."

The game was on.

Chapter 14

Kelly filled her lungs with the humid morning air as she exited the ship. "Another gorgeous day!" She placed her hand in the small of Natalie's back as they walked down the gangway, just to give her a little support in case she slipped on the incline, a gesture Natalie didn't seem to mind. In fact, Natalie had been quite familiar herself today, even fetching a second cup of coffee and casually delivering it to the bathroom while Kelly had finished her shower. She didn't dare return the favor when Natalie went into the shower, feeling certain she would get caught staring.

"Kelly, you really don't have to do this shopping bit just because I went snorkeling with you. I know how you hate this sort of thing."

"Are you kidding? I can't wait to finally see what this shopping fetish is all about. I feel like Margaret Mead going off on one of her cultural studies." She put her fist to her mouth and lowered her voice as if talking discreetly into a tape recorder. "The taller of the species is instinctively drawn to the decorative items with the horizontal stripes, while the reverse seems to be evident for those creatures of smaller stature."

"Very funny. Did you happen to know that, or was it just a lucky guess?"

"I'll never tell."

Natalie laughed. "I'm sure it seems silly, but it's our business to help women find the clothes that will make them look good. We have to look good too, or no one will want to take our advice."

"I don't mean to make fun of you, Natalie. Or Didi either. From what Yvonne tells me you have a very successful business and you both know what you're doing."

"We do. And the fashion part is all Didi, but I've learned to hold my own when it comes to dressing myself."

"I'll second that. You always look terrific."

"Thank you."

"In fact—and I realize that you realize that I don't know what I'm talking about—I think your clothes look better on you than Didi's do on her, but that's just my opinion."

Natalie smiled and looped her arm through Kelly's as they came to a stop at the end of the dock where they had arranged to meet the others. "What makes you say that?"

"Okay, you're definitely going to think I'm weird when I tell you this, but I actually do have an aesthetic eye. However, it's for architecture and interior structural design, not clothes. Some of the principles are the same, though, so I can't help but notice things."

"Like what?"

Kelly was pleased Natalie seemed genuinely interested in her thoughts. "Like that scarf Didi had on at dinner the first night we sailed. It really got my attention because the colors were the same as her blouse, but the pattern was different. But then I also noticed her belt, which had those same colors too, and a totally different texture."

"I do that sometimes…mix and match accessories."

"Right, but it's a different effect for you because you're taller." She placed one hand just above Natalie's breast and another at her waist. "It's okay to have two focal points in anything, but you never want them too close together. Didi's short, so that meant her focal points were only a few inches apart."

"You really noticed that?"

"I told you, I notice weird stuff."

"I think it's kind of amazing if you want to know the truth. With all of that in your head you probably have a better eye for what looks good than I do."

"I wouldn't go that far, but if you want to try on a million things today I'd be happy to tell you how nice you looked in all of them." Flirting didn't get much plainer than that, but before she could gauge Natalie's response, they were joined by the others.

"Let's go spend Yvonne's casino winnings," Didi said, slapping Kelly on the back. "You ready, Spike?"

Kelly decided it was a rhetorical question and swallowed her retort. The last thing she wanted was a petty squabble with Natalie's ex. Especially since her inclination was to kick Didi's ass.

"Knock it off, Didi," Natalie spat as she grabbed Didi's elbow and squeezed it hard.

"What'd I do now?"

"You know damn good and well what you did. Her name's Kelly, not Spike. And if you do that one more time, I'm going to make a scene in front of everybody."

Didi sighed. "She knows I'm kidding. Besides, she's a big girl. She can take care of herself."

"She's too polite to clean your clock, but don't push it, because I'm not." She dropped Didi's arm and strolled casually back to where the others were looking over a rack of colorful tops. "Anyone seen Kelly?"

"She's back there with Steph looking through the silk stuff."

To Natalie's surprise, it was Kelly pulling out the silk tops and holding them up for Steph's opinion. They were dressy, more like blouses than shirts, and not at all like something Kelly would wear. "Looking for something?"

"Yeah, I thought maybe I should break down and buy something that was actually formal-looking for dinner instead of winging it with my starched shirts."

Natalie frowned at their choices. "I'm not so sure this is you, Kelly." She took the blouse from Kelly's hand and held it up, looking around to see that no other customers were listening. "See how full it is? It's for people who want to hide their stomach. You don't want to do that."

"I don't?"

"No, because you don't have any stomach to hide. You need something that's sleek and tapered so it shows off your lines. What do you think, Steph?"

"I can see it. Something fitted."

"Right." Natalie rummaged through the racks and pulled out a navy top with darts that pulled it snug around the waist. "I'm not too sure about this one, but it's the only one here that might work."

When Kelly disappeared into the fitting room, Steph whispered, "I think she's trying to impress someone."

Natalie thought it more likely that Kelly was playing along just to get Didi off her back. But it didn't matter, because when she returned in the navy shirt, the response was a unanimous shaking of heads.

"I'm glad we all agree," Kelly said. "I would have been screwed if you guys liked it."

"We'll keep an eye out for the right thing."

"Whatever. I can always wear what I brought. Besides, I promised to carry your bags while you bought out the store. So hop to it."

Natalie and Steph busied themselves until Kelly returned from the fitting room in her own clothes. As they left the store, Yvonne met them on the sidewalk. "Didi sent me to get you guys. She's in the store across the street. She says she's found the mother lode."

"It must really be something if Didi likes it," Natalie said. "Let's go."

The moment they entered the store, Natalie knew exactly why Didi was so excited. Dozens of displays showed off cutting-edge fashions they wouldn't receive in Rochester until the late spring shipment. Didi and Pamela each had an armload already and were following an animated older woman as she showed them still more styles.

Kelly pointed to a mannequin perched high on a shelf. "That's what I'm looking for."

Natalie smiled and nodded. It was a dressy silk shirt with a high collar and wide cuffs. "Perfect. I can't wait to see it on you." She began exploring the racks and like the others, soon amassed a pile of items to try on.

Steph, found several outfits she adored. "It's times like these when I can almost understand what you find so appealing about Didi. The woman knows her stuff."

It was, in fact, that realization over eight years ago that first drew Natalie to Didi. She had stepped out of a fitting room to check her look in a full-length mirror when a very attractive blond salesclerk boldly laid a hand on her butt and told her she needed a tighter skirt to show off her figure. Natalie had been nearly floored, until Didi nonchalantly collected several examples and had her try them on. In a matter of minutes she was transformed from an ordinary corporate clone to a fashion plate.

Natalie smiled at the memory of the dinner invitation she had gotten as she was signing her credit card slip. She had accepted without even the slightest bit of hesitation, just as she did the night of passionate lovemaking that followed. Didi Caviness had literally swept her off her feet.

From their first night together Natalie was a new person, filled with the self-confidence that had eluded her since her college days when Theresa had left her for a woman more elegant than she knew how to be at twenty-one. With Didi's love and guidance, she had become the woman she always wanted to be. If only their passion had survived.

"Looks like that shirt must have fit her," Steph said.

Natalie looked up to see Kelly smiling and flashing a thumbs-up sign.

"I should go try some of these things on." As she passed the sales counter, she stopped in her tracks to listen to the exchange.

"What do you mean it isn't for sale?" Kelly demanded. "It was on the rack. It has a price tag on it. I have money. What more is there?"

Didi and Pamela emerged from the fitting room with their potential purchases, hundreds if not thousands of dollars worth of clothing and accessories. "Can I set these here?" Didi asked, spreading her things across the counter.

"The shirt is not for sale," the clerk said tersely, her earlier enthusiasm no longer on display. She reached for Didi's pile and began folding the items for checkout.

Natalie stepped forward. "What's going on?"

The salesclerk looked Kelly up and down with obvious disdain.

"Forget it, Natalie," Kelly said, her normally soft eyes blazing with fury. "I'll see you all back at the ship." She stormed through the racks and out the front door.

"What was that all about?" Didi asked.

"Let's get out of here," Natalie said as she grasped what had happened.

"Fine. Let me just pay for this."

"Leave it. We'll take our business elsewhere."

The clerk ignored her and began scanning the items Didi had stacked on the counter. "This one is ten percent off," she said cheerily.

Natalie spun Didi around. "If you spend one nickel with this bigot, I'll never speak to you again."

"What are you talking about?"

"She refused Kelly service because of how she looked."

145

The clerk jutted her chin out defiantly. "Fine, you can tell your friend to come back. I will sell her the shirt."

"You can keep your shirt, and everything else. It's obvious you don't want business from lesbians." She dropped her items on the counter and marched out with the others in tow. A quick scan of the street revealed no sign of Kelly. As they gathered on the sidewalk, she braced for a tantrum from Didi, who surprised her with casual indifference.

"She didn't waste any time getting out of here," Yvonne said.

"Do you blame her?" Natalie turned to the group. "Thank you all for standing up to that. I'm proud to call you my friends."

"All for one and one for all," Didi quipped sarcastically.

"Especially you."

"You threatened me. What choice did I have?" She grinned and nodded toward another shop. "Let's try our luck somewhere else."

Natalie didn't feel much like shopping anymore, but she didn't want to let the others down after they had come through for Kelly. She followed them from store to store, grasping Steph's forearm at regular intervals to check the time on her watch.

Kelly exhaled slowly as she pulled the barbell behind her head. With practically everyone ashore in St. Lucia, she had the run of the weight room and a burning need to let off steam. There was no better way to channel her irritation. What happened was bad enough, but the worst part was that Natalie and the others had seen the whole thing and were probably embarrassed by it. Didi was undoubtedly having a field day with it.

She finished her reps and wiped the sweat from her neck and chest. Her muscles would be screaming tomorrow from this abuse.

Yvonne walked past the window and abruptly stopped. "So this is where you're hiding. Natalie's been looking all over the ship for you."

"Just chilling. Sorry I ran off." She spun the towel in a twist and hung it around her neck. "I was so close to losing my temper with that woman. I didn't want to ruin everybody's fun."

"Yeah, well…you may have held on to your temper, but Natalie sure let go of hers. She ripped that woman a brand-new asshole and marched us all out of there without buying a thing."

"You're kidding. Even Didi?" She listened in disbelief as Yvonne described the scene. "Wow. I didn't mean to cause all that trouble. It wasn't really that big a deal to me. I just felt bad for dragging all of you into it."

Yvonne slapped her on the shoulder. "I'm going to tell Natalie I found you. She'll probably come around."

"Tell her I'll be back in the cabin in about an hour. I think I'm going to go sit in the steam room awhile."

She returned to her locker and traded her clothes for a large bath towel. She was tempted to go in nude, but the way her luck was running, half the women on the ship would suddenly decide they needed a steam bath. Sure enough, about ten minutes into her bath, the door opened and a figure emerged through the fog.

"Kelly?" It was Natalie, wearing one towel around her body and another on her head.

"This is a nice surprise." Her pulse rate agreed.

"God, it's like Mississippi in here."

She chuckled and slid over on the bench. "I didn't expect you to come looking for me."

"I was worried about you."

Kelly liked the idea of Natalie being concerned, but not over this. "I told Yvonne it was no big deal. It was embarrassing, but I can't let people like that get to me. I left so there wouldn't be a scene."

Natalie chuckled. "Well, there was one anyway."

"So I heard. Yvonne said you and that woman had a smackdown."

"We did. And it cost her a couple of thousand dollars in sales because I made everybody put their stuff back."

"I don't think anyone ever stood up for me like that. It was wonderful." And very sweet of her to come into the steam room wrapped only in a towel. Kelly would have sworn the temperature had shot up ten degrees.

"It made me mad. She had no right to treat you that way."

"Of course she didn't. But people in the islands aren't really accepting of gays. I found that out when I was stationed down here. It's not their culture...except in Key West. It's like a little oasis."

"You're too forgiving for your own good. Nobody would have blamed you if you had decked her."

Kelly chuckled. "I felt like it, if you want to know the truth. But I know what people see when they look at me." It was hard to focus on their conversation as she watched the sweat pour down Natalie's neck into the funnel of her cleavage. "I know I have a choice. I can grow my hair longer and put on a little makeup... wear Capri pants and eyelet tops like yours...put on some dangly earrings. Then I won't shock so many people. But none of that stuff feels like me. I'd rather be who I am and put up with people like that. I try not to get upset about it. It's their problem, not mine."

Natalie blew out a deep breath and put her hand on Kelly's bare shoulder. "I don't know what those other people see when they look at you, but I see someone who's beautiful inside and out."

"Thank you." Kelly wouldn't let herself read too much into that. She knew the difference between someone who was "beautiful" and someone who was "beautiful inside and out." Still, it was one of the nicest things a woman had ever said to her, and because the woman who said it happened to be Natalie Chatham, it was that much more appreciated.

"I don't know how you stand this heat." Natalie hitched up her towel and stood. "I should go back to the room and get ready for dinner. We're getting together for drinks in the observation lounge at five thirty."

"I'll meet you there. I brought my stuff to shower and change in the locker room." She followed Natalie to the door and stopped. "Thanks for coming down to talk to me."

"Friends do that."

"And this friend promises not to worry you by running off again."

"Then I guess we won't be needing that electronic ankle bracelet I picked up today."

Kelly couldn't resist a wink. "Hang on to it just in case. You never know when something like that could come in handy."

The timer on the steam shower ticked off its final seconds and went silent as the water droplets settled on the tile. Kelly gave it another whirl and returned to the bench for a few more minutes of heat and solitude. She was touched that Natalie had been concerned enough to seek her out and especially that she had engineered a protest on her behalf.

At the same time, she was mildly disappointed at what she had read between the lines. Natalie seemed to be laying out her feelings, and they were purely in the realm of friendship. Anything more had been a ridiculous pipe dream on her part, one that made too much of holding hands, Wave Runners and morning coffee.

She dragged herself from the steam room to the shower and washed away the salt of her sweat. Her dress clothes for the night were in her locker. The black slacks she had worn the other night had held their crease, and looked sharp. She smoothed her white tank top over her torso just as another woman entered the locker room and did a double-take at the Ladies sign on the door. It was all Kelly could do not to flash her tits. Instead, she turned her back and put on her new silk shirt, the one she had purchased at another store only moments after storming out of the first one. It was ordinary for the most part, but the lightweight leather jacket that had covered it on the mannequin was what sold it. She had a feeling Natalie would like it. Hell, she bet even Didi would like it.

Chapter 15

Steph slid into the large round booth next to Natalie, who was nursing a glass of white wine. "Just a ginger ale, please," she told the waiter.

Natalie raised her eyebrows. "Ginger ale?"

"You know how I am. Too much booze zonks me out, and Yvonne said if I fell asleep on her tonight she was throwing me overboard."

"It has the opposite effect on the pair next door to me. They just get loud."

Steph shuddered. "I bet that's hard to listen to."

"Actually, it's hard not to listen to, but Kelly picked me up some earplugs. Works wonders."

"Did you see Kelly? Is she okay?"

Natalie waved a hand dismissively. "She's fine, like it never happened."

"I find that hard to believe. Are you sure she isn't just putting up a brave front?"

"I really think she's okay. I looked all over for her when we got back and thought for sure I'd find her brooding in the bar. Yvonne said she was taking a steam bath, so I went down there to see about her. It made my skin feel great, by the way. We need to put that on our list." She stopped talking as the waiter delivered Steph's drink. "Anyway, Kelly says she's used to people treating her like that, and it's their problem, not hers."

Steph was looking at her with a teasing smile.

"What?"

"You and Kelly took a steam bath together?"

"We just—" She should have kept that detail to herself. "We had on towels."

"That sounds kind of sexy."

You have no idea. Natalie felt the beginnings of a blush, and panicked as Yvonne entered the lounge. Kelly was probably only moments away. "Time to talk about something else."

"Like what?"

"I don't care. Road kill." She scooted over to make room for the new arrivals. "That looks gorgeous, by the way," she said, fingering the material of Steph's new dress, a black shift with a silver chain belt.

"Thanks. Pamela has a good eye."

Indeed she did, Natalie thought. And with a gift for matching the style to the woman rather than herding all ages and body types into the fashion of the day, which was Didi's strategy. Didi believed women needed to adapt to the new styles, or risk being seen as old-fashioned. That didn't leave a lot of room for self-expression. Zero room, in fact, for women like Kelly.

Natalie watched the door, wondering what Kelly had in store for their formal night. If Didi dared to make a rude remark, she was cruising for a bruising. No way was she going to sit by and let Kelly be ridiculed again, not even in jest.

Didi and Pamela appeared in the doorway and scanned the room. They both wore outfits they had purchased in St. Lucia—Didi in a cream-colored silk pantsuit and Pamela in a light orange cocktail dress—and looked sensational. Didi detoured toward the bar to place her drink order and Pamela squeezed into the booth.

"Pamela, that color looks good on you. Brings out your tan."

"Thank you, Natalie. Apricot's always a risk for me with my skin tone. It would look fantastic on you, but then with your coloring, practically anything would."

It occurred to Natalie that Pamela always managed to say something sweet and make it sound genuine. Didi could take a lesson on that. "That's very kind of you."

Didi sat down and glared at each of them one by one. "I don't want to hear one word about it. Is that clear?"

Natalie covered her mouth to stifle a gasp. The skin around Didi's eyes, which had been swollen and burned yesterday, had begun to peel...hideously, in large flakes that bared red splotches on her eyelids and cheeks. The makeup she had worn to hide it only made it worse, calling attention to the contrast. "Does it hurt?"

"Not a word," Didi answered gruffly. "Let's talk about something else. What's the show tonight?"

"I'm not sure," Steph said, "but I hope it's ap*peal*ing." She pressed a fist to her lips to hold in her grin.

"Yeah, something *eye*-catching," Yvonne added, also choking back a laugh.

Steph continued, her face contorted comically. "I just hope they don't try to *slough off* something on the *flaky* side."

Everyone suddenly erupted in laughter, even Pamela, which left Didi fuming. "Oh, yes. You're all very fucking cute. Now you can kiss my ass."

"Lighten up, Didi," Natalie said. "It is what it is. You might as well laugh about it."

Didi made a face. "This whole trip has been a disaster. Whose idea was this anyway?"

"Mine," Yvonne said. "And I have to admit you've been the poster child for bad luck. We should make you wear your lifejacket all the time just in case."

"And I should probably have my own food tester."

Natalie laughed along, until a familiar figure in the doorway drew her attention. Everyone turned in unison as Kelly approached the table, looking positively dashing in black pleated slacks with a lightweight leather jacket. A thin black tie hung loosely from the open collar of a light blue silk shirt, the tiny mother-of-pearl buttons giving the whole look a subtle feminine twist. Her hair sported just a hint of gel, enough to give it lift and texture. On Kelly, it wasn't just the fashionable androgynous look. It was exactly who she was—and Natalie thought it was fabulous.

"Don't everybody speak at once," Kelly said, pushing her hands in her pockets and rocking back on her heels.

"Come sit by me," Natalie said when she found her voice.

"And when she's done there, she can sit by me," Steph whispered, leaning into Natalie's ear.

Kelly breathed an inward sigh of relief that her choice for formal night had apparently passed muster, even with Didi, who had snidely congratulated her for pulling off that "look." The compliment had surprised her, so much that she refrained from asking about the unsightly red, flaky rings around Didi's eyes.

Only one opinion really mattered—Natalie's—and though she had yet to comment, Kelly was getting a nice vibe from the way she had looked her up and down. Now she hung back to walk with her from the lounge.

"They're taking photos again tonight," Yvonne said.

"Not of me, they aren't," Didi snarled. "We'll meet you at the table."

Natalie turned and fingered Kelly's jacket. "Didi was right," she said, shyly raising her eyes. "This is a really good look for you. You should get a picture."

"I'm glad you approve. For once I'm worthy of the company I've been keeping." She nodded toward the photographer's line. The Christmas tree was gone, a scenic backdrop in its place. "I'd be honored if you'd stand with me. That dress is too beautiful to look at only once, and so is the woman wearing it."

It was a cheesy remark, but it produced the smile she hoped to see, and they joined the line. An awkward silence, reminiscent of a junior high date, ensued as Kelly giddily soaked up the sensation of actually feeling as if—for the moment, anyway—they were a couple. Something had definitely shifted between her and Natalie in the steam room, and now there was an undercurrent that hadn't been present before. It was too early to read it, though, and Kelly didn't want to jump the gun and spoil what might be happening.

When they reached the front of the line, the photographer's assistant motioned for them to stand in front of the backdrop, a moonrise over the ocean. "Together?"

Kelly nodded, and allowed the woman to position them so that her hand rested on Natalie's hip. The woman placed Natalie's hand on top in an intimate pose and the photographer snapped off the photo. "You're going to like that one a lot," she said.

As far as Kelly was concerned, it would be her favorite photo of all time.

By the time they reached the table, Didi's mood had degenerated to the point that she was berating the waiter over the selection of entrees. In this light, Kelly could see the problem with her eyes and figured they were bothering her a great deal.

Yvonne helped Steph into her chair and took the open seat next to Didi. "You need to chill, Didi. That shit will clear up in a day or so, but we'll still have the same waiter."

"What's it to you, Yvonne?" she snapped.

"Shhh," Steph said, patting Yvonne's hand before she could respond.

Didi pushed her chair back. "And since they don't have anything decent on the menu tonight, I might as well go back to my cabin and order *chicken fingers* from room service."

Pamela started to rise, but Didi put a hand on her shoulder. "I don't need a babysitter."

Everyone exchanged uneasy looks as she stormed off.

"Sorry about that," Yvonne said.

Natalie shook her head. "It wasn't your fault. She can't stand having her face look like that."

"Yeah, but I should have known not to push her buttons."

"All of you coddle her too much," Pamela said. "When she acts like a brat, you should treat her like one."

The women exchanged quizzical looks and several began to chuckle. Steph even lifted her water glass in a mock toast, but Kelly waited to take her cue from Natalie, who was clearly not amused. She wasn't exactly rising to Didi's defense, but she wasn't piling on either.

"I feel sorry for her," Natalie said. "She's had nothing but bad luck this whole trip. You too, Pamela. Neither of you have been able to relax and have a good time, what with being stuck in your cabin and now a bad sunburn. I don't want to add teasing her to all that."

Pamela nodded sheepishly and laid her linen napkin on her plate. "I should probably go see about her. No matter what she said about not needing a babysitter, we all know she didn't mean it."

"See if you can get her to come to the show tonight."

Kelly also felt sorry for Didi tonight, but not enough to let her tantrum ruin their whole evening. What worried her most was that the episode would dampen Natalie's mood, which had been cheerful up to now.

Not only had she had been in good spirits, she was making a real show of cozying up—but now that Didi was gone, there was no need for the pretense.

Yvonne patted her stomach as she sat down in the theater. "My diet starts the day I get back to Rochester."

Steph hooked her arm through Yvonne's elbow. "Don't talk about either one of those—diets or Rochester. I still have five more days of vacation."

"Fine, but in my next life, I want to be able to eat like Kelly."

Natalie had taken the seat beside Steph, saving the aisle seat for Kelly, who tugged at her tie as she sat down. "You can eat like her if you'll get up and run four miles every morning like she does. I think she actually likes it."

"One mile would use up my whole energy quota for the week," Steph said. "Did you guys get a look at that moon?"

"It's full tonight," Kelly said. "Hey, look who's coming in. Do we have two more seats?"

Natalie grinned as Pamela and Didi took seats directly in front of her and Kelly. Pamela had obviously worked some magic on Didi's mood. "Glad you could make it, girls."

Kelly leaned forward and tapped Didi on the shoulder. "I didn't get a chance to say thanks for sticking up for me today at that store. I appreciate it."

Didi looked uncomfortable at the acknowledgment, giving Kelly only a weak smile. It was possible she felt guilty, Natalie realized, since it had taken threats to get her to go along. Guilt was a new emotion for Didi, and Natalie was mildly impressed. What moved her even more was Kelly's gesture of thanks, considering she had been on the receiving end of quite a few snide insults from Didi. Most people in her position would carry a giant chip on their shoulder, but as she had said in the steam room, she didn't dwell on criticism when it came to her appearance or sense of style.

Readying for the show, Natalie faced the stage and burrowed into her seat, suddenly aware of a cold stream of air blowing onto her neck and shoulders. "I must be sitting under the air conditioner vent."

"Here, take this." Kelly removed her leather jacket and wrapped it around her shoulders. "How's that?"

The leather was cozy from Kelly's body heat. "I hate to take your coat. What if you get cold?"

"Then I'll bask in your warmth," she answered with a smile.

"I was about to take it off anyway."

Didi must have overheard the remark, as she turned and gave Kelly a sidelong look that Kelly matched with an impertinent wink.

As the curtain went up, Natalie turned her attention toward the stage. But no matter how much she tried to concentrate on the dancers, her thoughts kept going back to Kelly. The polite compliments that flowed freely now seemed more like flirtations, especially compared to three days ago when she agreed to help make Didi jealous. She definitely poured it on when Didi was around, but tonight it seemed as if everything she did was genuine.

The number ended and Natalie joined in the applause. When the second song began, she took advantage of the slanted angle of their seats, which let her discreetly study the object of her ruminations. Kelly sat casually, her legs crossed in the way a man would sit, with her ankle resting on her knee. Her hands, long and slender, rested on her thighs.

Another round of applause.

There was something magnetic about Kelly—it was that raw, animalistic appeal Steph had described. She was probably a fantastic lover. That sculpted ass...all those muscles. Natalie felt a jolt between her legs as she imagined their bodies sliding together beneath the sheets.

"Are you enjoying the show?" Kelly asked suddenly as the crowd erupted.

"Yes, very much."

No, she shouldn't give in and have an affair with her on board the ship, because that wasn't fair to Kelly. Kelly might want more than just a fleeting night or two of hot, steamy fun. Natalie couldn't do that to either of them, not as long as the question of Didi remained unsettled. And not as long as the logical side of her kept popping up and saying Kelly wasn't her type.

Two more songs...or three...or seven. Natalie lost count. Before she knew it, they had reached the finale and everyone was on their feet showing their appreciation. Didi and Pamela scooted quickly out of the theater without even saying goodnight, probably so Didi could get out of the crowd before the lights came up.

"You want to go to the lounge for a drink?" Kelly asked. "Or if you'd rather, we can go up on the deck and look at the moon."

Natalie automatically hooked her hand through Kelly's arm as they started out. What she craved was a chance for the two of them to be alone again, to see if there was anything behind the flirtations, or if she was imagining all of it. It was nice to be on the receiving end of someone's attention for a change, even if she didn't do anything about it. "I wonder if we can see it from our balcony."

"Only one way to find out."

Once inside their cabin, Kelly led the way through the sliding glass door to find the balcony bathed in moonlight.

Natalie couldn't resist peeking around the edge of the divider, though she wasn't surprised to see the curtain drawn in the room next door. She rested her elbows on the rail and pulled the leather jacket tighter around her shoulders. "It's absolutely gorgeous out here."

"I'll say."

She turned to see Kelly gazing directly at her. "You're not looking at the moon."

Kelly laughed softly and looked away. "The moon has serious competition tonight."

"If you're trying to make Didi jealous, she isn't out."

"The fact that you're beautiful doesn't have anything to do with Didi."

Natalie soaked up the flattery, feeling almost giddy to be the object of Kelly's attention. "You're very sweet to say so."

"I was sweating bullets about wearing this tie tonight. I thought it looked okay, but I wasn't sure what you would think."

"You look dashing." What Kelly looked was sexy, but Natalie couldn't bring herself to say so. Instead, she brazenly trailed her finger along Kelly's collar.

"Thank you." Kelly intercepted her hand and lifted it to her lips for a soft kiss. "That didn't have anything to do with Didi either."

Natalie found herself locked in a questioning gaze as Kelly's hand came to rest on her hip. For a fleeting moment, she thought Kelly might kiss her.

"I want to ask you a serious question," Kelly said.

"Watch out. You might get a serious answer."

"Why do compliments make you so uncomfortable?"

Natalie felt a wave of uneasiness just from talking about it. "I don't really get a lot of those, especially since Didi and I split up."

"Did she tell you how beautiful you are?"

"I could always count on her to tell me when I looked good… and when I didn't."

"I don't mean your clothes. Did she ever tell you that your eyes were brighter than the moon?" She tipped Natalie's chin upward. "Or that your laugh made her heart flutter?"

She felt the shift of their emotions as their faces inched closer. Their lips met in a gentle kiss, but then Kelly pulled away as if uncertain. Natalie looped a hand around her neck and drew her back for another, the second one deeper as their mouths opened and their tongues mingled. She reveled in the feel of the powerful arms that enveloped her, and was ready to surrender to what her body had wanted all evening when suddenly the door opened on the next balcony.

"You should come see this moon, Didi. It's lovely."

Natalie abruptly pulled away and Kelly turned to rest her elbows on the rail, their moment lost.

"Hi, you two," Pamela said cheerfully. "Romantic, isn't it?"

"Quite," Kelly said.

Natalie's hands shook as she gripped the rail. "Kelly and I were just talking about how much we enjoyed the show tonight. Did you like it?"

"I loved it." Pamela looked over her shoulder as Didi joined her.

"I can't believe we're at sea all day tomorrow and the weather report sucks," Didi said, leaning around the divider. "What do you say, Nat? You want to hit the duty-free shops down on Deck 5 and see if they've marked anything down?"

No, she didn't really want to do that. "Sure, that sounds like fun."

"That's a great idea," Pamela interjected. "We should try to get there at one when they open so we can get the best selection."

Didi practically spat. "I thought you were going to watch the art auction at one."

"I don't want to go by myself. I'd rather be with all of you. That's what you said this whole trip was about, me getting to know your friends."

When Didi turned away from Pamela and smiled lamely in their direction, it sparked a trace of sadness in Natalie. It was increasingly clear the bloom was off the rose for the May-December couple, and while there was a measure of providence in Didi finally realizing that she and Pamela were poorly matched, Natalie took no satisfaction from seeing her former lover unhappy.

Kelly cleared her throat, as if reminding the group of her presence. "If you'd like some company, Pamela, I'll go with you. The art auction sounds a lot more interesting than shopping."

Pamela leaned around Didi with a wide grin. "That would be fantastic. These two can fight over the markdowns while we watch the big spenders."

"Should be fun." Kelly patted Natalie's shoulder like an old friend and turned to go back inside. "I'll see you all in the morning."

Natalie roiled with both jealousy and ire. Hadn't they been kissing only moments ago? Hadn't she been imagining the feel of Kelly's bare skin next to hers? And now Kelly was making a date to spend the day with Pamela.

She said goodnight and went inside, where Kelly had pulled off her tie and loosened the buttons on her shirt. "You're going with Pamela tomorrow?"

Kelly shrugged. "Looks like things are working out exactly

the way you planned. You and Didi…all alone. Isn't that what you wanted?" The nonchalance in her voice was a dramatic contrast to her whispered intimacies only minutes earlier.

"Did I misunderstand what just happened? You told me that didn't have anything to do with Didi."

"It didn't, at least not for me. But you just made plans to spend the day with her, and I know that's what you were hoping for, so I'm not going to complicate things for you."

"And just like that you take it all back?"

Kelly smiled faintly and shook her head. "I'm not taking anything back, Natalie. Every word I said to you was true, and that kiss meant something to me. But I'm not going to take advantage of a full moon and a few sweet words when it's obvious I'm not the person you really want to share those things with. I saw that look on Didi's face. She's ready to ditch Pamela, and this is exactly the chance you've been waiting for."

Natalie had seen that look too, but the moment she realized Didi was back within her grasp, she had become surprisingly ambivalent, her expected giddy triumph nowhere to be found. "What if I'm not all that sure I want Didi back? If I did, would I have been out there kissing you on the balcony?"

Kelly dropped her slacks and carefully hung them in the closet. Standing in only her tank top and briefs, she was tantalizing, especially now that Natalie had felt her rock-hard body up close. "I need for you to be sure. A roll in the sack with you would be lovely, but I'm greedy about this, because I want all the feelings that go with it too. I happen to care about you, and I don't want to start down this road and have you change your mind later because she's the one you really want."

But what if she couldn't decide now? Couldn't they test the waters? Natalie wasn't averse to sleeping with someone and sorting out the feelings later—that's exactly what she had done with both Theresa and Didi—as long as testing the waters meant more than just sex. She wanted at least to feel that lovemaking might lead to something meaningful. "So as long as I still have feelings for Didi…"

"You and I can only be friends."

Natalie sat on the end of her bed and pulled off her heels. If she thought too long about sleeping with Kelly, she probably wouldn't. Sexual attraction was fleeting. Except now, when Kelly was prancing around in her underwear. "Why does everything in my life have to be so screwed up?"

Kelly laughed and disappeared into the bathroom. "A bunch of women wanting you…that's what you get for being so damn sexy. All of us should be so screwed up."

Kelly was glad they had set this routine early on in the cruise. As soon as it became apparent that Natalie's bedtime bathroom rituals took thirty minutes to her five, they agreed that Kelly would go first so she could go on to bed. Most nights, she was asleep by the time Natalie finished. That wouldn't be the case tonight.

For the next thirty minutes at least, she planned to beat herself over the head for passing up what might have been the most glorious night of her life. There was no mistaking Natalie's response to their kiss. She had wanted it, and if the way her body had melted into Kelly's was any sign, she would have welcomed even more.

The problem with that was tomorrow. She would have gladly taken a chance had Natalie not jumped at the offer to spend the day with Didi. That wasn't the sort of thing a woman should want to do on her first full day as someone else's lover.

As frustrated as Kelly felt lying in bed alone, she was proud of herself for showing self-control in the face of enormous temptation. Even more than Natalie's body, she wanted her heart.

Chapter 16

Natalie peered over the rack of clothes to see Didi rifling through the tops on the other side. By the look on her face, she wasn't finding anything she liked. That was too bad, because they practically had their pick of all the sales items since the rough weather was keeping most passengers in their cabins during their day at sea.

Why on earth had she agreed to spend her day in a stupid store? Not only had the invite completely derailed things with Kelly last evening, it had spoiled a chance to laze around with her in the stateroom all day. Something might have happened, something that was suddenly a whole lot more interesting than wresting Didi from the mess she had made for herself.

As she sidled around the rack, she noticed the small adhesive patch affixed behind Didi's ear. "What exactly do these things do?" she asked, gesturing with her finger.

"They're supposed to release tiny doses of medicine that keep me from throwing up all over the ship."

"I hope it works, at least as long as I'm with you. You and the nurse should be on a first-name basis by now."

"Dagna. She's from Norway, and I think she's into girls."

"Why do you think that?"

"Just the look she gave me when she saw Pamela and then realized our beds were pushed together."

"Hmmm." Natalie held up first one outfit, then another, not finding anything she couldn't live without.

"That one's you, Nat. Good color."

"You think so?" The lime green top had a plunging neckline and was short enough to leave her midriff exposed. Two years ago she would have purchased it solely on Didi's recommendation. "I think it's better suited to someone twenty years old."

"That's the whole idea. Who wants to dress like their mother?" Didi scrunched her nose in obvious distaste as she continued to peruse the rack.

Natalie didn't want to look like a senior citizen, but there was lots of space between that and a teenager. "Pamela has a wonderful eye. She found nice things for everyone yesterday."

"You mean the stuff we all put back?"

She bit back an indulgent sigh. "My point was that Pamela went to every rack and pulled out just the right things. She really knows her stuff."

Didi harrumphed and planted her hands on her hips. "Are you saying I don't?"

"Don't get your back up with me. I never said you didn't know your stuff too."

"You implied it."

Natalie noticed a nearby shopper looking up, and she lowered her voice. "I did no such thing. I was trying to give your girlfriend a compliment."

Didi scowled and buried her nose into the rack. "I think my

164

days with Pamela might be numbered. Every now and then she says something and it hits me just how young she is."

And how old you are, Natalie thought, not letting herself take the "end-of-days" reference too seriously. Didi made lots of noise when she was annoyed about something, but most of it was bluster. "I thought that was one of the things you liked about her."

"Oh, don't get me wrong. She's nice to look at...and she's very hot in bed."

"Please, spare me the details."

"Sorry. If it makes you feel any better, I'm finally starting to realize that the sex thing isn't all it's cracked up to be. I know that was an issue for us." She gave Natalie a sheepish look. "Okay, it was an issue for me."

Natalie stepped into the corner, well out of earshot of the shopper. "It was important to me too. But we never should have let it become the deal breaker."

"Sex wasn't the deal breaker and you know it," Didi said, her voice rising with irritation. "It was you lying about it."

Gritting her teeth, Natalie replied, "I am not going to have that conversation here. If you want to talk about it like two adults, let's at least go somewhere private."

Didi glanced around the store and shrugged. "There isn't much here anyway. I'd invite you back to my stateroom, but I've seen enough of it to last me a lifetime."

"Let's go up to the observation lounge," Natalie suggested. Maybe if they finally cleared the air once and for all on why they had broken up, the other pieces would fall into place and they could get on with whatever they were meant to do next. Ignoring it for the past two years hadn't worked at all. She turned out of the store and started forward down a corridor.

"Not that way. The art auction's down there. Let's go around."

"It's quicker." Besides, that's where Kelly was, and Natalie wanted a chance to wave at her.

"I don't want Pamela to see us. She might want to come

along, and then we couldn't talk about anything."

If Didi couldn't even bear to pass by Pamela in the audience at the art auction, things were worse than Natalie had thought. She followed Didi up the stairs to the top floor, where they settled into the same corner booth she had shared with Kelly a few nights earlier. A steward took their drink order, which Didi signed for.

"When did you start drinking beer?" Didi asked.

"I had one the other day when I was out on the boat with Kelly."

"You'd better not make a habit of it. When was the last time you saw somebody with a wine gut?"

"I'm not drinking a whole keg," she answered sharply. The constant criticism was tiring. "Besides, I'm on vacation. I can do whatever I want."

The waiter delivered their drinks and Didi offered hers in a toast. "To dry land."

Natalie pulled her bottle back. "Some of us are having a good time."

"A little sympathy, please. I've never been so miserable in my life."

It was hard not to feel sorry for her—food poisoning, sunburn and now, seasickness—but Natalie had a feeling those were only the superficial problems. She guessed the situation with Pamela was eating at her. "Besides getting off this ship, what would it take to make you happy?"

Didi sighed. "I've never spent this much time with Pamela before. She's a lot easier to deal with on just the weekends."

"Aren't you glad I didn't let you move the business to New York?"

"That has nothing to do with Pamela. New York is where the action is. That's always been my dream and you know it."

Natalie held up her hand to stop the direction of the conversation. "We agreed not to talk about it until we got home."

"You brought it up."

"My mistake." She sipped her beer and nervously began to peel the label. The subject they had broached in the shop was still lurking in the back of her head. "What we were talking about earlier…I just want to say one more time—I know I've told you this before—that I didn't lie to hurt you. In fact, it was just the opposite."

"I don't want to talk about that. It happened. I'm over it."

From where Natalie was sitting, that was the biggest lie of all. "We've started this conversation a dozen times and we never get past the part where you call me a liar. Is that all you're really interested in?"

"Would you believe I really don't even care about it anymore?" She didn't wait for Natalie to answer. "Okay, maybe it still bothers me a little bit. The mistake I made was thinking it had to do with sex. Now I realize it was just a symptom."

Natalie couldn't wait to hear where this was going. "What do you think it had to do with?"

"A couple of nights ago I sort of borrowed your little trick. I got bored with it and wanted to get it over with."

She felt her face redden, which it did nearly every time she thought about what had caused their huge blowup. If only she had lied when the subject came up and Didi had asked her point-blank.

"Anyway, that's when it hit me there was more to it than just the sex part. I figured you must have been pretty unhappy with me all along if you had to fake your orgasms."

Natalie shuddered. "I wasn't unhappy. And I only did that a few times. I just…I just wanted to make you feel good. I shouldn't have done it. I'm so sorry."

"And I probably shouldn't have made such a big deal out of it," Didi said dismally.

Natalie felt a wave of relief at finally having the chance to apologize, and she sensed that Didi did too. She lightened her tone and managed a smile. "Though why you have to carp about every little thing I do is beyond me."

"It's just my way of showing affection," Didi answered with a smirk. "I wouldn't do it if I didn't care."

"That isn't true. You do it to Kelly and I know you don't feel any affection for her."

"She's all right. She sure looked good last night."

"Didn't she, though?" Natalie's stomach knotted nervously as she heard the enthusiasm in her voice. It wouldn't do for Didi to pick up on that sliver of interest she felt for Kelly. "I was really glad to see you come back down for the show."

"Yeah, well…the alternative was being stuck in that stateroom again."

Natalie nodded. "It must feel like the walls are closing in."

"It's not that. I've already run out of things to talk about with Pamela," she grumbled. "We have sex just to kill time."

"I doubt Pamela would appreciate knowing you feel that way about it."

"Is that what it was like for you, Nat? Were you bored with it?"

She squirmed uncomfortably, knowing she couldn't avoid such a point-blank question. "I was never bored with you, Didi. I just got to a point where I didn't care much about myself. I was more focused on you." There was a whole lot more to it than that, but Natalie kept the details to herself. The last three years of her life were a shining example of how honesty was not always the best policy.

Didi twirled her glass and looked around the lounge, as if checking to make sure no one could hear her. "There's a pretty good chance I'll break things off with Pamela when we get back home. I don't know what I was thinking."

Natalie leaned back and folded her arms, reminding herself that Didi was notoriously fickle when it came to what she wanted. "Maybe things will settle down when we get off the ship and things go back to normal."

"I don't know, Nat. I care for Pamela, really. But she's one of those touchy-feely types, always wanting to cuddle and talk about feelings. You know how I am about stuff like that."

She knew too well. Didi didn't mind displays of affection,

especially in public for all to see, but once behind closed doors she wanted her space. Sometimes she thought what Didi really wanted was not a girlfriend, but an escort.

"Anyway, thanks for letting me dump about it. I've always felt like I could count on you to be there for me."

Natalie nodded and flashed a weak smile, suddenly aware that something monumental had shifted. This was what she had wanted all along, for Didi to forgive her and to realize that Pamela was wrong for her. But now with the door opening for them to get back together, she wasn't as excited as she had expected to be. In fact, she was surprisingly unsettled by the idea.

Kelly listened with curiosity as Pamela queried the ship's expert on the impressive collection of limited edition lithographs. She seemed genuinely interested in acquiring a piece, and made several notes in a small tablet she carried in her purse.

"For a fashion designer, you sure seem to know a lot about art," Kelly said.

"My stepfather is an artist. He works at MoMA." Pamela must have noticed her blank look. "The Museum of Modern Art in New York. He works in restorations, but he loves to talk about the displays and exhibits. I try to walk through there every chance I get. He gets a big kick out of showing off the new stuff."

"So you have a chance to learn from an expert."

"Yeah, and it's a nice way to spend a little time with him, especially when I can talk my mom into coming in from Long Island to join us. I don't get to see my folks much now that I'm running back and forth to Rochester."

It was impossible not to like Pamela, and just as impossible to understand what she saw in a woman like Didi when she could probably have her pick of any lesbian in New York. She had everything going for her—looks, intelligence, charm and a sweet personality that contrasted sharply with Didi's dour disposition.

"Oh, look. They have champagne," Pamela said, darting across the gallery.

Kelly caught up to her just in time to refuse a glass. "It gives me an awful headache. I paid dearly for my extravagance on New Year's Day."

"At least you got to go out. We were still stuck in our cabin."

"That's too bad. You and Didi have had a rough trip."

Pamela shrugged. "I shouldn't complain. We need this time together. It's hard when you live in two different cities."

"Sounds like Didi's really jonesing to move the business to New York."

"I wish she would. Then we could get a place together and stop this crazy back-and-forth every weekend."

Kelly nodded mindlessly, thinking Pamela seemed more certain about their future than Didi. If Didi's miserable expression last night were any indication, her loving relationship with Pamela was on the downward slope. From the outside, it was tough to see why anyone would let someone like Pamela get away. She was gorgeous to look at, but unassuming, and from what little bit Kelly had seen, she had a very pleasant personality. Anyone who could tolerate—more than that, cheerfully accommodate—someone as cantankerous as Didi was a special person. "You guys have been together for what? Six months?"

"Officially. We met about a year ago at a fashion show in New York and started e-mailing and getting together—just as friends, you know—whenever she'd come to town. I've always had a thing for older women, and I fell for her"—she snapped her fingers—"just like that."

"I can sure see why. Didi's a very attractive woman."

Pamela fanned herself. "You're telling me. But she was still trying to sort out things with Natalie. Once she realized Natalie would never move to New York, she gave up on her."

"Going to New York is really that important to her?"

"I don't think Natalie quite understood how much. They probably would have gotten back together again if she had been willing to move. But I'm not complaining. Her loss is my gain."

Kelly couldn't help her curiosity about why someone like Pamela would be attracted to Didi, but she was too polite to come right out and ask the question. "I was surprised to see you two at the show last night. Didi was pretty upset when she left the dining room."

Pamela started toward the auction area, where chairs were set up before a podium and easel. "She just needed a little stroking. No one would ever believe this about her, but Didi's very insecure."

"You're right. That's the last word I would have used to describe her." Kelly took the aisle seat as Pamela slipped into the row. "She always seems so sure of herself."

"Didi's very sure of what she knows. She has lots of confidence when it comes to the fashion business, but that doesn't translate to being sure of herself. She worries all the time about her hair, about her skin—you name it. No matter how often I tell her how beautiful she is, it's never enough."

Kelly thought back to the question she had asked Natalie the night before, whether Didi had built her up with sweet words. "And what about Didi? I bet she tells you those things all the time."

Pamela chuckled and shook her head. "It's not her style. I don't know why, but she doesn't give out much in the way of compliments unless she had a hand in it, like picking out something for me to wear. Lucky for me I don't have issues about that sort of thing. I'm pretty happy with myself, and I can usually tell that Didi's proud to have me on her arm. I don't need to hear it from her lips all day."

That explained why Natalie was so uncomfortable with attention. She hadn't been on the receiving end with Didi either.

"*Ladies and gentlemen, our first item up for bid...*"

Pamela turned her attention to the auction.

Though Kelly had said she would wait until Natalie had settled the matter of Didi once and for all, that didn't mean she couldn't nudge it along. As the auctioneer droned on, she began to formulate a plan.

A new game was on.

Natalie put the finishing touches on her makeup and checked the bedside clock. The auction should have finished an hour ago. Since Kelly hadn't returned, she used the extra time alone to freshen up, something she didn't normally do in the afternoon unless they were dressing for dinner. She was only doing it today because—yes, she could admit this to herself—because Kelly noticed and appreciated how she looked.

Why was she taking so long to come back to their room?

No sooner had the question run through her mind than she heard the sound of a key card in the door. She hurried to the couch and picked up the daily update, feigning to read.

"Hey, Natalie! Did you and Didi buy out the store?"

"We didn't see much. We spent most of the afternoon in the observation lounge. How was the art auction?"

"Interesting. I had no idea Pamela was so smart. She knows all about art, even more than some of the people working the auction. Turns out her stepfather…"

The words were like white noise as Natalie watched Kelly kick off her sandals, empty her pockets and stretch out on her bed. Off and on all day, she thought of how she felt when Kelly's lithe arms had enveloped her last night as they closed in for a kiss. There was something vastly different about kissing Kelly, a sensation she had never gotten from either Theresa or Didi. She couldn't put her finger on—

"Do you like it?"

The question jarred her, and she tried to play back the last bits of what Kelly had said. Her best guess was something having to do with art. "Who doesn't?"

"I didn't used to. My father had no use for it. Art to him was one of those landscapes you bought at the furniture store to hang over your couch. I took an art appreciation class at the community college in Buffalo and guess what happened? I wound up appreciating art."

"Maybe we can take in something at ARTWalk this spring."

"That would be nice." Kelly propped up on her elbow. "I really like Pamela. She's pretty down-to-earth for someone working and living in the middle of such a dynamic industry. And you would expect a woman as pretty as her to be stuck up about it, but she isn't."

Natalie didn't like the flavor of these new revelations. For one thing, it bothered her to think Kelly just threw around compliments about pretty women, and that her words the night before had been just ordinary platitudes. More important was the possibility that Pamela might have turned Kelly's head.

"I heard the weather's supposed to be better tomorrow," Kelly said. "Any idea what you want to do on the private island?"

"What are our choices?" Only moments ago, she had seen the description of activities in the daily update, but her mind hadn't processed any of it.

"They have an adults-only beach. It's supposed to be quiet and relaxing. I doubt Didi would be up for anything in the sun, but Pamela probably would. We could get an umbrella like we did back on Antigua. As long as we don't let Didi—"

"Maybe we should do something by ourselves. The cruise is almost over and we haven't really had a chance to get to know each other."

Kelly sat up and rested her forearms on her knees, a barely perceptible smile emanating from her lips. "I'd like that. Just us."

"Just us."

Natalie drew in a deep breath as a warm flush crept up her neck. Kelly's smile had gotten bigger, and now she was sporting one of her own.

Chapter 17

Kelly peered over the balcony to watch the tenders shuttle passengers to the private island. "We'll get to ride in the lifeboats today, Natalie," she shouted through the open door.

Natalie appeared beside her, dressed for another beach day in her swimsuit, shorts and a beach wrap. "Nice to know they all float."

No doubt about it. Kelly had stumbled onto the perfect plan, and it was coming together perfectly. Pamela had unknowingly provided the missing piece, and was also lending a sense of urgency for Natalie to make up her mind once and for all to move on to something new.

"Don't forget your shades," she said to Natalie as they started for the door.

Natalie spun around and plucked her sunglasses from the bed.

"Looks like this will be our last chance to get some sun before we go back to the dreaded ice and snow."

Didi had pouted through dinner the night before when the others talked about their day of sun and relaxation on the private island, so much that Natalie had offered to shop with her in Nassau on their last day in port. Kelly promptly responded by asking Pamela if she had any interest in a carriage tour of the island. When she agreed, Natalie twisted Didi's arm to give up the shops and tag along. That was all the confirmation Kelly needed to know she was on the right track.

Her strategy for winning Natalie was two-pronged. First was to show a hint of interest in Pamela, which had probably been the catalyst for Natalie's suggestion that they go it alone today on the private island. Second was to take advantage of her new insight into Natalie's dynamic with Didi, one that suggested she might enjoy being on the receiving end of the attention for a change.

Kelly had observed Didi's habit of complimenting clothes rather than people, and wanted to send a different message. "Speaking of sunglasses, that teal swimsuit really brings out your eyes. They're gorgeous anyway, but they seem extra bright next to that suit."

Natalie's beaming smile told her she had struck the perfect chord. "I think it's the sun, which I'm starting to think I can't get enough of."

They ran into Steph and Yvonne on the steps.

"You guys just missed Didi and Pamela," Steph said. "Didi's slathered in sunscreen and has on an enormous hat."

To Kelly's disappointment—and Natalie's too, from her look of annoyance—their day alone was now a group outing.

"Let's go. They're saving us a place on the tender. Oh, and thanks for the books, Kelly."

Natalie glanced between them with confusion. "What books?"

"I ran into Jo this morning and she had finished two more books, so I got a couple of Steph's and swapped them."

"You're addicted to that stuff, aren't you?"

"What can I say? I'm a sucker for romance."

Kelly brought up the rear as they walked down to Deck 2 and out onto the platform to board the tender. She doubted that Didi's motivation was being with all of them. If her behavior of the past couple of days was any indication, the one she wanted to be with was Natalie.

Her theory panned out when they reached the boat and found Didi and Pamela on a long bench saving the four seats between them. Didi immediately gestured for Natalie to take the seat next to her. Rather than sit on Natalie's opposite side and compete with Didi for her attention, Kelly scooted in next to Pamela at the other end, leaving the middle spaces for Steph and Yvonne. "I'm glad you decided to come along," she said loudly enough for Natalie to hear. "Our time with friends will be over soon."

"I doubt that," Pamela replied sweetly. "I think we'll see lots of each other once we get home."

"I want to come to the city so you can show me around all the art museums."

"Wouldn't that be fun?" Ever the charming hostess, Pamela leaned around and invited Steph and Yvonne to join them.

Natalie frowned, but then her face lit up. "Kelly, if you're ever interested in touring the Eastman House, I'd love to go. It's one of my favorite museums."

Yes, her plan was coming together. "Just name the day, Natalie. That sounds like fun."

They reached the island and set off en masse to the adults-only beach, which was situated by a peaceful cove. Didi quickly claimed a shaded hammock, and Yvonne and Steph dragged several beach chairs so they could all sit alongside.

Kelly darted off to the vendor's hut and rented two foam rafts. By the time she returned, the others had already ordered drinks from a passing waiter.

"I got us a couple of beers," Natalie said.

"Great. And I got us a couple of escape pods," she said, holding up the rafts.

"You read my mind."

Kelly led the way into the warm, clear water carrying both of the rafts. "I know we put on sunscreen, but we'll still have to be careful not to burn. It would be a shame for you to cover that nice tan of yours with blisters and peeling skin."

"Like someone else we know?"

"Precisely."

"You really enjoy Pamela, don't you?"

Though the question seemed to come out of nowhere, Kelly knew better. Natalie was bothered by her conversation with Pamela on the way to the island. "Honestly, I think she's one of the nicest people I've ever met."

Natalie frowned and grabbed one of the rafts. "I know. I've tried not to like her, but I can't help it."

Kelly chuckled and took mercy on her. "But if I had to choose only one woman to spend time with, it wouldn't be Pamela."

"No?"

"No, I'm pretty happy right where I am, thank you. I've stolen the prettiest woman on the beach from all her friends. Now I'm going to tie our rafts together and set us adrift. Does that sound all right with you?"

Natalie smiled and stretched out on her raft, sucking in a breath as the water hit her belly. "I wanted this to be a day for just us."

Kelly fell across her raft too, maneuvering so they were floating face to face, barely a foot away. "So did I. Now that we're all alone out here, why don't you entertain me? Tell me what's on your mind." She rested her chin on her hands.

"I think Didi's about to break up with Pamela."

A sick feeling enveloped her, and she let the words float along with them for several seconds. "That's what you wanted, isn't it?"

"I used to think so." Natalie stared at her fingers as they trailed gently through the water. "I expected to be a little more excited about it. Instead, I just feel sad for her."

"Sad enough to go back to her?"

Natalie reached out to grasp the edge of Kelly's raft to stop her from floating away. "I've always been there for her…whatever she said she needed."

"Has she been there for you, Natalie?"

"Mostly…but not always. We were pretty happy a long time ago, but I've started to think we'll never get that back." There was a distinct tone of melancholy in Natalie's voice, but also a hint of resolve. "I think I could persuade her to give up New York, but why should I keep her from that if it's what she really wants?"

"New York is just a small piece of this. The real question is whether or not you love her, and if you want to spend your life with her."

Natalie looked up with sad eyes. "Yes to the first. No to the second. I'm always going to love her, but I think we're both better off if we can just be friends and business partners."

Kelly wanted to smile at her own good fortune, but it gave her no pleasure to see Natalie so glum. "What about the New York thing?"

"Maybe if she breaks up with Pamela, it won't be such a big deal."

If Pamela was right, Didi's dream of moving her business to the city wouldn't just go away. But it might be easier to resolve if Natalie could disentangle her emotions and make the best decision for the store.

"There's the guy with our drinks," Natalie said. "I'd rather float around out here, but Yvonne paid for our beers, so I guess we should get them while they're still cold."

"Stay where you are." Kelly slid into the water and pushed both rafts toward shore. Only when they reached knee-deep water did she stop to help Natalie stand.

Natalie grabbed her wrist as they walked toward their friends. "Why don't we get our drinks and take a walk down the beach?"

"I have a better idea. You wait here and I'll run these rafts up there and get our beer." Kelly's idea was to hurry off before anyone asked to come along.

Natalie stared at Kelly's retreating figure. Somehow, in the last eleven days, board shorts on a woman had become sexy. Or maybe it was the twitching muscles in Kelly's calves as she plowed through the sand. No, it was the way said shorts hugged that very tight butt. Or the broad shoulders...the air of confidence...the total package.

With every minute that passed, Natalie became more convinced of what she wanted—and what she didn't want. In the last twenty-four hours, she had imagined what it would be like to get her old life back. Thanks to Didi's none-too-subtle overtures, her feelings about a rejuvenated relationship had been quite vivid. Each time she took a mental step in that direction, she found herself filled with doubts and misgivings. Going back to Didi meant a return to a life that was dull and unfulfilling—for both of them. They had invested enough of their lives in each other. Their love was safe forever, but the romance was over.

From her stance near the shore, she grew anxious to see Didi trying to climb from her hammock as if to come along. But then Pamela put a hand on her shoulder and she fell back.

Moments later, Kelly was handing her a beer and steering her in the opposite direction. "We almost had company."

"So I saw."

"It's curious that Pamela doesn't seem to be jealous. Didi isn't making any secret that she wants to be wherever you are."

"Didi's a complicated person. She's probably sending Pamela other messages too. She needs to manage all the pieces around her." Natalie took a sip of her beer as they waded into the gently lapping water. "That probably makes her sound like a control freak, but she isn't like that. She just doesn't trust people to have her interests at heart, so she micromanages everyone close to her."

"It must have been hard not to feel trusted."

Natalie felt a wave of shame in thinking Didi had been right not to trust her after all. But it wasn't fair to Kelly to mention that and not elaborate on the humiliating details. "I understood why she did that, even if I didn't always appreciate it." They walked in silence for several minutes, until her curiosity got the best of her. "You got quiet all of a sudden."

"I was trying to figure out how to say something without sounding like just another person trying to tell you what to do."

She laughed softly. "I guess if I stopped letting people lead me around by the nose, that wouldn't be an issue."

"I promise I won't try to do that." Kelly took a long pull on her beer. "I was just thinking it was only a couple of days ago that you wanted Didi back. Now you're saying you don't, and while a part of me feels like jumping up and down, the other part is worried about you rushing into things, or out of things, as the case may be."

She exhaled with relief, glad that Kelly had just confirmed she was still interested. On the other hand, she was embarrassed to have her erratic emotions on full display. "I'm not usually this wishy-washy. It's just that I realized I didn't really feel the way I thought I did. I guess I just wanted something familiar."

"It happens like that sometimes. A woman's prerogative is to change her mind. When you think about it, it's amazing a couple of lesbians can ever agree on anything."

"Do you do that too? You want something so badly that it's all you can think about, and then when you get it, it's not as nice as you thought it would be?"

"I think that's where they get that saying about the grass always looking greener on the other side of the fence."

"Maybe that's it. Somebody came along a couple of days ago and showed me that the grass on this side could be pretty green too." She looked up to see Kelly break into a grin. Those dimples were adorable. "I don't know why I went off and killed a whole day with Didi yesterday. I guess I'm just in the habit of doing whatever she says. What I really wanted was to spend the day with you."

"Just like I really wanted to be with you instead of Pamela."

"Next time, just step on my foot or something."

"I hope there are lots of next times. So does this mean I can relax and be charming again? I've been trying to hold it in."

Natalie laughed heartily. It was nice to be rid of their serious tone. "I bet you couldn't hold it in if you tried."

By this time, Kelly was walking backwards in front of her, sporting a flirtatious smile. "No more than you can stop turning heads."

She looked at the other beachgoers, none of whom were looking their way. "I think you're imagining things."

"You're certainly turning mine."

Natalie slogged through the water with Steph until they were waist-deep. "Let's see if we can lie down on these without falling into the water like a couple of klutzes."

"How did you manage before?"

"Kelly helped me. But I can't ask you to help because you're the only one I know who's clumsier than I am."

"Thanks so much." Steph fell onto her raft awkwardly and wiggled until she was in the center. Though her long curly hair was tied back, a stray ringlet soaked up the water like a sponge. "They're all watching us, just waiting to laugh."

"I know." Natalie straddled her raft and leaned forward until she was prone. "Ha! Made it."

"Wow, this is the life. Thanks for coming out here with me."

"I'm surprised Yvonne didn't want to come."

"She does, but I needed to talk to you first. I have good news and bad news." Steph craned her neck to peer past Natalie toward the shore.

Natalie groaned. "I don't want any bad news."

"You're getting it anyway. When Pamela and Yvonne went to pick up the towels, Didi told me she's on to your little charade with Kelly. I asked her why she thought it was a charade and she said there was no way you'd ever be interested in somebody like Kelly. She thinks you're being a shit for using her like that—and by the way, Yvonne said the same thing until I told her Kelly was in on it."

The news wasn't as bad as she had feared. In fact, it was of no consequence at all, since she had been straightforward with

Kelly. She didn't care what Didi thought about it. "What's the good news?"

"That it worked. She said, and I quote, 'I'm starting to think getting back with Natalie would be the best thing for everyone,' unquote."

"Hmm." The good news in combination with the bad news made it all very bad news. Now she had to send a new message to Didi that she wasn't interested anymore, and the only way to do that was to tell her flat out.

"That is good news, isn't it?" Even Steph was having a hard time sounding enthusiastic.

"I suppose she knows you're out here telling me all this."

"Yeah, she wanted me to talk to you. She wants to wait until we all get home to break up with Pamela, but she asked me to let you know so you wouldn't have to hang out so much with Kelly."

"So I wouldn't have to. That's pretty funny." Natalie laughed softly and shook her head. "What if I want to?"

A knowing smile spread across Steph's face. "I knew it." She splashed water on Natalie's back. "You and Kelly."

"Not officially, but I'm coming around. You were right."

"Of course I was right. Didi might know fashion, but I know hotness. Tell me everything."

"There's nothing to tell, except I discovered the other night that she's a very good kisser." Natalie wasn't ready to commit her feelings about Kelly to words. "She's different. I don't really know what it is."

"She's a top. You've never been with a top before."

"Pfft! I think tops and bottoms are a bunch of bunk. I like women who like being women, not ones who want to be men."

"That's not what a top is. Do you think Yvonne wants to be a man?"

"Of course not."

"Trust me, Yvonne is a top, and I wouldn't have it any other way. That doesn't mean I don't take over once in a while, but I like having her be the aggressor most of the time, and she likes it too."

"A partnership is supposed to be equal, though. Didi and I didn't play roles."

"Because you're both bottoms. That's what made you equal. I'm surprised you didn't both die of Lesbian Bed Death. That's what happens when nobody takes charge."

"There was nothing wrong with our sex life." Even as the declaration left her lips, she knew it to be a lie. "It wasn't fabulous all the time, but at least it was regular...or semi-regular. And it was—" She started to say satisfactory, but that was the biggest lie of all. "Okay, so it wasn't all that great. To tell you the truth, it was pretty flat, especially after the first year or so."

"Which one of you initiated sex?" Steph asked in a tentative voice.

Natalie sighed and contorted her face. "I can't believe we're talking about this."

"Come on, Nat. We've been best friends for eighteen years. We used to talk about sex all the time."

"That was back when it was fun and interesting. Now it's just another thing to stress about."

"It shouldn't be that way. Are you sexually attracted to Kelly?"

Did lustful twitches in her loins count? "I think so."

"And Didi?"

Natalie turned her head to see the others on the shore. Didi was lying in the hammock, gazing out in their direction. "It isn't a fair comparison."

"Right, because Kelly's new and exciting. But if Didi isn't pushing your buttons anymore, you might as well just be friends, right?"

"I suppose." That was exactly what Didi had said two years ago when they broke up. Back then, Natalie had thought she had lost interest in sex. Now it seemed she had only lost interest in sex with Didi.

"Are you going to say something to Didi, or do you want me to?"

"I guess I will. I'm not going to rush into anything with

Kelly, but I don't want Didi to think I'm out there waiting in the wings."

Steph began to paddle away from shore. "Okay, I'm done with you now. Will you go back to the beach and send my girlfriend out here?"

"Not that you're trying to get rid of me or anything."

Chapter 18

On the balcony, Kelly shielded her eyes from the sun as they rounded the tip of the island and headed for the open sea. Even with the whole group in tow, her day with Natalie on the ship's private island had been almost perfect, the best of it being that Natalie was no longer interested in getting back with Didi. The missing piece was whether or not this was the right time to pick up where they had left off the other night. She had a feeling it was, but thought it best to proceed slowly, not because she was worried Natalie would change her mind but so they could avoid any missteps. She wanted more than just an onboard fling, and she hoped Natalie did too.

Natalie emerged through the sliding door dressed for dinner in a casual tropical blouse with slacks and sandals. A tan sweater hung about her shoulders, its arms tied across her chest.

"Very nice."

"You like it?"

"Yes, but you could make a potato sack look good." She nudged the deck chair back to make room for both of them to stand at the rail. "I can't believe we've been out here for over a week and you still have things you haven't worn."

"I brought too much. I'll probably have to change three times a day from here on out just to get through all my stuff."

"I hope I get a chance to see your winter wardrobe when we get home." It was a lame way to broach the topic, but at least it was benign. If Natalie wanted to talk about what was next for them, the door was open.

"I'm counting on it."

Kelly turned so they were face to face, relishing Natalie's faint smile. "Does that mean what I think it means? Am I going to be able to charm you into a date when we get back to the frozen north?"

"Is that what you want?"

"That's just the beginning. I'm hoping for a lot of dates." She tugged Natalie's head toward hers and delivered a soft kiss. "I don't want to rush things, though. If I get too charming, you'll have to call me down."

"I'll grant you a little leeway in that department."

Their eyes met in a sultry gaze that might have led to another kiss had Didi not suddenly appeared on the balcony next door.

"You two ready for dinner?" From the smile on Didi's face, she relished every single chance she got to disrupt their private moments. Now that she was on to their jealousy scheme, she would probably be even more annoying, at least until Natalie set her straight.

"Sure, see you in the hall," Natalie answered as she went back inside. "I need a few minutes with Didi."

"I'll tell her to wait for you, and I'll walk up with Pamela." Kelly stopped at the door and turned. "Be sure, Natalie."

"I am."

Natalie took a deep breath and opened the door to the hallway.

Didi was leaning against the wall with her arms folded, wearing what looked like a satisfied smile. "I take it you got my message."

"I did." She held her tongue until an older couple passed by. "You looked like you were enjoying yourself in that hammock. We used to have one of those in our yard in Mississippi, till the neighbor's dog chewed the rope on one end and my poor Aunt Maureen fell on her behind and dumped a whole glass of ice tea on her Easter dress. Mama said the dog didn't have anything to do with it, that—"

"You're rambling, Nat. What did you think about what Steph said?"

Natalie couldn't believe she had walked into this conversation without planning exactly what to say. It was no simple matter to explain that she didn't want their old relationship back again, nor did she want a new one, even on different terms. At a complete loss for words, she shook her head.

"What's that supposed to mean?"

"It means I've been thinking about it, and I believe we're better off as friends."

Didi flashed an irritated look before plastering on a smile. "That's exactly what I want too—a lover and a partner who is also my friend. I was wrong, okay? I admit it. We should have chilled just a little bit and gotten back together a year ago, but then Pamela came along. Call it a midlife crisis or whatever. I was an idiot, but I'm over it."

Natalie couldn't argue with that, but there was nothing in Didi's declaration that told her their life would be better than before. And even if there had been, she now had a new piece of information in the form of Kelly Ridenour. Actually, it wasn't only what she saw in Kelly. It was what she saw in herself, which was a hunger for a different dynamic, one in which she didn't constantly feel pressure to impress. "I'm not the same person I was two years ago...or for that matter, a week ago."

"Look, if you're worried about Pamela, I promise we'll cool things until we get back and I'll break up with her as soon as the plane lands. I just don't want to ruin her trip, you know?"

As usual, Didi wasn't listening. "This isn't about Pamela. It's not even about you. It's about me. I don't want to go back to what we had."

Didi caught her elbow and they stopped at the entrance to the dining room. "So what do you want? What do I need to change?"

"Nothing, Didi. You're a wonderful person just the way you are, and so am I. But we don't go together anymore." She forged ahead to their table without waiting for further argument. If Didi wouldn't listen, she would have to find another way to make it clear they were finished. The obvious answer was to be more open about her new feelings for Kelly but now that their attraction was no longer a charade, she didn't feel right about using Kelly to make her point.

Kelly held the door against the stiff wind as Natalie stepped out onto the Promenade Deck. "It's cool out here. We must be getting farther north."

Natalie pushed her arms through the sleeves of her sweater and hooked her hand around Kelly's elbow. She had been quiet through dinner, and declined the invitation from Steph to take in a movie.

"You okay?"

"Fine." Her face was expressionless.

"How did your talk with Didi go?"

Natalie shrugged. "I talked, but that doesn't mean she listened."

So was Natalie quiet because Didi had pleaded her case and gotten to her, or was she frustrated that disentangling was going to be more difficult than she thought? "I don't think anyone takes no for an answer the first time. They always think they can change your mind if they say or do just the right thing."

"Didi should know better. She's been working on me to move

to New York for a whole year and I haven't budged."

Kelly hoped that meant she wasn't budging now, because if she showed the slightest hint of being receptive to Didi's pleas, she would have to back off and give them the space to try to work things out. "I don't want to pull on you, Natalie. I meant what I said about not rushing things. I'm not going anywhere, and if you need some time to sort this out, you should take it."

"I'm walking with you—not Didi—on the Promenade Deck and holding your arm."

"Yes, you are."

"I spent most of the day floating around with you—not Didi—in a romantic lagoon. And if I'm not mistaken, it was you I kissed earlier on the balcony."

Kelly was picking up on the pattern, and she smiled at Natalie's roundabout way of reassuring her.

"On top of that, I'm thirty-seven years old, which is old enough to know what I want, when and with whom."

"Yes, ma'am." They reached the back of the ship, where the waning moon cast a rippled streak toward them. Kelly wrapped her arm around Natalie's waist and guided her to the rail. "I believe that's our moon."

"What makes it ours?"

"This." Kelly dipped her head and waited for Natalie to meet her lips. When they came together, she folded Natalie into her arms and pulled her close. The delicate, womanly feel of her body sent a shockwave directly to her core, and she heated up quickly.

Natalie must have felt it too, because her back arched into the embrace as her arms slithered around Kelly's neck.

The sound of footsteps broke their kiss but not their hold on one another. Locked in a fiery gaze, they were barely aware of another couple passing. Kelly could see her desire mirrored in Natalie's face. "Do you have any idea what kissing you does to me?"

"I think I do." She stepped back and reached for Kelly's hand. "Let's go back to our room."

Natalie's pulse quickened when Kelly latched the door and turned to reveal a lustful look. Within seconds, she found herself swept up in strong arms with Kelly's mouth descending onto hers. The sensations darted from one place to another as her body awakened to the hands that streamed from her hips to her shoulder blades. The instinctive grinding of her hips encouraged the exploration and erased for both of them any fleeting doubts about where they were headed.

The seconds turned to minutes as their kiss grew more intense. Kelly's lips left hers and traveled to the soft skin below her ear, sending a shiver up her spine. She dropped her head back and guided the hot mouth to her throat.

"You smell so good."

Natalie made a mental note of which cologne she had dabbed behind her ears and in the hollow of her neck. Whatever Kelly liked was her new favorite.

Kelly had to know what she was feeling, but she seemed to be holding back as if waiting for something. Permission... submission...Natalie didn't care if it was a mission of mercy as long as they didn't stop. Finally, she felt a tug on her zipper and responded in kind, making quick work of three buttons on Kelly's shirt.

"This would be so much better in bed," Kelly said.

Natalie stepped out of her dress and waited self-consciously for Kelly's appraisal, which came in the form of a low whistle. She would buy more black lace to wear with that cologne.

"Natalie Chatham, you are one beautiful woman." Kelly followed her to the nearest downturned bed, which happened to be Natalie's, dropped her trousers and shed her shirt. Her nipples peaked against her white tank top.

As Natalie lay back on the bed, Kelly straddled her, sliding one arm underneath to cradle her back. More kisses followed, now with Kelly lying almost on top of her. Never in her life had she been kissed so thoroughly, and never by someone who seemed impervious to her other urgent needs.

Natalie lowered her hands to Kelly's hips, marveling at the

rock-hard muscles beneath her fingertips. None of the other women she had been with had felt this way, nor had they moved over her with such authority and intent. She shamelessly writhed upward for more contact just as Kelly's mouth left hers to start again down her neck.

Spiraling with want, she grasped the hem of Kelly's tank top and pulled it upward. Kelly obliged, breaking contact to remove it and toss it aside. Natalie caught only a small glimpse of her small brown nipples before Kelly lowered herself to continue her attentions.

"Please touch my breasts," she murmured, guiding Kelly's hand to her lacy, strapless bra.

Kelly worked her way downward at an excruciating pace, finally trailing her tongue along the top of her breast. The hand under Natalie's back effortlessly released the clasp, and the other slid the bra from between them as Kelly returned to her mouth.

The sensation of their warm breasts together sent Natalie climbing even higher. She was on the verge of begging for more when Kelly finally took a breast in her hand and squeezed.

"I've never touched anything so perfect." Kelly used every part of her hand—her fingertips, her palm, the backs of her knuckles—to caress her stiffened nipples. Finally her lips took over and she drew a taut nipple between her teeth.

The jolt traveled instantly to Natalie's clitoris, which she began to grind against Kelly's leg. She was literally moments from her climax when Kelly sensed her urgency and shifted her leg to the side. "I have to touch you."

Natalie groaned at the loss of contact, but the sensation evaporated instantly. Kelly's fingers were sliding under the band of her thong, which meant her secret swirl wasn't going to be a secret much longer. Inch by inch, the lacy elastic slithered from her hip...to her thigh...and to the floor.

"So lovely," Kelly murmured, her fingertip following the trail of the sculpted swirl into the wetness below. Lower it crept, until it firmly pressed against the base of Natalie's vagina as if gathering its forces to breach the wall. Then it tracked upward along the cleft of her labia, stopping just short of her clitoris. Again. And again, the most exquisite torture imaginable.

"You're driving me insane." The rest of her body felt paralyzed as she concentrated on Kelly's touch. When Kelly's mouth found hers once again, the sensations intensified, now darting in a circuit from her center. She turned her head for air, but Kelly stayed close, their lips only millimeters apart as their breath came in shallow rasps. Finally Kelly slipped inside her and the sublime quiver began. "Oh, God…"

Kelly murmured something, but Natalie didn't hear. She was subsumed with powerful shockwaves that made her bury her face in Kelly's neck as she cried out.

"…beautiful…" Kelly brushed her lips along her chin as she withdrew her hand.

Natalie had craved each impulse, and even in the wake of her climax, her center still popped like a live wire. She suddenly became aware of her hands, which were tucked inside Kelly's briefs, gripping her tight butt. What on earth did a person say at a moment like this? Thank you? Who knew?

Instead of using words, she tried to show her feelings with another kiss, this one smoldering for more than a minute. When they finally broke, she found Kelly searching her eyes. "That was amazing."

Kelly opened her mouth to respond, but then shook her head. "I don't even have words for it."

"I'm still throbbing."

A warm hand tenderly enveloped her mound and she stirred upward.

"More?"

Natalie shook her head. "No, I can't. I just want you to hold me." She fingered the elastic of Kelly's briefs. "Take these off."

Kelly complied and pulled the covers up around them as she snuggled close.

"I think we're not finished," Natalie said as she stroked the newly exposed skin. "Your ass is like a rock."

"It's a runner thing."

"Magnificent," she said, feeling the curves and cleft. "How would I go about making you come like I just did?"

Kelly laughed softly and kissed the tip of her nose. "I guess I'll have to make a little more noise next time."

"What does that mean?"

"That I came already, about ten seconds before you did."

Natalie's mouth opened in shock. That was the most amazing thing she had ever heard. "I wasn't even touching you."

"But I was touching you. That's all it took," she said, nibbling gently on Natalie's earlobe. "You excite me like nobody ever has. So you can have your way with me again, or we can lie here just like this until we fall asleep. I couldn't possibly be more content than I am right now."

Natalie had never made love before with someone who seemed to take her pleasure from giving it. The invitation to have free rein was tempting, but so was lying in her arms in the warmest afterglow she had ever experienced.

She stared as Kelly emerged from the bed, her nude body sleek and ripped. Piece by piece, she collected their clothing and spread it neatly on the couch. "It's a habit from being in the navy. I hate to iron." Then she turned out the lights and crept back into bed.

"You have an incredible body."

"Nothing compared to yours, lady. I've been fantasizing about that ever since our first day at sea when you came out on the pool deck in your swimsuit."

Natalie chuckled and gently pinched her rib. "You have not."

"I have so. I was watching you from behind my sunglasses so you wouldn't see me. I got jealous when that redhead Aussie woman started hitting on you."

"Julie…I didn't come on this cruise to have a fling." She went silent as the magnitude of what she had just done struck her. This was how it always started—sex first, with love to follow. Neither she nor Kelly had ever said what this meant, but she hoped it hadn't been just a sexual thing.

Kelly nuzzled her neck. "Good. I hope that means you want more than a fling."

"Mmmm." Natalie relaxed and smiled to herself, thinking that Kelly had read her mind. It was way too soon to put words to this new feeling, but she liked where it was headed, and gave Kelly a warm, reassuring squeeze.

The slow, even breaths signaled Natalie's restful sleep.

Kelly wasn't so lucky, left awake and wondering why her question had gone unanswered. Maybe Natalie hadn't realized it was a question. Her only response had been a hug, which Kelly would have relished had it not seemed like a dodge.

No matter what happened after tonight, making love with Natalie had been one of the most wonderful experiences of her life—sweet, satisfying and filled with promise. While she wanted to believe it could lead to mutual love, the cold hard reality was that she and Natalie had very little in common. Few things could be so different as construction and fashion. In fact, her only real understanding of fashion was that Natalie looked fantastic in everything she wore. That didn't mean she wasn't willing to learn about the important things in Natalie's life, though it was hard to imagine developing a real interest in it beyond what mattered to Natalie.

Despite their differences, one thing they had going for them was chemistry, especially if tonight was any indication. The question was whether or not it was enough to seed a lasting relationship. In some ways, it was the most important piece, because if Natalie felt the chemistry too, it was motivation to work for more. But it was also the most fleeting, the easiest to let go, since it could totally vanish once they left the romantic setting they currently shared.

She closed her eyes and tried to imagine their lives one month from now…three months…a year. It made a nice fantasy to see herself hanging sheets of plastic in the doorways at Natalie's house in preparation for gutting the kitchen. In her mind's eye, Natalie would watch her with excitement and interest as she showed off her construction skills. They would share an ice-old beer and trade kisses as they talked about the new fixtures and designs. Then she would take Natalie's hand...

Chapter 19

Natalie stirred, grasping at once that she was alone in bed. Several times in the night she had awakened to find herself comfortably draped across Kelly's chest, wondering what the morning would bring. Then she would sigh, snuggle closer and drift off to sleep again, secure in Kelly's strong embrace. She was convinced this was a wonderful new thing, a chance to build a relationship with someone who valued her for the person she was, no matter what she wore or how she looked.

Upon finding Kelly gone, she grew uneasy. Yes, she ran most mornings. And yes, she usually brought both of them coffee so they could relax together in their room or on the balcony a few minutes before facing the rest of the world. It was sweet that she did that every day...but after what they had shared the night before, it would have been nice today to wake up in Kelly's arms.

Kelly had said she wanted more than a fling...or something like that...and that's what Natalie wanted too. In her life, she'd had only two sexual encounters that she considered flings. Both had been fun, but emotionally empty. She had expected more this time. It was too soon to be taken for granted, and that's how she felt about Kelly leaving her on her own this morning.

It wasn't as if she didn't have misgivings of her own. They were as different as night and day. And then there was the image of them together in public, her ultra-femme look to Kelly's butch persona.

It must have been her hormones at work, or just the fact that she hadn't had sex in over two years. No matter what had caused her to set all her judgment aside and give in to her lust, this thing with Kelly probably had zero chance to turn into a relationship. It was true that with Theresa and Didi she had established a pattern of sleeping with a woman first and then working to build a relationship based on physical attraction. That wasn't going to happen here, no matter how good the sex with Kelly had been... and it had been very, very good. Sexual chemistry wasn't enough to overcome her misgivings.

Her mind made up, she swung her legs out of bed and went immediately to the bathroom, where she gasped in horror at the makeup smudged around her eyes. It wasn't like her to go to bed without washing her face and applying the usual two layers of moisturizer. With the door cracked so she could listen for Kelly's return, Natalie went through the motions of putting herself back in order—a face scrubbing, a quick shower, and a once-over with her toothbrush. Finally fit to face the day, she emerged, increasingly irritated about Kelly's prolonged absence. What was she doing that was taking so long? Maybe she was feeling sheepish about last night too, and now she was out there running off her frustrations, anxious about coming back to the room.

A breeze wafted the curtain and Natalie suddenly realized the balcony door was open. She cinched her robe around her waist and peered out to find Kelly stretched out in a deck chair, eyes closed, barefoot and wearing last night's briefs and tank top. Clearly, she hadn't gone for her morning run at all.

Natalie felt a shiver run up her back as she studied the long, languid form. Only a few hours ago, it had been a sinewy mass of energy, intent on bringing her pleasure. Those hands, now hanging limply from the arms of the chair, had been alive and in command of her body, as if they had known exactly what she needed. Her center pulsed in response to her wandering thoughts, and she consciously shook them away. This situation called for a little self-control. "Kelly?"

Kelly's eyes shot open and she straightened up in her chair, a brilliant smile bursting onto her face. "Hey, I didn't hear you get up."

"You've been out here all morning?"

"Yeah, I woke up a while ago. I was afraid you'd open your eyes and find me staring at you, so I got up and came out here. You want me to go get coffee?"

"You didn't go for your run?"

"Are you kidding? No way was I leaving today. It was all I could do to tear myself out of bed so I wouldn't wake you up."

It was amazing how quickly her emotional pendulum had swung, from blissfully happy when she first awoke to irritation and doubt when she thought Kelly had gone. Now she found herself beaming like a lottery winner.

"So what about the coffee?"

Natalie eyed her up and down. "I don't know if the rest of the ship is ready for you in your skivvies."

"Are you complaining about my attire, or is this how you flirt?"

She lifted her eyebrows and smiled. "The only reason I'd complain about your underwear would be because I wanted you out of it."

Kelly grasped the belt on Natalie's robe as she pulled herself out of the chair. "Did you like the blue ones I had on yesterday? Those are my favorites."

"They were very nice. In fact, I was thinking of getting some for myself."

"No, no. Women like you are the reason they make silk and lace." Kelly parted the robe daringly and slipped a hand inside. "And there's nothing I like better than removing silk and lace."

A wave of heat rushed through Natalie as Kelly pressed her body against her skin. Their slow grind began anew and they met in an easy kiss, with Kelly nibbling gently at her lips. "Where did you learn to kiss?"

"This isn't kissing," Kelly answered. "I'm making love to your mouth."

Natalie was so focused on the feel of Kelly's lips and tongue that she was barely aware of being out in the open half naked. Her robe fell completely apart as Kelly cradled her bottom. "I'm thinking we should carry this back inside."

"Sorry. I can't help myself, especially now that I know all about this glorious body of yours. I'm thinking room service might be a good idea for breakfast."

"And lunch," Natalie answered, tickling the downy hair at the small of her back. "And maybe dinner."

"If we don't get off this balcony, I'm going to devour you right here."

Natalie pulled away and cinched her robe, struggling to get a grip on her desires. "Who knew you were such an animal?"

"I'd be a whole zoo if that's what you wanted."

She drew a deep breath as Kelly stepped back and stretched, a move that exposed not only her taut stomach, but the snug fit of her briefs. When she stepped aside to let Kelly through the door, she was startled by warm lips against her temple, which refueled the sensations she had almost managed to tamp down.

"I should probably grab a quick shower. I won't be but a minute," Kelly said as she removed her top and briefs and tossed them into a laundry bag in the closet. Then she disappeared into the bathroom.

Natalie collapsed on the couch and buried her face in her hands. She had no self-control at all. So what?

Something was off a bit about Natalie this morning, but Kelly couldn't quite put her finger on what it was. Morning-after awkwardness wasn't unusual, though, and this didn't seem like more than that. Fortunately, Natalie seemed more relaxed now than when she had first gotten up.

"You can have that last muffin," Natalie said as she propped her feet on the balcony rail. They had polished off most of their basket of bread, a tray of fruit and a large pot of coffee.

"I'm stuffed. Room service was a great idea. I wish I'd thought of it."

Natalie popped her playfully with a linen napkin. "Very funny. I'm surprised you didn't want to get out of the room for a bit."

"What could possibly interest me out there when I could stay here with the loveliest woman on the ship?"

"You can stop flirting now, you know. After last night, I'd say it's quite unnecessary."

"Who says I'm flirting? I'm just finally saying all the things I've been thinking since we met."

"And what were you thinking through that silly charade of trying to make Didi jealous?"

Kelly dropped her teasing smile. "I only agreed to help you because that's what you wanted. I'd much rather have you be happy with me."

Natalie looked away, shaking her head. "I hate to be the one to tell you this, but I'm not the prize you seem to think I am."

"That's my call." She scooted her chair closer and took Natalie's hand. "As far as I'm concerned, you're the biggest prize there is. This is probably going to sound weird, but I feel like I can be myself with you. Actually, it's more than that. I feel like I can be the person I want to be. I like how we go together."

The smile on Natalie's face as she nodded said she knew it too. "I like the way I am with you too."

"How are you with me? What is it you feel?"

"You pay attention to me. I feel very…I don't know, you make me feel good about myself."

"You should, Natalie. When you take my arm, I feel like the

envy of everyone here."

Natalie was blushing demurely, but obviously enjoying the compliments. "You know, the people closest to me call me Nat."

"That's what I want to be, close. Like really close."

They held their gaze for a long, steamy moment until Natalie squeezed her hand. "I think we ought to get off this balcony."

Kelly scooped up the remnants of their breakfast and followed her through the glass door. She continued on to set the tray outside for pickup, and placed the Do Not Disturb placard in the lock. By the time she returned, Natalie had pulled the curtains for privacy, leaving a gap to allow sunlight into their room. She was sitting on her unmade bed, and had loosened the tie on her robe.

"Feeling...sleepy, Nat?"

"Come here, you."

Kelly dropped to her knees and slid her arms inside the robe to feel the warm skin. "You are irresistible."

"I want to touch you. Will you let me do that?"

"I'm all yours." She pulled her tank top off and tossed it on the other bed. To that, she added her shorts and briefs.

As she stood naked, Natalie eyed her up and down with obvious pleasure. "You have the most amazing body." She shifted and motioned for Kelly to lie down. Then she shed her robe and stretched out beside her.

"I can't imagine anything feeling more fantastic than this." Kelly couldn't stop herself from running her hand along Natalie's hip to cup her bottom.

"I want you to relax. I didn't get a chance to do this last night." She ran her hand gently across Kelly's stomach, stopping short of stroking her breast. "What do you like best?"

"Whatever you do." She sucked in a breath as Natalie raked her fingernails across her nipple. "I could go for that."

Natalie's mouth found hers and they dissolved in a kiss. A warm hand traveled from her breast to the hollow of her throat and back again, but their lips never parted.

It was all Kelly could do to remain submissive under the

tender onslaught. Natalie had taken the kissing lesson to heart, and was exploring her mouth with her lips, tongue and teeth. Finally her hand ventured lower to tickle the stiff hairs of her mound and she instinctively parted her legs. At the first touch, she realized she was wet and ready.

Natalie recognized her response and slid her fingers through the slick folds. "I should have known this part of you would be hard too."

Before Kelly could respond her lips were crushed in another kiss, this one strong and demanding. The stroking quickened as their passion flowed, and she pressed upward for more contact. Both of them moaned rapturously as Natalie plunged her fingers inside and her thumb grazed the clitoris. Kelly was torn between the desire to push Natalie's hand deeper or to clutch her round bottom in an effort to draw her body even closer. Her own needs won out and she found herself rubbing Natalie's hand to urge it on its intimate quest.

Natalie was panting furiously in a rhythm that matched her strokes, her open mouth only millimeters from Kelly's ear.

The first deep impulse rippled from within and slowly built to a powerful clenching of her walls. "Oh, God. Feel me...feel what you do."

"Kelly..." she whispered. Natalie gripped her in a tight embrace, burying her face into her neck.

Kelly was sure it was more of an emotional gesture than a physical one, and stroked Natalie's head reassuringly. "I don't want to scare you half to death or anything, but if you want to make love with me like that for the next fifty years, you certainly may."

Natalie smiled as the credits rolled on the sappy dog movie she and Kelly had found on the ship's family entertainment channel. Their only foray outside the stateroom—a walk around the Promenade Deck to allow the cabin steward to freshen their room—had been cut short by a sudden storm that was now a driving rain. The weather had sent them back to their stateroom after all, where they again gave in to temptation.

The movie had been a pleasant way to rest and pass the afternoon. When she had offered her lap as a couch pillow, Kelly took her up on it. Now she was fast asleep, and Natalie had no choice but to sit perfectly still through the next movie. Not that she minded. Being close had its own rewards.

Her fingers brushed the hair just behind Kelly's ear. It was soft and baby fine, like worn satin. She would never have guessed that "soft" would have described so many things about Kelly—her hair, her skin, her lips, and most of all, her touch. But that wasn't what had made their lovemaking so thrilling and satisfying. Even more than all the physical sensations was the way Kelly had whispered sweet words of endearment, phrases that had made Natalie feel like the most special woman in the world. And the fact that Kelly had climaxed again from her own excitement…Natalie had heard of such a thing, but until last night had doubted it could actually happen, let alone with her.

Sex had never been like that for her before. It wasn't that she had never had a powerful climax. But those came mostly at her own hand, and after a lot of practice. The main difference with Kelly was finding herself the object of someone's lust. Neither Theresa nor Didi had shown the hunger for her that Kelly did. Both of them had been focused either on their own satisfaction or their sexual prowess and skill. From the moment she and Kelly had kissed last night, she felt it was all about her.

"What are you thinking about?"

Natalie was startled by Kelly's voice, and unnerved by the twinkling blue eyes that seemed to be reading her prurient thoughts. "I'd better plead the Fifth on that one."

"Hmmm…you make it sound so interesting. Sure you don't want to elaborate?"

"I'm very sure." Despite her efforts to distance herself from her thoughts, her hand still stroked Kelly's hair. "I can't get over how soft your hair is. I wish mine was like that."

"No, you don't. Yours is so thick and wavy. And I love the color."

As usual, Kelly had managed to turn the conversation into a stream of compliments. "You're always so good for my ego."

"I'm also house-trained."

"If only you could cook."

"I can learn. What's your favorite dish?"

"Anything with shrimp. But you don't have to worry about cooking, because I like to do that."

"And I like to eat. Don't you see what that means?" Kelly sat up and grinned. "We're made for each other. It would be a perfect life."

Natalie laughed aloud. This line of playful banter carried none of the seriousness of their afterglow chat, but the message was the same. Kelly wanted this to last. "And what would you be doing while I was slaving over a hot stove?"

"I'd be busy laying tile somewhere or up on a ladder wiring a new light fixture."

"Are you really serious about doing all this work at my house?"

"If you want me to."

"I'm not even sure I can afford you." Natalie caught herself staring as Kelly stood and stretched, again showing off her flat stomach. "We'll have to go over your skin—I mean your rate. That's what I meant to say…rate." She covered her face as it heated up.

"You're welcome to go over my skin if you like, Natalie." She inched her shirt upward. "Just say the word."

Natalie fanned herself. "Boy, it got warm in here all of a sudden."

"That's because you need ice cream. I'll run up to the stand and get some."

Natalie's eyebrows went up and down suggestively. "And what are we going to do with this ice cream?"

"It's hard to say. The possibilities are endless."

Chapter 20

Bursting with energy, Kelly bounded up the stairs to the ice cream parlor. Funny how a day spent lying around lazily would be the best time she'd had so far on the cruise. No question about it—she and Natalie were both feeling something special.

"Where's the fire?"

She turned at the familiar voice and waited as Yvonne caught up. "Hey, stranger! What are you guys up to today?"

"I've been in the casino all afternoon losing the eighty dollars I won last night. Steph went back to bed after lunch with one of those books your friend swapped for her. That was a lifesaver, by the way."

"Yeah, Jo thought the same thing. She didn't know what she was going to do for the last three days without a new book. Have you seen Didi or Pamela?"

"Not since this morning. They were in the picture gallery looking at all the photos from dinner the other night."

Kelly smiled as she remembered her pose with Natalie. "I forgot about those. I'll have to go find ours."

"I know it's there, because Didi found it. Just don't be surprised if she gave you a set of horns and a moustache."

"Why would she do that?"

"You tell me. Maybe she noticed the breakfast tray outside your stateroom this morning and the Do Not Disturb sign."

Kelly chuckled uncomfortably. "So much for keeping things low-key." She wasn't particularly embarrassed for the others to surmise how she and Natalie had spent their morning, but it made her ill at ease to hear that Didi was upset about it. This was a special time for her and Natalie, and she didn't want Didi to spoil it with a tantrum. More than that, she didn't want Natalie to suddenly have second thoughts just because Didi had decided to reinsert herself into the picture.

Yvonne nudged her with an elbow and gave her a knowing wink. "So what's up? Are you guys an item, or just having fun?"

Kelly was uneasy about sharing too much, though it was too late to try to pretend nothing had happened. "I can't speak for Natalie, but it feels like the real deal for me. We'll just have to take it one day at a time and see where it goes."

Yvonne shook her head. "I'm just glad you finally hooked up. I made a bet with Steph that you would, and now she's going to have to pay up. Good thing, since I lost all my money at the craps table."

"Glad we could help."

"I have to warn you, though. Steph's been awfully patient about Didi, but she won't sit by again and watch her best friend rot in another bad relationship. She'll kick your ass."

"She won't have to. I plan to worship Natalie for as long as she'll let me."

"Natalie deserves that. But Didi's got her head so screwed up right now she probably doesn't even know what she wants. I just hope Natalie doesn't jump back into that fire if Didi snaps her fingers."

That was Kelly's fear too. "So what exactly happened between them anyway?"

Yvonne shook her head. "Nobody really knows. Something pretty embarrassing for Natalie, I'd say, because she didn't even tell Steph what it was. All she said was that honesty wasn't always the best policy. We don't have any idea what she meant."

That was pretty much all Natalie had told her also. "Whatever it was, Didi was a fool for letting her go. Women like Natalie don't come along every day."

"She's a sweetie. It's a shame the only two women she's ever been with thought they were the center of the universe." Yvonne began to walk backward toward the stairs. "I need to go break the news to Steph that my luck ran out in the casino, but she owes me money. See you at dinner."

Kelly studied on Yvonne's words as she moved up in the line for ice cream. Maybe it was time for Natalie to get a taste of being at the center of someone's universe.

Natalie inhaled deeply as she slid the door open and stepped out on the balcony in the cool air. The rain had stopped for the moment, but the sun was nowhere to be found. No sooner had she positioned herself at the rail than the door opened from Didi and Pamela's suite. "There you are," Didi said tersely. "I was beginning to wonder if you remembered the rest of us were here too."

"Kelly's gone to get ice cream. With this weather, it's been nice to relax inside."

Didi scowled. "Yeah, we've been listening to you two relax. Did you realize you were putting on a show, or was that the whole point?"

Natalie felt her cheeks redden, but Didi's indignant tone made her more angry than embarrassed. "You're one to talk. At least now you know what it's been like for us having to listen to you two."

"So is that what this was about? You thought you'd get back at me by acting like a couple of dogs in heat?"

"Don't flatter yourself. What I do with Kelly has nothing to do with you."

"Bullshit." She rolled her eyes. "You've been parading around here all week on her arm making sure I saw every little touch and smile."

Natalie was pretty sure Steph had confirmed the charade, or at least hinted at it, so there was no use denying that it had been her intent up until a couple of days ago. "That's how it started. I thought seeing me with somebody else would make you miss what we used to have, but then..." She looked over her shoulder in case Kelly had come back already. "I've had so much fun with her, Didi. I understand now what it is with you and Pamela. You needed to be with somebody who could give you what I couldn't. I guess I needed that too."

"So do you fake it with her too?"

The words cut her to the bone, and she turned abruptly to go back inside.

Didi reached around the barrier and caught her wrist. "I'm sorry. I just had an urge to hurt you."

"You did."

"I don't know why I said that."

Natalie knew why. It was because it was never far from the surface, a constant reminder of all the things that had gone wrong in their relationship. If she'd had it to do over again, she would have held onto her lie—that Didi was the best lover in the world. After all, that's what Didi had cared about, not that she had expressed her love intimately in a way that brought them closer together.

"I just want you to realize that you can do a lot better than Kelly."

"I'm not so sure of that." Natalie knew Didi still loved her, and she wanted to believe she had her best interests at heart. "I've never met anyone quite like her."

"Humph. You know lots of men, Nat."

208

A surge of ire filled her, but she held it in check. "Believe me, she's all woman."

Didi shuddered visibly and moved closer, as if suddenly worried Pamela would overhear. "All I'm saying is that people are going to look at you two and think that's the kind of woman you like. Is that what you want?"

"Why should I care what people think? It's nobody's business but my own."

"It's everybody's business when you work with the public like we do. How are we supposed to sell women's fashion when our customers see you with somebody in a hard hat?"

"Not everybody judges people by how they dress."

"More bullshit. You can't tell me you weren't put off when you first saw Kelly. You stood right here on this balcony and said she looked like a man."

"That's not quite the way I put it." She vaguely recalled the conversation, and admittedly had been taken aback. "I remember being a little surprised at first but the more I've gotten to know her, the more I like what I see. We all have to be ourselves. She's comfortable with who she is and so am I."

"But you don't seriously think she's attractive?"

She couldn't tell if Didi's question was serious or challenging, but she had vowed never to lie to her again. "She isn't glamorous like you or Pamela, but she makes me feel like a goddess."

Didi sighed and looked out to sea. "I could do that for you, Nat."

"Didi, I—"

"Hear me out. I'm going to break up with Pamela when we get home Friday night, no matter what else we decide. What happens after that is up to you. If the New York thing bothers you that much, we'll drop it. I'd rather be in Rochester with you than anywhere without you. Is that what you want to hear?"

It was what she had wanted to hear three days ago, but everything had changed since then. Besides, she doubted Didi would stick to her conviction. "I'm all for dropping the New York part, but don't do that out of some pledge to me. Do it because it makes more sense for our store to stay and grow in Rochester. I don't want to risk everything we've built by moving somewhere that chews up new fashion stores and spits them out."

Didi glanced behind her again. "Forget the store. Just promise me that we'll get things back the way they used to be." She must have seen Natalie's incredulous look because she quickly added, "Only better."

For Natalie, it was a moment of truth, admitting aloud to the woman she had loved for most of the last eight years that she was moving on. "I can't make that promise anymore. Things have changed, and not just for me. We both want what we had a long time ago, but that isn't going to happen. We're different people now, and that's why we fell apart to begin with."

"That's not true. We fell apart because you stopped being honest with me."

"No, the biggest reason is because I wasn't honest with myself, because I talked myself into believing that what we had was enough. It wasn't, because I wasn't happy and neither were you."

"How do you know I wasn't?"

"Because it was so easy for you to let me go, Didi. You wanted more than I was giving you, or maybe you wanted less. All I know is that our sex life was just a symptom of things not being right."

"So you're running off with Tammy Toolbox now?" Didi tipped her head toward the door behind Natalie.

Natalie rolled her eyes, resisting the urge to snap back. Didi was only lashing out because she felt her grip slipping. "I don't know exactly what we're doing."

"Boy, you can say that again."

"That's not what I meant and you know it. I meant that I don't know what's going to happen." This time, she gave her a scolding glare. "Look, I care about Kelly. She's opened my eyes to a side of me I never knew existed. Maybe she's the one, Didi." Her breath hitched as the words left her lips and Didi's face fell. "Or maybe not. Once we get back to Rochester, I might slap myself in the head and say, 'What were you thinking?' All I know is this feels fantastic, and I have to see it through."

It shocked her to see Didi wipe away an actual tear. "Fine, Nat. You do whatever you have to do. But when this turns out to be a flash in the pan, I'll still be here. That's how I know what we have is real love, and you ought to know that too."

She took Didi's hand and squeezed it hard. "Listen to me. If there's one thing I can promise, it's that I'm going to love you for the rest of my life, no matter what happens to either of us. Nothing about Kelly or anyone else will ever change that."

"So will I ever get another chance?"

Natalie felt pity at her desperate plea. All Didi wanted was a lifeline, something to hold onto until she came to terms with the reality that it was over. Still, Natalie couldn't bring herself to say something that wasn't true just to soothe Didi's feelings. She had learned the hard way that it was better not to say anything at all.

The sound of the heavy glass sliding behind Didi announced Pamela's arrival on the balcony.

Didi never turned back to acknowledge her presence, instead, mouthing her words silently. "I love you, Nat."

Natalie squeezed her hand again and stepped back inside.

Kelly pushed her wet hair against the grain to give it lift. The result was a disheveled look, which was exactly what she wanted, since Natalie had complimented it the night she had worn the outfit with the tie. Anything to please.

"Does this look all right?" Natalie asked as she appeared from behind in the mirror. She was dressed casually in Capri pants and a long-sleeved rayon shirt, the latter bunched at the waist with a woven belt she had bought in San Juan.

"You look fabulous."

Natalie poked her in the back. "You didn't even look."

"I didn't have to. You always look fabulous." She turned and eyed her up and down, twirling her finger to get Natalie to spin around. "I was right."

"I'm sure if I've done something wrong, Didi will let me know."

Kelly grabbed the door frame as the ship pitched to the side. "Feels like we're in for another rough night."

"The TV said fifteen-foot swells. Good thing we don't get seasick."

"Like some people," Kelly said, tipping her head in the direction of the cabin next door. She handed her dolphin necklace to Natalie. "How about helping me with this? My outfit needs a focal point."

"You're making fun of me."

"I am not. I'm showing off the only thing I know about fashion." The ship's daily planner called for a casual dinner, so Kelly wore her usual tank top underneath a white shirt, and chinos. "Maybe when we get to Nassau tomorrow we'll cut out of our carriage tour and you can help me pick out a tropical shirt to wear on our last night."

"The tour only lasts a couple of hours, so we should have time to do both." Natalie finished fastening the necklace and reached over Kelly's shoulder to finger the pendant. "It's not too late to change your mind and do something in the water. It's your last chance."

"It's your last chance to shop too, and I want to be with you."

"And, in this case, with Didi and Pamela."

"As long as you're there, it won't matter."

Natalie studied her with clear curiosity. "Why on earth would you give up something fun to come shopping with us? You hate to shop."

Kelly held the door as they headed out to dinner. "I've decided to broaden my horizons."

As they passed a long mirror at the entrance to the dining room, Natalie caught the smile she knew she had been sporting all day. And why wouldn't she be smiling? In the past twenty-four hours, she'd had five orgasms, and not a single one from her own hand.

"I think we're late," Kelly said, guiding Natalie to the table

212

with a hand in the small of her back.

"That's because you kept pulling me back to bed," she whispered naughtily.

"You're lucky we're here at all."

"You call that lucky? I was going to ask for dinner in a doggie bag."

When they reached the table, Natalie noticed Didi had switched places with Pamela and was now sitting next to Yvonne instead of Kelly. If it was meant as an insult, it wasn't particularly subtle, and she deflected it by taking Kelly's seat instead of her own.

Kelly smiled across the table at Didi as she pushed Natalie's chair in. "Are you holding up all right with all this rocking and rolling?"

Didi looked past her directly at Natalie. "Those pants are nice on you, Nat. They're the ones from the spring show two years ago, right?"

Natalie eyed the empty highball glass in front of Didi's plate, thinking it had to be at least her second to account for the stilted cadence in her voice. "That's right. I love how they fit."

"I love how they fit too."

Natalie glanced uncomfortably at Pamela, who didn't seem troubled by the remark. Perhaps it had been an innocent observation after all, instead of the brazen overture she had first perceived. When she glanced back at Didi, she noticed a bandage on her thumb. "What happened to your hand?"

"Burned it on my curling iron," she grumbled.

The wine steward suddenly appeared and presented a bottle of cabernet sauvignon for Didi's inspection. She nodded, and he worked the cork and proceeded to pour six glasses.

"I thought we ought to celebrate since we only have one more day on this damn ship," Didi said, slurring faintly.

Natalie shook her head and sighed. There was no denying it had been a miserable trip for Didi, and it was perfectly understandable she would be ready to celebrate its end. "To good friends," she said, lifting her glass in Didi's direction.

"And to lovers," Didi added. She slapped her glass to Natalie's carelessly, sloshing her wine so that it splashed on both Pamela and Natalie. "Oops."

Pamela pushed back quickly and tried to mop her lap with her napkin. "Uh-oh, this is going to stain."

"I'm sorry. Did I get you too, Nat?"

"Just a little. I think I can wash it out if I hurry. Come on, Pamela. There's a ladies' room right outside the door." Moments later she entered the restroom with Pamela on her heels. "Looks like Didi got an early start on happy hour."

"Poor thing," Pamela said, scrunching her nose as she saw the reflection of the stain on her top. "Everything that could go wrong on this trip has. Food poisoning, sunburn, getting seasick, and now, burning her hand. I think if Emerald gave her a voucher for a free cruise she'd drop it in the shredder."

"I'm sure she'll be glad to get home." Natalie dabbed a wet paper towel to a wine spot on her pants.

"I hate to say this, but I think my top's ruined. I'm going to run back to our cabin and change. I'll be back in a few minutes."

Natalie was impressed at how Pamela had kept her cool after such a careless accident, and even more that Didi's antics were getting under her radar. "I'll let the others know."

"How's it going, Spike?" Didi asked, her face fixed in a smirk.

"Not bad," Kelly answered. It was obvious Didi was drunk, and Kelly felt no desire to pile on to her obvious misery. "It's supposed to be nice weather in Nassau, so maybe the seas will calm a bit as we get closer."

"You having a good time with Natalie?"

From her tone, Kelly got the distinct impression it wasn't a friendly question, and her patience was wearing thin. "Great. In fact, I'd say it was perfect."

"Enjoy it while it lasts. She's just playing a game with you. When we get back to Rochester, it'll all be over."

Yvonne shook a finger in Didi's direction. "Knock it off, Didi.

And go easy on the wine before you fall over in your plate."

"You stay out of this. It's not your fucking business."

"I don't care whose business it is," Steph interjected. "You're drunk and you don't know what you're talking about."

"The hell I don't. You heard what Natalie said. 'Might as well be with a man.' Wasn't that it?"

Kelly flinched inwardly at the words and studied Steph's reaction. It took only seconds to realize Didi was speaking the truth.

Steph was clearly flustered. "She didn't really mean that, Kelly. It was just…"

Yvonne spoke up. "Natalie hasn't been around butch women much. I think she was just a little surprised at first."

Didi drained her wineglass and banged it on the table. "That's what she really thinks of you, so don't go fooling yourself into believing you're more than just a fuck. The woman hasn't been laid in two years. She told me today while you were off fetching ice cream that she has no idea what she's doing with you. And for your information, she also said she loves me, and nothing's going to change that."

Kelly got a sick feeling in the pit of her stomach. As much as she wanted to dismiss Didi's drunken rant, there was just enough plausibility in her words to make them stick. When she saw Didi look up and smile, she knew Natalie was behind her, and she wanted nothing more than to leave them all here quibbling about who said what.

"My spot came out, but Pamela wasn't so lucky. She had to go back to the room and change."

Kelly resisted her natural inclination to help Natalie with her chair.

"Why's everyone so quiet?"

"Didi's been running her mouth," Yvonne groused.

"About what?"

Didi shrugged, feigning innocence. "I just told Kelly what you said this afternoon, you know, about getting home and slapping your head because you didn't know what you were doing."

Natalie's face turned beet red, and she glanced nervously in Kelly's direction. "That is not what I said."

"Come on, Natalie. You said if you were going to be with someone like that, it might as well be a man."

"I did not." She grabbed Kelly's hand under the table. "I might have said I thought she was a man the first time I saw her, but that's because she was standing behind Yvonne and I couldn't see her very well."

"Bullshit. Can't you be honest just once in your life?" Didi looked over at the others. "You guys heard her say that, didn't you?"

Yvonne glared across the table. "Didi, you're such a bitch."

That was all the confirmation Kelly needed, and she wriggled her hand free from Natalie's and stood. "I'm sure there's probably some debate about the semantics, but I think I got the gist of it."

"Hey, Nat. Did she know you were faking? Did you tell her you did that?"

Kelly didn't wait to hear the answer.

"I can't believe you'd be so mean," Natalie said, her voice shaking with fury. "I hope you're proud of yourself."

"Did I say one thing that wasn't the gods' truth?"

She wanted to throw her wine in Didi's face, and would have if Steph and Yvonne hadn't been trapped in the middle of the spectacle. She stood and leaned menacingly across the table. "How's this for some truth? When we get back to Rochester, we'll sit down with the lawyers and accountants and draw up the papers. I'll sell you my half of the store, and you can take it and move to New York. Better yet, why don't you move to Mississippi...or Timbuktu?"

Didi tossed her chin defiantly. "Aw, come on. I just saved you all the trouble of telling her to get lost. You know as well as I do that she's not good enough for you."

"What I know is that after ten days, she knows me better than you ever did because she cared enough to find out. You never cared about anyone but yourself." She threw her napkin on her plate and leaned closer to deliver her parting shot in a low, venomous hiss. "And for your information, I don't have to fake it with her because she's a thousand times better in bed."

Chapter 21

The inside cabins were black as pitch, but Kelly's backlit watch showed a few minutes after seven. They had been in port for a while because the ship's engine had gone perfectly still about an hour earlier, and moments ago she had heard a muffled announcement that the gangway was open. She tightened her shoelace and groped in the dark for her sunglasses.

The figure in the other bed stirred. "Hey, mate. You can turn on the light if you need to."

"Sorry if I woke you up. I really appreciate you letting me crash here."

Jo sat up and turned on the bedside lamp. "No worries. Julie's trying to squeeze in every last second with her new lady friend, so she probably won't be back until it's time to pack."

"You've been on your own a lot."

"Doesn't bother me. I mean, if I was here with a girlfriend or something, I'd want to be with her all the time, but I don't mind being by myself with Julie. I want her to have a good time."

"Who knows? Maybe next time you take this trip, you can talk Sarah into coming along…pushing the beds together…"

Though she grinned with embarrassment, it was clear she liked the idea very much. "Only in my dreams, mate."

"You need to start living those dreams, Jo. You can't keep letting life pass you by."

"Yeah, well. You're not exactly living yours, or you wouldn't be bunking down here with me."

"I lived them, but they didn't last." Kelly gathered her small bundle of belongings and stuffed them inside her gym bag. "No regrets, though."

"So what are you going to do today?"

"I was here a few years ago when I was in the navy and I remember a coastal road that goes all the way out to the airport. I thought I'd take a nice long run and clear my head. I'll come back about noon and round up my gear before my roommate gets back."

"Stow it here if you need to. And there's a pretty good chance Julie will sleep with her lady again tonight."

"Thanks, mate." Kelly liked using the friendly Aussie moniker. "I may have to take you up on that."

"So what happened with you and Natalie? Last time I saw you, things were looking up."

"Yeah, I thought so too. Turns out we were looking at different things."

"Sorry it didn't work out."

"Me too, but like I said. No regrets." She stowed her tidy bag in the closet. "I'll pick this up later."

Hardly anyone was stirring in the hallway as she made her way to the exit on Deck 2. The tours would leave around eight, which meant Natalie and the others were probably at breakfast. She had plotted half the night about strategies to avoid further

219

contact. It would be nice if it worked out for her to stay with Jo again, but she was prepared to sleep in one of the lounges if she had to—anything to keep from seeing Natalie again.

She followed the signs to Bahamas Customs and flashed her passport and key card. Then she exited the row of shops along the pier and began to run. If the map was right, it was twelve miles to the airport and back. That would give her a good workout and put her back on the ship well before Natalie returned from her carriage tour.

"…She didn't sleep here. I have no idea where she went, but all of her things are still in the drawers." Natalie paced as far as the phone cord would allow. "No, you and Yvonne should go on to Atlantis. No reason for anyone else to be miserable. I'm going to wait right here for her to come back."

She hung up and started out onto the balcony so she could watch the passengers depart. She doubted Kelly would leave the ship alone, but it didn't hurt to watch for her. A loud knock on the door stopped her short. The cabin steward usually tapped gently and announced his presence, so that could only mean one thing—Didi had awakened, hung over and filled with remorse for her rude behavior. Too damn bad.

But it was Pamela, not Didi, on the other side of the peephole. "What on earth happened last night, Natalie?" Her face was a mask of worry.

"I'm afraid you'll have to get that story from Didi…if she can even remember it. People as drunk as she was are lucky because they're spared most of the memories." She left the door open for Pamela to follow her inside.

"She never said a word about it last night, but I knew something was wrong. I let her sleep it off, and then told her this morning that I'd had enough of her acting like she could do whatever she wanted, that this was my vacation too. She left while I was in the shower."

"Look, I really like you and I don't mean to be rude about this. I know I haven't exactly been gracious toward you because, frankly, I was jealous. But believe me, I'm over all that. You can have her with my blessing." She didn't owe Pamela the level of honesty about Didi's intentions to dump her when they got back to Rochester. Didi would have to do her own dirty work on that one.

"I knew you were jealous, Natalie. And I could tell you were trying to get under her skin by hanging all over Kelly, but I figured you might as well take your best shot. If you're the one she really wants, it's better for me to find that out now. I love her with all my heart, but I want her to be happy, no matter what happy is."

Natalie sighed and slumped onto the couch. Pamela was a better person than all of them, and more mature to boot. "Good luck. I promise I won't make any more trouble for you."

"Thank you. So will you help me find her before she does something totally stupid, like leave the ship and fly home without her things?"

"I'll help you find Didi if you'll help me find Kelly. She left during dinner and I haven't seen her since."

"So that's what it was. Didi shared one of her little fashion critiques about Kelly."

"It was a good bit worse than that, but you've got the general picture."

Pamela started for the door. "I'm going to walk around the ship and see if I can find either one of them. And I'll leave Didi a note to come talk to you if she comes back to the room."

"I don't really want to talk to her, Pamela. Whatever else needs to be said is between the two of you."

They traded grim looks. "It must have been quite a scene. I'm sorry I missed it."

"I wish we all had missed it."

The run was just what Kelly needed, a chance to punish her body and take her mind off the events of the night before. How on earth had she ever convinced herself that someone like Natalie would find her attractive…or even acceptable? She knew her own limitations. Women were charmed by her adoring, chivalrous doting, not by her looks. The beautiful ones—women like Natalie—were well out of her reach.

She had been running along the beach road for nearly an hour, and a low-flying plane signaled her proximity to the airport. In a perfect world, she could walk onto a plane that would take her to Miami, where she would meet the ship once the others had disembarked. Then she would collect her belongings and take a late flight back to Rochester alone. Her hopes of making friends were dashed. No way did she want to be part of a social circle that included the likes of Natalie and Didi. Where did those people get off passing judgment on everyone around them?

She had expected such behavior from Didi, but it crushed her to find that Natalie had been a part of it too. Apparently, deception was her forte. If what Didi had said was true, their lovemaking had probably been a sham too.

Of all things to enter her head as she pounded along the crushed shells that lined the roadway, making love with Natalie was the last thing she wanted to think about. If indeed she had faked her body's response, she was quite the actress. The low moans and twitching torso…her breathless kisses and thrashing hips…and her throbbing inner walls.

It wasn't possible, she realized. Even the best actress in the world couldn't make her vagina spasm like that.

Kelly smiled with satisfaction that Didi had been wrong about that. Just because Natalie had faked it before didn't mean—

Her left foot suddenly found a hole that was deep enough to turn her ankle. "Ow!"

She hobbled a few feet to the line of porous gray coral that separated the road from the beach. This was definitely bad news. She was as far from the ship as she could possibly be, and it was Natalie's fault. If she hadn't been so focused on the vivid memories of making love, she would have seen the hole and stepped over it.

Several minutes passed and the pain lessened, but after a few test steps, it was clear she wouldn't be running anymore today.

Out of options, she started the slow walk back to the ship, wincing each time her foot bore weight. If she persevered at this rate, she would cover the six miles in...about a day and a half.

Natalie peered over the rail at the familiar figure in the distance. It was hard to believe Didi would go shopping in Nassau as though she hadn't a care in the world. It was some consolation that by her posture she looked miserable as she made her way back to the ship with her bags.

Still no sign of Kelly. She was probably hiding out on the ship somewhere, since she hadn't been among the adventure tourists and she certainly wasn't shopping or taking the carriage tour. Pamela had walked every deck several times in search of both Kelly and Didi and had finally given up. Now it was after two, and only an hour or so before all were due back on board.

She stepped back inside and dialed the number for the cabin next door. "Thought you'd want to know that Didi is coming back onto the ship right now, and she's carrying a load of shopping bags. She ought to be up here in a few minutes...No, no sign of Kelly. I think I'm going to walk around and look for her myself."

Didi would be coming up the elevators at mid-ship, so Natalie turned aft to avoid her. Kelly could be anywhere, so she started with a full sweep of the ship's common areas. She half expected to find her in the observation lounge on the top floor, since that had been a regular watering hole. But the lounge was empty and she continued through the fitness center, checking the exercise room, the spa and the steam shower.

As she crossed the pool deck, she spotted a familiar face in a shaded deck chair. "Hi, there, Jo."

The young woman nodded and smiled, apparently pleased to see Natalie. "I've been hiding out here reading all day. I feel like I'm on my own private ship."

"I'm really sorry to disturb you. I was wondering if you'd seen my friend Kelly. I've been looking for her all day." From Jo's bemused look, Natalie knew instantly that she knew something.

"Where is she?"

"I'm not really sure she wants you to know."

Natalie snatched the novel from Jo's hands and jumped back. "If you want to know how this story ends, you'll come clean."

Jo sprang from the deck chair to swipe at her novel. "Hey, give me that."

"Tell me," Natalie demanded, holding the book over the pool.

"She said she was going for a run to clear her head, and she'd be back by noon to get her gear out of the room."

Natalie shook her head. "She never came back. I've been watching for her from the balcony."

"I'm telling you, she had on her trainers with shorts and a tank top. She said something about a coastal road out to the airport that she knew from when she was here in the navy."

Ten minutes later, Natalie was climbing into the backseat of a taxi. "Is there a road that runs along the shore to the airport?"

"West Bay Road," the old man answered in a song-like cadence.

"Let's take that. I'm looking for a friend who's out running for exercise."

They wound through the traffic of Nassau's shopping district, finally emerging on a two-lane highway that paralleled the shore. Natalie looked left and right for signs of a runner, all the while checking the clock on the dash anxiously to be sure she got back to the ship on time. As they approached the airport, she realized the futility of her search. Kelly must have sneaked back aboard somehow, because a runner this far out with only thirty minutes before boarding had zero chance of getting back on time.

"I guess we should turn back. She doesn't seem to—"

"Is that your friend?"

She followed his eyes to a lone figure sitting on a rock at the edge of the water and her heart lurched. "Stop the car."

Unfortunately, the water along the shore was too warm to stave off the swelling. With mounting concern, Kelly examined the blue hue of the puffy skin below her ankle. It wasn't the worst sprain she'd ever had, but she could cross running off her list for the next two or three weeks.

And by her watch, she could cross cruising off as well. The gangway was going up in about thirty minutes and she had no way of getting back to the ship. Waving down a passing taxi wouldn't do her any good, since she didn't have any cash. No taxi driver would trust her to come back and pay after going through customs to get back on the ship.

As backup plans went, hers sucked, but it would have to do. Once she reached a point where she could walk again, she would head back to the airport and call her brother collect. He would probably gripe about it, but with some cajoling would front her the cash to purchase her ticket to fly back to Miami tonight. She could sleep in the terminal and catch the early departure for Rochester, long before the others disembarked. That meant leaving her belongings behind, but at least she had her passport. If Natalie thought to gather up her things, she could collect them from Yvonne later.

Somehow, she would have to get word to the group that she was fine. Though she didn't want to talk to any of them right now, it was cruel to make them worry. Maybe the airline would pass on a message.

A dark blue taxi abruptly slid to a stop in the gravel. She briefly toyed with the notion of throwing herself upon the driver's mercy and begging for a ride back to the port, but the more she thought about it, the more she liked the idea of going back by plane and avoiding Natalie and Didi.

Then the back door opened, and the last person on earth she wanted to see—next to last, actually, since had it been Didi, she might have gotten up and started running again—crawled out and started walking toward her. Kelly spun around on the rock to stare out to sea. The footsteps stopped only inches behind her.

"I'm so sorry, Kelly. I don't even know where to start."

"It's okay. Let's just forget it."

"No, it isn't okay and I'm not going to let this go." Natalie's hand came to rest on her shoulder. "I said something ignorant and judgmental the first time I saw you, and I'm ashamed of that. But you taught me a lesson. And whether you believe it or not, I started learning it the first time we sat down and talked. I know now that it's not about how a person looks. What matters is what they're like inside."

Kelly bristled with frustration. "That isn't all that matters. This may come as a shock to you and your friends, but I happen to like the way I look. My hair, my clothes...believe it or not, I do these things on purpose. I don't care if people accept me, but I expect the person I'm making love with to actually like those things about me, not overlook them."

"I do like them," she said plaintively, walking around to look her in the eye. "You turn me on like nobody ever has. Didn't I show you that?"

When she realized Natalie was stubbornly waiting for her answer, she nodded weakly.

"What Didi said...I did that with her, and I got caught, because she asked me one time if I ever faked it, and I stupidly told her the truth. Looking back on it, I wish I'd lied and made her think she was the most perfect lover in the world. But I didn't fake anything with you."

"I know you didn't."

"Kelly, you've shown me things about myself that I never knew before. I feel like a totally different woman than the one I used to be, and I love it." She sat on the rock, forcing Kelly to scoot over. "I like us together. I like the woman I am when I'm with you."

"I like the woman you are too," Kelly admitted, feeling the full force of her emotions as she began to let go of her anger and humiliation. "You make me want to give you the world, Natalie. I'd do anything—grow my hair out...whatever—if that's what you really needed. All you have to do is ask."

Natalie shook her head. "No, I mean it. I'm falling in love with the real you."

All of Kelly's defensive posturing died inside as Natalie

confessed her heart, and she allowed her hand to be taken. "If that taxi driver sees us holding hands, he's liable to drive off."

"There are worse things than being stuck with you in the Bahamas." She stood and gave Kelly a gentle pull. "But maybe we should come back here another time and do that on purpose. Right now we've got about twenty minutes to get back to the dock."

Kelly shook her foot and gingerly worked her sock into place. "I had a little accident. You're probably going to have to help me back to the ship."

Natalie flashed a look of alarm and bent down to examine her injury. "What happened?"

"Just a sprained ankle. I was sitting here already planning another way to get home, because there was no way I could get back to the ship." She hitched an arm around Natalie's waist and allowed herself to be led to the waiting car. With Natalie's declaration that she was falling in love, the sting of her flippant words was gone. "It's a good thing I'm gimpy. If I could stand on one leg, I'd probably have to kick Didi's ass."

"You let me worry about Didi."

Chapter 22

Natalie dumped her toiletries and filled the plastic bag with ice from the bucket in their tiny wet bar. By the time they got back to their room, Kelly was expressing optimism that the sprain wasn't as bad as she had originally thought, and packing it in ice for an hour or so would help minimize the swelling.

She opened the door to the bathroom and stared brazenly at Kelly in the shower. "What a body. You're going to have to show me what you do to look like that and help me get in shape."

Kelly looked over her shoulder and grinned. "Oh no, you don't. You have the curves in all the right places, and soft spots I can bury my face into. I better not catch you lifting any weights."

Natalie snickered, remembering Kelly's response when she had teased about buying some briefs like hers. It was wonderful to be with someone who liked the woman she already was. "I fixed you an icepack. I think we should order room service so you can rest."

"I don't think either of us will be getting much rest tonight, but room service is a great idea."

"Are you saying you have other things in mind?"

"Definitely. We have to make up for last night."

"We're going to have lots of time for that, you know."

"Good, because I'm going to need lots of time with you." She spun the dial and turned off the water. "Good as new."

Natalie held out a towel and frisked Kelly's short hair. Then she methodically patted her dry from head to toe. "I should call Steph and tell her we won't be at dinner."

"Have you talked to Didi?"

"She called a few minutes ago and asked me to meet her out on the balcony, but I told her I wasn't ready to talk to her yet."

"You ought to go, Nat. You'll feel better if you get it behind you."

"I'm afraid of what I'll say. I've put up with her constant critique for eight years, but I've never known her to be as cruel as she was last night. And I can't believe she said that last part in front of everyone. There are some things you like to think will always be private."

"She was drunk and she felt things slipping away. All she wanted was to break us apart, and I almost let her do that." Kelly slipped on her robe and hobbled carefully to the couch. "Lucky for me, you didn't."

Natalie fetched the icepack and helped her prop her ankle on a small stack of pillows. "You really think I should talk to her? I'm not up for another fight."

"If it feels like that's going to happen, you can walk away. I'll be right here staring at this picture." Kelly craned her neck for a kiss as she reached for the photo of the two of them from formal night. "Just knock on the glass if you need me and I'll hop out there and rescue you."

"What would you do?"

"I don't know. Moon her?"

Natalie laughed heartily, imagining Didi's shock at such a gesture. She hated to give up her good mood for a confrontation, but Kelly was right. Settling things once and for all would make her feel better, even though a part of her wanted Didi to stew a bit longer. But she owed it to Kelly and Pamela both to officially end things with Didi once and for all.

The sound of voices from the adjacent balcony surprised her, not because Didi and Pamela were talking, but because they seemed to be talking amiably. She listened as Didi cheerfully related her shopping experiences from earlier in the day while Pamela laughed. Natalie finally cleared her throat and poked her head around the divider. The conversation abruptly stopped.

Pamela smiled at her and stood. "I think I'll go start packing."

"I'll be there in a minute," Didi said. "I can help you with that big suitcase."

Natalie had the urge to clean her ears. Didi helping?

Didi left her deck chair and sauntered casually to the rail. "I guess it's back to the grind tomorrow."

"And to the snow."

"I forgot about that part. Maybe Pamela and I should cash in those vouchers and just stay on the ship. You game?"

Natalie shook her head. "I can't. I've got a lot to do when we get back."

"About the store, Nat...why don't we sit on that for a while? Maybe you're right about New York. We could always try opening a Manhattan location down the road, but we should keep the main store in Rochester. You can keep all the business operations—"

"I thought you wanted to buy me out."

"I don't. I had a brain fart or something. I never really wanted you out of the business. I just thought if I pressured you about it until it drove you nuts, you'd move with me. I can't run this store without you. You're the reason it's been successful. You've worked hard and made all the smart decisions. Sometimes I need you to save me from myself."

This was a new experience, listening to Didi praise her strengths while admitting her own limitations. "That's not true. You're the one who understands how to merchandise. And you always know exactly what's going to be hot two years from now. It's amazing. After eight years of seeing you every day, and I still can't even dress myself."

"Sure you can, Nat. You always look like a million bucks. I'm sorry I didn't tell you that enough." Didi folded her hands and gazed out at the open sea. "I'm sorry for lots of things, but especially for last night. I was drunk, but that's not an excuse. I deserve whatever you want to do, but please don't stop loving me."

It was bittersweet to hear Didi finally saying some of the things she had always wanted to hear, now that she had Kelly to tell her again and again. "It's over for us, Didi."

"I know that part's over, but I couldn't stand it if you weren't in my life anymore. No matter what happens or where we go, I'm always going to need you to love me. And I'm always going to love you back, even if it's someone else who makes you happy."

"And if it's someone you don't approve of?"

Didi looked at her sheepishly. "Sorry about that too. I knew you were falling for her. I saw how she practically worshipped you, and that's when I finally realized what an idiot I was. I never gave you that because I always expected you to do those things for me."

"I never needed to be worshipped, Didi."

"No, but you deserved it. I was too selfish to see that. I wish I had told you how lucky I felt to be the one you loved."

Natalie fought a well of tears, thinking she had never felt closer emotionally to Didi than she did right that minute. "I kind of wish you had too. I always felt lucky to be with you. But sometimes I felt like you sucked all the light out of the room... that you didn't leave any for the rest of us."

"You had your own light, Nat. You were always the prettiest, and you didn't have to work at it like I did." She looked behind her and tipped her head toward the door. "Pamela must be nuts, because she thinks I'm worth holding onto. Lucky for me she likes old hags."

"You're not an old hag, Didi. You have a classic beauty that never ages." This was an old habit for both of them, Didi disparaging herself and Natalie building her up. "Just don't go too long without telling Pamela those things, because she needs to hear them too."

"I think I'm off to a good start. I slipped off the ship this morning to buy her some very expensive diamond earrings. I would have gotten you something too, but I didn't think I could handle watching you pitch it in the ocean."

Natalie chuckled and shook her head. "I'm not sure I could ever get angry enough to throw diamonds overboard." Her anxiety waned as several seconds of comfortable silence passed, and she turned to give Kelly a reassuring wave.

"I've got to tell you, Nat—and please don't get mad at me—but you and Kelly...that surprises me."

"It surprised me too at first, but that's how I knew it was something special. She just broke through everything I thought I knew about myself."

"Yeah, I guess I can see it. There's something about her."

She liked to think Didi was being truthful, instead of just trying to smooth things over. "I hope you'll get to know her. I want all of us to be friends."

"Are you sure she wants to be friends with me?"

"I think so. She's a better person than you are," she added teasingly.

"That doesn't take much."

Natalie bit back the instinct to respond, thinking maybe just once she would let Didi wallow in remorse. "We're going to skip dinner tonight. Kelly sprained her ankle and she's having some trouble getting around."

"Is she okay?"

"I'm sure she'll be fine. We'll see everyone at breakfast tomorrow." She held out her hand and Didi gave it a squeeze.

"I love you, Nat."

"Love you back."

Kelly zipped her duffel and set it outside the cabin door with Natalie's luggage. Between the two of them, they had only one small bag to carry off the next morning, a welcome relief for her bum ankle. "That's it. Hard to believe twelve days went by so fast. I'm ready to go again."

"Believe it or not, that's what Didi said."

"After all she's been through? I would have thought she'd sworn off ships forever." Natalie hadn't shared much about her conversation with Didi, though she had seemed relaxed and settled ever since their talk. "I take it you got everything sorted out?"

"More or less. I think she'll apologize to you eventually."

"It's not necessary."

"It is if we're all going to be friends one of these days." Natalie pulled her onto the couch. "Would you be okay with that? Being friends with Didi, I mean."

"Sure. Why not?"

"I just wondered. She hasn't treated you very well."

"What matters to me is how she treats you." Kelly took advantage of their proximity to slide her fingertips inside the waistband of Natalie's pajama bottoms. "And how I treat you."

"And how often you treat me," Natalie added with a tantalizing smile. She turned and leaned backward into Kelly's chest.

"Now you're talking." Kelly continued her sensuous strokes inside the pajamas, trailing her fingers over the swirl of Natalie's pubic hair. "It's going to be hard to get used to not seeing you every day."

"Who says we won't? If you ask me, it's sort of silly to make love with somebody and then try to pretend you're taking things slowly."

Though everything about their relationship felt right, Kelly had tried to keep her expectations from running wild. She liked that Natalie seemed to take for granted the fact that they were now a couple. "I hope we'll take years to get to know each other, but that doesn't mean I don't want to sleep with you every night."

Natalie dropped her head back on Kelly's shoulder and sighed. "You can't move in until you build me another closet. Those Victorians must have worn the same clothes every day."

"You certainly know how to motivate. I'll have that closet finished by the end of next week."

Another set of hands slid under the waistband to cover hers. "That feels so nice."

"I could do this all night." Kelly dipped her fingers lower to tickle the smooth skin of her labia, wondering if Natalie would let the hair grow back after her waxing. "How long do you think you could stand me touching you like this without making you come?"

Natalie reached lower and parted her labia. "How long can you touch me like that without touching this?"

"Good point." The folds were already wet and warm, and Natalie began to undulate in response to the slow strokes. "This is the most exquisite feeling. Are you sure you won't let me do this all night?"

"I'm...just a few more..." Her hips arched upward as she heaved.

"Wait for me."

Natalie groaned in protest, but Kelly withdrew her hands and slid off the couch and to her knees. She worked the pajamas to the floor and eyed the glistening softness, which Natalie held open for the touch of her tongue.

"Oh...God."

It was all Kelly could do to stay clear of the swollen clitoris, knowing Natalie would come almost instantly and this luxurious feast would be finished. When she could stand it no more, she closed in on the nub, sucking it gently between her teeth.

Natalie exploded, muffling her scream with the back of her hand.

Kelly nuzzled the warm flesh and kissed it all around. "Yes, I definitely want to take my time getting to know you."

Chapter 23

Kelly tightened her watchband as she waited at the door for Natalie. "I hate having to put this thing back on."

"So did I, but not nearly as much as I'm going to hate wrapping in that heavy coat to get off the plane in Rochester. I already miss the warm weather."

"What I'm going to miss is that twin bed. Next time we sleep together, we won't even touch each other."

"Oh, yes we will." Natalie stepped into her closed-toed shoes, and dropped her sandals into their carry-on bag. "And just in case you have other ideas, the next time we sleep together will be in my bed tonight."

"Yes, ma'am."

"How's your ankle?"

"Not bad if you like big and blue, but I can walk okay. I'll have to figure out how to keep it elevated on the plane." They started down the hallway toward the breakfast buffet, their last meal aboard ship.

"You can put it in my lap."

"Hmm. Too bad it wasn't my hand that I sprained."

"Or your tongue," Natalie whispered.

"You naughty girl!" By the time they reached the terrace, Kelly's ankle was aching, and she made a mental note to avoid stairs for the rest of the day. She couldn't afford to miss work after being gone for two weeks.

"Hey, mate."

Kelly whirled to see Jo sitting with her sister. "I'll catch up in a minute, Nat." She dug into her pocket for the coral necklace she had bought the day she and Jo had gone for the bike ride. "I was hoping I'd see you."

"Looks like things worked out for you and Natalie."

"They sure did. Lucky me."

Julie nodded in Natalie's direction. "That's quite a lady you have there. I gave it my best shot, but she wouldn't give me the time of day."

"From what I hear, you landed on your feet with a certain nurse."

"A nurse who's coming all the way to Brisbane for six weeks when she gets her break in March," Jo added proudly.

"Here, Jo. I have something for you." Kelly dropped the coral necklace into her hand. "Take this back to Sarah and tell her how you feel. If it brings you half as much luck as it brought me, you'll have a new sweetheart."

"Aw, mate." Jo grinned and held up a hand for a shake. "I'm just crazy enough to do it. Good luck to you."

"And to both of you." Kelly spotted Natalie at the buffet and quickly joined her. "Did you find a table?"

"Steph and Yvonne are sitting out in the sun."

"Any sign of Didi and Pamela?"

"Steph said they left the ship early on one of those shopping excursions. Figures, huh? They'll meet us at the airport."

Kelly wasn't terribly surprised that Didi was avoiding them. "I'm just going to get a cup of coffee. See you at the table."

"You go on. I'll bring it."

Steph and Yvonne were grinning smugly when she arrived to sit.

"What's up with you two?"

"Yvonne's sitting here gloating."

"Why do I get the feeling this has something to do with me?"

"The first time you showed up in her clinic for physical therapy, she came home and told me she'd found the perfect woman for Natalie."

"Is that a fact?"

Yvonne buffed her nails on her shirt. "I could tell you were just what Natalie needed. It just took a few days for her to realize it."

"From what you all said the other night, I didn't make a very good first impression."

Steph craned her neck to look past Kelly's shoulder as if to make sure Natalie was still at the buffet. "Back when we were in college, Nat was this close"—she held up her thumb and forefinger to indicate a space of only a few millimeters—"to hooking up with one of Yvonne's softball teammates, and she happened to look a lot like you."

"KT treated her like a queen," Yvonne added, "and Natalie ate it up."

"But then Theresa came along, and Nat got it in her head that she wanted a femme girlfriend instead. So for the past fifteen years she's been hung up on women who have to be the center of attention and she's never gotten the chance to enjoy that for herself."

Kelly nodded and stood as Natalie started toward their table. "I'll make up for all of that."

"Just keep her smiling like she is today. It's nice to see."

Indeed it was, and even nicer when Natalie bussed her cheek as she sat down.

Natalie scanned the departure lounge anxiously for any sign of Didi or Pamela. The boarding process would begin in just a few minutes, and they were in danger of missing the plane.

Kelly sat with Steph and Yvonne in a row of chairs along the windows, her swollen foot propped on their carry-on bag. "Relax, Nat. If they miss this flight, there will be another one in a few hours."

"There they are," Steph said.

Didi and Pamela were hustling toward the gate, arm in arm and all smiles. Natalie hurried out to meet them. "You two had me worried."

"You wouldn't believe the shops at Bal Harbour," Pamela gushed. "We're coming back when we have more time."

Didi dropped her overloaded shopping bag at her feet. "That's right. Maybe next year we'll stay here while you guys take the cruise from hell without us."

Pamela smacked her arm playfully. "It was not the cruise from hell. I think it turned out pretty well."

From what Natalie could see, the vacation had ended beautifully for Didi and Pamela, who were holding onto one another like new lovers. "You made it just in time. They're about to call first class."

"Where's that gimpy girlfriend of yours?" Didi asked.

"Who are you calling a gimp?" Kelly called out.

Didi walked over to where the others sat. "I owe you an apology, Kelly, and I suppose it ought to be as public on this end as it was on the other."

Natalie studied their faces and smiled to see a mischievous spark between them.

"I'll let it pass this time, but if it happens again I'll hold you down, shave your head and dress you in cargo pants."

Didi nodded, not showing even a hint of humor. "Now that's what I call a threat."

"Ladies and gentlemen, at this time, we'd like to invite our first class passengers to board for Philadelphia."

"That's you," Natalie said. "Think of us when they bring you that tenderloin for lunch. We'll be back in the cattle car fighting over a sack of peanuts."

Didi handed over their boarding passes. "Take these and give us yours. Kelly will be a lot more comfortable up front and she can use the footrest."

Natalie's jaw dropped at the gesture, which she might have refused if not for Kelly. "That's so generous of you. We both appreciate it."

"You know how I am...always putting others first."

Once the words sank in, it was all Natalie could do to keep from snorting. That was more than she could say for Steph and Yvonne.

She held onto Kelly's arm as they started down the jet bridge. It was amazing to think that only twelve days ago she was at a crossroads in her life and didn't even know it. Now she was on a path she could walk for a long time—maybe even forever—with someone who made her feel like the center of the universe.

**Publications from
Bella Books, Inc.**
The best in contemporary lesbian fiction

**P.O. Box 10543, Tallahassee, FL 32302
Phone: 800-729-4992
www.bellabooks.com**

WALTZING AT MIDNIGHT by Robbi McCoy. First crush, first passion, first love. Everybody else knows Jean Harris has a major crush on Rosie Monroe, except Jean. It's just not something Jean, with two kids in college, thought would ever happen to her. $14.95

NO STRINGS by Gerri Hill. Reese Daniels is only in town for a year's assignment. MZ Morgan doesn't need a relationship. Their "no strings" arrangement seemed like a really good plan. $14.95

THE COLOR OF DUST by Claire Rooney. Who wouldn't want to inherit a mysterious mansion full of history under the layers of dust? Carrie Bowden is thrilled, especially when the local antique dealer seems equally interested in her. But sometimes secrets don't want to be disturbed. $14.95

THE DAWNING by Karin Kallmaker. Would you give up your future to right the past? Romantic, science fiction story that will linger long after the last page. $14.95

OCTOBER'S PROMISE by Marianne Garver. You'll never forget Turtle Cove, the people who live there, and the mysterious cupid determined to make true love happen for Libby and Quinn. $14.95

SIDE ORDER OF LOVE by Tracey Richardson. Television foodie star Grace Wellwood is not going to be golf phenom Torrie Cannon's side order of romance for the summer tour. No, she's not. Absolutely not. $14.95

WORTH EVERY STEP by KG MacGregor. Climbing Africa's highest peak isn't nearly so hard as coming back down to earth. Join two women who risk their futures and hearts on the journey of their lives. $14.95

WHACKED by Josie Gordon. Death by family values. Lonnie Squires knows that if they'd warned her about this possibility in seminary, she'd remember. $14.95

BECKA'S SONG by Frankie J. Jones. Mysterious, beautiful women with secrets are to be avoided. Leanne Dresher knows it with her head, but her heart has other plans. Becka James is simply unavoidable. 14.95

PARTNERS by Gerri Hill. Detective Casey O'Connor has had difficult cases, but what she needs most from fellow detective Tori Hunter is help understanding her new partner, Leslie Tucker. 14.95

AS FAR AS FAR ENOUGH by Claire Rooney. Two very different women from two very different worlds meet by accident—literally. Collier and Meri find their love threatened on all sides. There's only one way to survive: together. $14.95